MURDER SO SINFUL

To NHRHS Students,
Follow your dreams,
no matter where they
may lead!

Eileen Curley Hammond
Class of '74

MURDER SO SINFUL

A Merry March Mystery

Eileen Curley Hammond

Twody Press

Cover designed by SelfPubBookCovers.com/ Bravo Covers

This book is a work of fiction. Names, characters, places, and incidents either
are products of the author's imagination or are used fictitiously. Any
resemblance to actual persons, living or dead, events, or locales is entirely
coincidental.

Eileen Curley Hammond
Visit my website at www.eileencurleyhammond.com

Printed in the United States of America

First Printing: Aug 2018
Twody Press

ISBN-978-1-7325460-1-1

Library of Congress Control Number: 2018909012

AUTHOR'S NOTE

Writing is a solitary pursuit. Luckily so many people in the writing community are willing to give of their time. In particular, I would like to thank young adult writer Jenna Grinstead, Eric Henderson, and the Columbus, Ohio, Sisters in Crime chapter.

Jenna, I appreciated your insightful comments and gentle nudges when I needed to take it up a notch. I also appreciated your willingness to answer my endless questions. Eric, your time and keen gift of logical flow was always welcome. And, to my friends in Sisters in Crime, I appreciated the experiences you created to make us better writers.

Miranda, of Editing Realm, was an amazing resource with her encyclopedic knowledge of punctuation and grammar, as well as her ability to spot superfluous text. The story became crisper and far more readable because of her.

My family pitched in as well. Thank you to my sister, Carol, sisters-in-law, Debbie and Linda, and brothers, Pat and Mark. I was also blessed to have uncles for whom writing is their stock in trade, specifically Kevin (a playwright) and Jim (an industry newsletter editor). All of you provided valuable guidance, feedback, and hugs—virtual and otherwise—when I needed it most.

And last, but most important, thank you to my spouse. I appreciated your willingness to listen to my endless stream of non sequiturs and your sense of humor.

For Mom.

CHAPTER 1

"I'll be right there." I hung up the phone, grabbed my purse, and ran out the door.

When I shut the garden gate, Nancy Piedmont waved from her front porch next door. "Hi, Merry. Some to-do at the church, huh?"

I paused in mid-stride, my eyes widening. In our small town, news traveled almost before it was made. Continuing my half trot, I tossed over my shoulder, "Yes. I'm on my way there now to pick up Jenny. And she better have a darn good explanation."

Hurrying toward the church, I practiced my deep breathing. That not working, I counted my blessings, like in that Christmas song. Neither lowered my increasing blood pressure. It spiked when I ran past a small clutch of people near the graveyard. They were cleaning off the coffin and loading it back into the hearse. Thank heavens Frank hadn't fallen out. I needed to send flowers, some baked goods, and definitely a nice card for Edna.

Racing up the rectory steps, I yanked open the door and stormed into Father Tom's office. "Jenny, how could you?"

She jumped.

Father Tom waved me into the seat next to him and put his hand on my shoulder, motioning for me to be silent. "Jenny?"

Jenny stared at her feet, as if wishing they would dance her far away. She looked up. Father Tom continued to stare at her with his kind brown eyes and waited.

"It wasn't my fault," she said.

He sighed. "It never is."

"It seemed like such a good idea at the time. We were cold and late. The hearse was running. Who knew that Old Man Schaffer was ready for his final resting place? We were totally shocked when we peeled out and realized the back doors were open." Her eyes widened. "I've never seen a casket bounce like that."

Father Tom shook his head. "It was even more surprising for Mrs. Schaffer and her family. Luckily the casket's landing was cushioned by the wet grass and only slid ten feet."

Unable to control myself any longer, I yelled, "How could you do that? What were you thinking?"

Jenny flinched and moved closer to Father Tom. "Cindy and I had ballet this afternoon, and afterward, Mrs. Twilliger was supposed to pick us up."

"Yes, I remember."

"Well, she didn't. We texted her twice, and she never answered. So we started home. Cindy needed to get ready for her date with Michael and didn't want to be late. Plus, it was really cold. When we saw the hearse, we decided it would solve both our problems. We thought since Cindy's Uncle Jim let her borrow it for Halloween, he wouldn't mind if we borrowed it again." She shrugged. "How were we supposed to know it was already occupied?"

"It was parked in front of the church! Why else would it have been there? And just because someone is generous enough to let you borrow something once doesn't mean you have free access forever. You know better than that." I frowned. "Where's Cindy?"

"Her dad picked her up. And, boy, was he mad."

I rolled my eyes. "Not a surprise."

"He was finalizing a sale on one of the cars when he got the call. He had to turn it over to another salesman and won't get the commission. He wasn't happy."

Clenching my teeth, I stood. "Father Tom, thank you for your help, and thanks for intervening for me with Edna and her family."

Father Tom's eyes shone. "Let me know if there is anything else I can do. I'll see you at Mass on Sunday. I expect I'll see you as well, Jenny."

"You can count on that. Plus, I'd appreciate it if you would think of a list of tasks Jenny could complete as penance. I'm sure she would be only too happy to volunteer." With that, I grabbed Jenny's hand and pulled her toward the door.

"Thanks, Father Tom," Jenny called out as I shut the door behind us.

I dragged Jenny the four blocks to the house, nodding as I went to friends who waved as we went by. As I came in the door, my phone rang. It was Patty Twilliger, my best friend and mother of my daughter's partner-in-crime. I held up my forefinger as a signal to Jenny that we weren't finished and answered. "Hi, Patty. What happened?"

"Had a flat and my phone was out of juice. Who knew the dynamic duo would go all *Grand Theft Auto* with a hearse on us?"

"I know. It's amazing. Luckily the Schaffers are not pressing charges. It's a good thing the girls have an otherwise excellent reputation."

"It's unbelievable all right. Standard punishment?"

"Definitely. I'll talk to you later." I hung up the phone and faced my daughter.

I shook my finger. "And now, young lady, you are grounded for two weeks. You know the drill. No phone, TV, or games while you're in the house and you only leave the house for school. Upstairs, please."

"Fine."

Jenny trudged up the steps, her shoulders slumping as if the weight of the unfair world pressed down on her. A tall, willowy blonde just coming into her own, she took after that rat, Drew. Damn, she had his blue eyes too. I was a sucker for blue eyes. I sighed. She was a good kid who had grown up fast since Drew went to jail four years ago. I normally thought of her as a very old seventeen, but sometimes, like today, she showed she had some real growing up to do.

When I walked into the kitchen, my stomach growled. I really needed to think about dinner. Opening the refrigerator, I saw we had some leftover lamb that could be paired with some frozen stir-fry vegetables. And I had a scant half cup of rice left in the pantry. Combined with some salad, it was dinner.

I stumbled over my two rescue cats, Drambuie and Courvoisier, as they weaved around my feet. Since they already had food, I let them out into the fenced garden while I prepared dinner. A glass of Pinot Noir was in order after this afternoon's exploits. I had just pulled out the cork when a text arrived.

"Forgot to tell you. New single man in town, and he is hot!" texted Patty.

"Who?"

"John Gordan, new superintendent of schools. They're introducing him tomorrow at back-to-school night."

"Not interested."

"You will be." She added some flame emojis for emphasis.

CHAPTER 2

The next morning, I rose early to stretch and lift some light weights. Exercising was not one of my favorite things to do, but osteoporosis would be worse. After a light breakfast with my grumpy daughter, she and I parted ways, me to work and her to school.

Jenny paused at the front door. "Don't forget, we have the school open house this evening."

"Mrs. Twilliger reminded me last night, but thanks." I hugged her as she twisted away. "I love you."

She glared but then relented. "Love you too."

A soft smile on my face, I strolled the three blocks to my office. I owned the company: the Meredith March Insurance Agency. As I entered, I asked my assistant, Cheryl, to give me a summary of what was going on. She told me about late payments, clients with recent life events I might want to recognize, and anyone who had submitted a claim that needed special handling. After that was my weekly staff meeting with sales associates to see who was on track and who needed assistance. That finished, I retired to my office to google John Gordan.

He had a sterling reputation, attended good schools, and was highly rated in his last school district. *I'm not interested. But it's always good to be prepared when meeting someone for the first time.* Unfortunately, there didn't seem to be a clear photo of him online, despite my checking several sites.

Deciding I should get back to work, I made phone calls to existing clients and some prospective customers. Time passed quickly, and before I knew it, I needed to go home and dress for back-to-school night.

As I walked, I mentally paged through my wardrobe. Even though I wasn't interested in Mr. Gordan, I still wanted to make a good impression. My normal work clothes were too formal, and my few cocktail dresses seemed way over the top. Opting for a pair of twill slacks, a soft gray turtleneck, and a more casual jacket, I ran into Jenny on the stairs. She did not criticize my outfit, so I figured I was good.

At the school, I first spoke with Jenny's math teacher, Dawn Peterson. "Is Jenny working up to her potential?"

"She's doing quite well, but I still believe she may not be applying herself as much as she could. I think she has a real shot at some of the "A" schools if she would just bring it home. This is her last year to make a splash."

"What would you like me to do?"

"Encourage her to spend more time working and a bit less time socializing."

"You got it."

I chatted with a few more of Jenny's teachers. Spying her biology teacher across the way, I started to walk over but stopped in mid-stride.

A tall, well-built man with his back to me said, "Yes, I heard about the hearse incident from several people. Now that I'm here, I can assure you there will be tighter controls on students. That and the school's partnership with involved, caring parents will make this type of hooliganism a thing of the past. Obviously, those kids had a very lax upbringing."

My temper rose, and I unconsciously edged closer to the discussion. When he finished his statement, he turned abruptly and knocked me over. Flat on my back, looking up at him, I was able to appreciate his good looks.

"I'm so sorry." He extended his hand.

I grabbed it, and he helped me to my feet. I brushed off my slacks with my other hand, my face burning.

He smiled down at me. "Forgive me. I didn't know you were standing there. Are you okay? Let me introduce myself: I'm the new school superintendent, John Gordan."

"That's quite all right." Heat rushed through my body. "I'm the lax parent, Meredith March." As I turned on my heel, I realized Patty was right. He was hot. Six foot one, obviously worked out, wavy brown hair, and, of course, deep-blue eyes. *Too bad this is ending before it began.* I stalked out of the school.

Patty caught up with me just as I was about to get into my car. "What's up? I was looking for you all evening, and just as I caught sight of you with John, you took off."

"That jerk! Does he think this is the Dark Ages? Does he think waterboarding students is an idea with merit? Does he have any idea how tough it is to be a parent today?"

"Hold on, girlfriend. Don't get yourself so riled up. What happened?"

"He said Jenny and Cindy had a lax upbringing."

"What? Seriously?" Patty's mouth gaped open. "How on earth could he know what kind of upbringing they had? He's only been here since breakfast!"

"He was talking about the hearse incident."

She looked at her shoes. "Oh. Well, that *was* bad."

"Are we bad parents?"

"No. We are good parents with kids who occasionally go haywire. And we are parents who need a drink."

I nodded. "My place?"

"Definitely. Patrick is still not talking to me after missing out on that sale yesterday. I figure I'll let him cool off a bit more before I go home."

We settled in on the sectional in my living room with glasses of Pinot Noir. It wasn't long before each cat found a lap and begged for attention, which we were only too happy to give.

Patty petted Courvoisier. "Good wine."

"From the Willamette Valley near Portland. Are we going to talk about the wine?"

"No, that's it on the wine conversation,"

"Thank God. How are the other kids?"

Patty had three other children, all boys. When I looked at her, I was amazed. She still fit into her skinny jeans but didn't deny herself the occasional donut. She had kind brown eyes that seemed to look deeper than most, long brown hair with a tendency to curl, and, most importantly, was fun and a great friend.

She looked at me impatiently. "They're crazy, but are we really going to talk about the kids?"

I shrugged. "No, we don't have to. What do you want to talk about?"

"You." She pointed at me. "I know your marriage to Drew was a disaster, but not all men are like that. At some point, you have to start trusting them again."

"Which part was the disaster? The fact that he ran a bogus money management firm and bilked most of our friends and neighbors out of their hard-earned cash? Or the fact that I was spectacularly unaware of it and his offshore bank account? Thank goodness there was still enough left in his account to repay everyone, or I would have had to move. I'm done. I'm never going to trust one of the male tribe again." Gulping my wine and then taking a deep breath, I continued in a calmer voice. "Let's talk about the kids instead."

8

"No. Let's continue this conversation. Other than the fact that John is a male and was wrong about our parenting skills, what did you think of him?"

"It doesn't matter because I'm not going to date anyone. However, if you insist on knowing my opinion, I thought he was kind of cute. But his views concern me. Plus, I don't think he was impressed with me either."

"Okay, John is out for now," Patty said in a conciliatory tone. "Who else piques your interest?"

"No man in this town, country, or world!"

Patty rolled her eyes. "It was four years ago. You need to get over it, Ms. Drama Queen. But, since I am your best friend with your best interests in mind, I will disregard your outburst." She paused to take a ladylike sip of her wine. "I may have someone for you. Not your usual type, but in view of your past that may be a good thing. Would you be open to a blind date? Patrick and I would come with you so in case you're bored we can talk."

"Why is me getting together with someone so important to you? Jenny and I are just fine."

"Jenny's going to leave for school in another year. I don't want you to be lonely."

"I won't be. I have the cats." Cuddling Drambuie, I kissed her on the head.

"So your plan is to be the crazy cat lady?"

"I don't think you can be a crazy cat lady with just two." Petting Drambuie, I cooed to her, "Don't listen to the mean lady. She'll be leaving soon."

Patty gave me one of her death stares.

"Okay, fine. If you want to fix me up, I'll come."

"Great!"

"And now you have to leave because I need to be up early for work tomorrow. You okay to go home on your own?"

"Yes, Mom, I only had one glass of wine."

After escorting her to the door, I went upstairs to get ready for bed. A light peeked from under Jenny's door. When I carefully opened it, a soft snore emerged. Picking up the book on the floor by her bed, I tucked the covers around her, turned off the light, and backed out quietly.

Entering my room, I started kicking myself. What was I thinking? Why on earth had I agreed to a blind date?

The sky was beautiful the next morning. It was clear blue with not a cloud in sight—a good omen. I was obviously wrong because when I checked my phone, there was a text from Patty: "We're on for Friday at eight. Fiorella's. Pat and I will pick you up." Adding insult to injury, she signed off with a smiley face. *Great. When will I learn?* Sighing, I woke Jenny up and prepared breakfast. When she sat at the counter, I told her that her math teacher said she was a social butterfly.

"Mom, I don't socialize too much!" Jenny protested.

"Every single report card my mother saved encouraged me to apply myself more and socialize less. Obviously, I never learned, so you may have a genetic problem." I smiled. "However, with work, maybe you'll do better than me and overcome it."

Jenny relaxed. "I'll try harder. Can we go to the lake this weekend?"

"No can do. You're still grounded." I winced. "Plus, I have a date on Friday night."

She perked up. "A date? With whom?"

"Not sure yet. Mrs. Twilliger is setting it up."

"A blind date?"

"Yes."

"I have full wardrobe approval."

CHAPTER 3

The week flew by. Arriving home on Friday, I smiled. My daughter left four outfits displayed on my bed. Unfortunately, the cats chose two of them to relax on while I was at work. Just in case they were helping me narrow my choices, I neglected to scold them. Selecting the sleeveless black dress—well-toned arms were a side benefit of my exercise regimen—I adorned it with a strand of pearls and a sage-green sweater. Some minor makeup repairs and I was finished. I went downstairs to wait.

Jenny looked up from her book and studied me. "Mom, for a short person who's fast approaching forty, you look beautiful." I gave her a dirty look. She laughed. "That sweater matches your eyes. Plus, green looks awesome with your red hair. Nice choice, Mom."

I curtsied. "Thank you for your assistance. I appreciate it."

"Where are you going?"

"Fiorella's."

"I love their eggplant parm! And their garlic bread is to die for. Hmm. Maybe you should lay off the garlic bread tonight."

"Don't get ahead of yourself. I haven't even met the guy yet."

"Here, take my mints, just in case." She tossed them to me.

Making a great catch, I slipped them into my purse. "Thanks."

A horn tooted. Jenny said, "Be home early, young lady."

Tossing a pillow at her, I blew her a kiss and shut the door.

I slid into the backseat. "Are you going to break down and tell me his name before we get to the restaurant?"

She smiled. "His name is Rob Jenson. I didn't want to tell you before because I knew you would google him."

"I wouldn't google him." I gave her an offended look as I surreptitiously took out my phone and typed in his name.

"Tell the truth. Do you ever not google someone?"

"No, but what are you hiding? Is he a mass murderer? Does he look like Quasimodo?"

"No to both. He's a reporter, he's very nice, and he's cute. Put your phone away; I can see you looking him up."

Rolling my eyes, I tucked my phone back into my purse. "A reporter? You know how I feel about reporters. You know what they put me through during Drew's trial."

"Yes, I do, but it's time to forget that. It was four years ago, and Rob wasn't even here."

I hit her lightly on the shoulder. "It's very tricky of you to tell me this after I'm already in a moving car."

"Yes, it is."

"And it's a good thing you picked this restaurant, or I'd be really mad."

"I know." A smile spread over her face.

We arrived at the restaurant, which was two towns over. The entrance was brightly lit with warm wood tones, but the interior of the restaurant had mood lighting.

"We have reservations under Twilliger," Patrick said to the hostess.

"The party joining you is at the bar. Would you care to join him, or would you like to be seated?"

Patrick glanced at us. "Why don't you both be seated, and I'll bring Rob over?"

Unsuccessful at trying to peer around Patrick to get a glimpse of my date, I gave up and followed Patty and the hostess to our table. Patty carefully sat me next to her facing where Patrick and Rob would come in.

She nodded toward the door. "Just in case you don't like him we'll be able to chat more comfortably." I smiled at her.

Patrick and Rob entered the dining room. Luckily our table was toward the back, so I was able to get a good look at him as they ambled over. He was tall, maybe six feet, and slender. He had wavy blond hair that was cut short and sported a well-manicured mustache. Darn, another weakness of mine—mustaches.

Patty and I stood and shook his hand, and Rob and I introduced ourselves. We exchanged pleasantries and then agreed to study the menu for a moment.

After ordering, Rob turned to me. "So what do you do for a living?"

"I run a property and casualty insurance shop. My job and daughter keep me pretty busy."

"March. That name seems familiar. Let me see... Wasn't there a guy named March who embezzled a lot of money from his clients a few years ago? As I remember, his wife got off scot-free. It always seemed a stretch that his wife didn't know anything about it."

"That would be me." I stared daggers at him. "And, regardless of what you and others might think, I didn't know anything about it. Plus, ex-wife is a better descriptor at this point in time."

A faint flush rose on his cheeks. "Sorry. I'm always putting my foot in it. I remember things and blurt them out without thinking. As Patrick and Patty may have told you, I'm a reporter, and snippets of information stick with me. I had no idea that was you."

"Yep, it's me." I shifted in my seat. "Do you always offend people within five minutes of meeting them?"

"Not normally. It usually takes me ten." He waited for a beat. "Just kidding. I hope you accept my apology."

"Apology accepted, with one caveat."

"What's that?"

"No more discussion on that subject."

"Done."

Patrick and Patty had been following the conversation like a tennis match. Now that it appeared the combatants had declared a cease fire, they tripped over each other to change the subject. Patty won. "So, Rob, do you have any children?"

Rob smiled. "No. I just haven't had the time. I reported globally, and although it was exciting, it was hard on relationships. Being a reporter is a lonely business. The travel started off being glamorous, at the end it was just tedious. I met so many people and experienced all sorts of different cultures. The unfortunate part was that it was all transient. I only call a few of the people I met friends. I'm not sorry I opted for my career; it's just that I feel so fortunate that I had the opportunity to buy the local paper here and set down some roots.

"My hope is to be able to focus on everyday human happenings and to form some lasting friendships."

The food arrived, and we all ate appreciatively. The rest of the evening passed pleasantly enough. At the end, Rob asked, "May I give you a lift home?"

I shook my head. "Thanks, but it's probably easier if I just bum a ride with Patrick and Patty."

"Should I read something into that?" he asked, his eyes questioning.

"No." I looked at Patrick and Patty. "Ready?"

We shook hands and went to our respective cars. As soon as the doors shut, Patty turned around. "Well?"

"Liked him, but what he said about the money Drew took smarts. Plus, he is a reporter..."

✳ ✳ ✳

The next morning, I threw a load of wash into the machine and started working out. The doorbell rang, and Jenny answered it. She said a quick "thanks," and the door slammed. A moment later, she poked her head around the corner. "Guess who got flowers? Someone must have had a good time last night."

I gave her *the look* and opened the card: "Sorry we got off on the wrong foot. Please accept my apologies." It was signed John Gordan. "Well, that was unexpected."

"Unexpected?"

"The flowers are from your new superintendent of schools."

"He's hot." She gave me a high five. "I didn't even know you knew each other."

"We bumped into each other at back-to-school night, literally."

Thanking her for bringing them in, I recut the flowers and put them in fresh water. Task accomplished, I texted Patty. "Need to talk."

"Fifteen minutes?"

"I'll call you."

After moving the clothes to the dryer, I finished my exercise regimen. Then I called Patty.

"What?" she answered.

"You'll never guess who sent me flowers."

"That's easy: Rob."

"Nope. John Gordan."

"Well, isn't that nice. I thought he wasn't interested, and as I remember, you told me you weren't either."

"Both potentially true, but it was nice he sent the flowers."

"And?"

"I know. What should I do? If I'm really not interested, I should just send him a nice note thanking him for thinking of me."

"Is that what you are going to do?"

15

"No. I've been thinking about it, and you're right. It's time for me to start going out with people again. And John is one good-looking man. I'm going to call him."

"Keep me posted, and good luck." With that, she signed off.

Calling the owner of the flower shop, I asked if she had John's number.

"You know, I really shouldn't do this, but since it's you..." She gave it to me.

Pacing the floor, I worked through what I was going to say and then dialed John. Getting his voice mail, I left a message: "Hi, John, it's Merry March. I called to thank you for the lovely flowers. If you'd like to talk, please call me back." I appended my number and hung up the phone.

About five minutes later, the phone rang. "Hello?"

"Is this Merry?"

"Yes, it is."

"This is John Gordan. I wanted to return your call and apologize again, first for knocking you over, and second for talking negatively about your parenting skills. Since the other night, I spoke with Jenny's teachers, and they all said the hearse incident was a one-off and not indicative of her normal behavior."

"Thank you for that. And thanks again for the beautiful flowers. I love the combination of daisies and lilies."

"I was wondering if you'd like to meet me for coffee at some point. I'm still in the middle of settling in, and it would be valuable to get your thoughts on the school system."

"I'd love to. When would work for you?"

"Does Saturday after next work? Nine thirty?"

"That would be great. I look forward to it. Should we meet at the Morning Pastry? I don't know if you've been there yet, but they have really good coffee."

"I look forward to seeing you there."

CHAPTER 4

Sunday morning, Jenny and I joined the Twilligers for the ten o'clock Mass. Father Tom's homily centered on respect and care of others, living or dead. Jenny and Cindy slid down in the pew, turning red. After the service, Father Tom told them their penance would be assisting in the next four memorial services. They graciously accepted as Patty and I shot them warning looks.

The next week at work was hectic, and on Wednesday Cheryl knocked on my door. "I hate to interrupt, but someone wants to move their insurance to us."

"Can't one of the sales assistants handle it?"

"I guess they could, but he asked for you specifically. And he's cute."

"What's his name?"

"Rob Jenson."

I smiled. "You better send him in."

A few moments later, Cheryl ushered Rob in and shut the door after him. I rose to greet him.

"Please have a seat, Rob. It's nice to see you."

"I wasn't sure you would want to see me again after the other night."

"Why?"

"Well, we got off to a shaky start, and then you decided to leave with the Twilligers instead of me."

"Is this off the record?"

He grinned. "Of course."

I shifted in my seat and studied my stapler. "The press was really rough on me four years ago when my ex-husband was arrested and sent to jail. They, like you, had a tough time believing I was unaware of what he was doing. I know it looked bad; after all, I run my own business. But I wasn't in on his scheme, and the authorities cleared me. I've had a sour taste in my mouth about the press ever since."

Rob turned red. "And I guess when I mouthed off it brought it all back."

"Yep."

"Again, I'm sorry, and I apologize for my press brethren as well."

I straightened and picked up a pen. "What brings you here today?"

"I need to change my auto insurance coverage, and everyone I asked said you were the best. I also wanted to tell you that I'm looking for a home in the nearby area and will need homeowners coverage then too."

"I can handle that for you and get you a discount. Let's walk through the paperwork."

At the end of the transaction, Rob gave me a pensive look. "I'd like to see you again. Any chance?"

"Give me a week or two to think about it."

"Okay, no pressure. I'll follow up." He winked at me as he left.

Later that night, I looked up some of his old news stories. He had a very distinct point of view, one I really liked. Then I looked up the newspaper's Facebook page. Rob's story about the standoff between Janet Tomlinson's cat, Ed Jenkin's dog, and the stepladder was really amusing, and I had to laugh. Maybe I was being too tough on the guy.

The following Thursday afternoon was the first penance for the girls: Jasmine Elderflower's funeral. Patty and I sat in the back to observe. They did a great job. They were properly solemn and respectful. After the service, we spoke quietly with some of the family members and offered our condolences. Jasmine died at ninety-five, and her wisdom and kindness had obviously been cherished by those who knew her.

Patty and I left and waited for the girls in my car. After chatting for a while, I glanced at my watch, surprised so much time had passed. Worried, I told Patty, "They should have been here by now."

The girls appeared and pounded on my door.

Jenny yelled, "Mom, open up. Something terrible happened."

Patty and I leapt out of the car. "What's wrong?" I asked.

"Cindy and I found a body, and Cindy cut her hand."

"That's not funny. We know Mrs. Elderflower is dead. What is it with you girls and dead bodies?"

"Mom, it's not Mrs. Elderflower. It's someone else, and they're not moving."

Patty bent over her daughter. "Cindy, how did you cut your hand?" She grabbed tissues from her purse. "Keep pressure on it. We'll go to the rectory so I can get a better look."

"We'll meet you there." I turned to Jenny. "Show me where you found the body." We ran back to the church.

"It was dark. We left through the side door, and we tripped over him," Jenny sobbed.

We rounded the corner. The outside light was on. Father Tom bent over someone, blocking our view.

I ran up to him. "What happened?"

"It's the postman, Ben Ford, and he's dead. I'm going to stay here with him. Go to the rectory and call 911." Father Tom leaned against the railing to shield the body and to support himself.

"Oh my God," I gasped. "Jenny, let's go!"

Dialing 911, I ran to the rectory, huffing as I told the dispatcher what happened. Jenny followed close behind me. When we got there, Patty was in the kitchen, holding Cindy's hand above her head while pressing on it with paper towels to stop the bleeding. Within a minute, we could hear the sirens.

Patty nodded at me. "I think she's going to need a stitch or two."

After a few moments, Father Tom joined us in the kitchen.

"Father Tom, do you have a bandage I can use for Cindy's hand?" Patty asked.

He took a quick look. "I'll go back out and get one of the EMTs."

He bustled back in with the EMT, and she confirmed Cindy would need stiches. She took Cindy and Patty into the other room, while we waited in the kitchen.

"Would anyone like some tea?" I asked.

"I think I need something a bit stronger." Father Tom made a beeline to the cupboard over the refrigerator, took down a bottle of whiskey, and poured himself a small glass. He took a long sip. "The police want us to wait for them in here." He waved the bottle at me. "Do you want some?"

I took him up on it, as I poured Jenny a cup of tea with plenty of sugar in it.

Patty came back in and opted for whiskey. "He wasn't that old, only forty-five. I hadn't heard he had heart trouble. It's such a shame to die that young."

Father Tom shuddered. "I may as well tell you. It wasn't a heart attack. Ben was murdered."

"Are you sure?" I asked. "Don't we have to wait for the coroner or something?"

"I'm fairly certain. He had a large chef's knife sticking out of his back."

Jenny gasped. I rushed to reassure her. "I know this is terrible, but the police will get to the bottom of it. I'm sure whoever did this was just passing through." I shivered. "And I'm sure that person is long gone now."

The door opened with a bang, and Detective Jay Ziebold entered. "I'm going to have to ask all of you some questions. Who was the first person to find the body?"

Jenny said, "Cindy and I did."

Frowning, he looked around the room. "Where's Cindy?"

"The EMT is finishing up putting stiches in her hand in the other room," Patty said.

"How did she cut her hand?"

Patty shrugged. "We don't know yet. It must have been when she fell."

He gave Patty a level look and then turned to me. "I'll start with you, Merry, and then Jenny. Merry, since Jenny is underage you may sit in when I question her, but you need to let her answer. Father, do you have another room we can use?"

"Yes, my study. It's just down the hall on the left."

The detective nodded to Jenny. "We'll be back for you in a few minutes."

He and I walked down the narrow hallway to the study. The detective had been part of our town's police force for at least fifteen years. He was stout, married to a really lovely woman named Barbara, and they had five boys. How she did it, I had no idea.

"Please sit." Detective Ziebold waited a moment for me to comply. "Start at the beginning. What happened, and what did you see?"

I told him what I knew, which wasn't a lot. He then told me to ask Jenny to join us.

"Jenny, start from the beginning. Why were you here today?"

"Cindy and I were helping Father Tom with Mrs. Elderflower's funeral. After the funeral, the family had a meal for friends and relatives in the basement of the church. We stayed to help serve and clean up, and then we left to meet our mothers in my mom's car."

"What door did you leave by?"

"The side door."

"What happened next?"

"Cindy was in front of me, and I turned to close the door. It was so dark out, I could hardly see anything. I heard Cindy fall over something at the bottom of the stairs, so I carefully edged my way down. My foot stopped on something, so I bent down and felt it. It was someone's leg! I hopped over it, and then I could see the rough outline of a body. And it wasn't moving." Jenny shuddered.

"What did Cindy do?"

"She screamed, and then we ran to my mom's car and pounded on the door."

"Were you together the whole time at the service?"

"No. Cindy said her stomach hurt, so she disappeared for a while. I thought she was in the bathroom, but when I went to check on her, she wasn't there."

"When was that?"

"I don't know. It might have been around three thirty? She came back just as we were cleaning up. I was going to ask her where she'd been, but I didn't have a chance to."

"Thanks, Jenny," He got up and flipped his notebook shut. "You and your mom can leave, but come down to the station sometime tomorrow to sign your statement. Please ask Patty to join me."

We passed Patty and Cindy on our way out and relayed instructions. I told Patty, "Call me tonight if you need me; otherwise, we'll talk tomorrow."

On the way to the car, we ran into Rob Jenson. He was standing just outside the crime scene tape. He frowned. "What happened?"

"I don't think I'm supposed to talk about it."

He escorted us back to our car. "There wouldn't be anything wrong with you giving me the bare minimum, would there?"

I sighed. "I need to get my daughter home, but if you must know, there's been a death, and since I'm not sure if they've notified the next of kin, I think I'll stop there."

"Got it." He made a quick note on his phone. Finished, he looked up. "You must be Jenny." Smiling, he held out his hand to her. "I'm Rob Jenson. I run the local newspaper now."

She shook it. "Were you my mom's blind date the other night?"

"Yes."

"Hmm." She turned, climbed into the car, and shut the door.

"What did that mean?" he asked.

"She's seventeen. I have no idea. I have to run now."

As I got into the car, Jenny said, "He's cute."

"But?"

"He's a reporter, and we don't like reporters."

"True. The jury's still out on him, though."

She shot me a look and curled up in the passenger seat.

"Are you okay?"

"No. Somebody's dead, and I found the body." She rested her head on the window.

I gave her shoulder a squeeze. "Let's talk more about this when we get home. We'll get into our jammies, have some soup, and turn the fire on."

We drove the rest of the way in silence. When I turned into the driveway, Nancy Piedmont waved at me to come up to her front porch.

I patted Jenny's hand. "I'll be inside in a moment."

I crossed the driveway to Nancy's house, taking a moment to admire the collection of mums that framed her walkway.

"What happened to Ben?" she asked.

I marveled again at the speed news traveled. "Not sure yet. We'll likely know more in the coming days."

"But you found him."

"Actually, Jenny and Cindy did. I'm sorry, Nancy, but I'm not supposed to discuss it. I'm sure we'll know more in the morning. It's so sad." I pointed to her front garden. "Your mums look terrific; I love all of the different colors. They blend together so well and make a terrific accent to your burning bushes."

Pleased, Nancy followed my gaze. "It's some trouble, but it's great to have such vibrancy before winter sets in."

I gave her a quick hug. "Jenny's upset, so I need to be getting in."

I hurried to my door. She called after me, "Let me know what you find out."

"Will do." I shut the door behind me.

Jenny was upstairs changing, so I took a moment to inventory the soup in the freezer. This occasion required something substantial. Taking out some potato and leek with bacon, I put it on the counter for a moment to defrost enough so I could get it into a microwave bowl. Then I grabbed some frozen rolls and preheated the oven. Checking the wine fridge, I pulled out a Merlot, opened it, and took a few gulps almost before the wine hit the glass. With the kind of weeks I'd been having recently, I was going to need to make a wine run.

Hurrying upstairs to take off my makeup, I changed into my comfy jammies. By the time I returned, Jenny had the soup in the microwave, rolls in the oven, and the fire on. Giving her a long hug, I grabbed my wine and sat on the sofa in front of the fire. I patted the seat next to me, and she sat.

I put my arm around her. "This is better, isn't it?"

She gave me a pointed look. "Yes, but it's better for you because you're having wine."

I jumped up. "I can fix that by making you some of my killer hot cocoa." I stopped dead in my tracks. We both stared at each other. "Probably the wrong way to phrase that, but one hot cocoa with marshmallows and whipped cream coming up."

CHAPTER 5

The next day, I called Patty. "How's Cindy's hand? And how did your interview with the police go?"

"Her hand is bothering her, as expected, but it looks better. The interview with the police was odd."

"What do you mean?"

"He kept asking Cindy if she and Jenny had been together the whole time. She told him they had, but he just wouldn't leave it alone. He wants to see us again this afternoon down at the station. He says they have some more questions."

"Um."

"What does *um* mean? Um what?"

"Jenny told him Cindy had a stomachache and left to use the bathroom for quite a while, but when she went to check on her, she wasn't there."

"That's strange. I'll ask her what happened before we go down there. How is Jenny doing?"

"She's been a bit quiet."

"Dead bodies are a hard thing to process at seventeen. Actually, they're a hard thing to process at any age."

"True. What do you think happened?"

"Hard to tell. Who would do something like that? It can't be anyone we know."

"We can hope. Need to sign off. I'll call you later."

The rest of the day I focused on work. Needless to say, there were a lot of questions from the staff on the murder and from clients who were curious. I handled it as best I could and finally left for the day. Remembering that I was meeting the new superintendent of schools the next morning, I puzzled about what to wear as I strode home. As I turned the corner to my street, my eyes widened slightly. Nancy Piedmont was on her porch again. *Does she ever get cold sitting there?* I waved. "Hi, Nancy."

She huffed. "I can't believe you didn't tell me about Ben Ford. I had to find out from my cousin Melissa."

"The police told me not to talk about it, so I didn't."

"Murdered. In our little town. Makes you think about your own safety." She shivered, and her eyes darted around. "Why Ben? He wouldn't hurt a soul. And he was such a good postman. He kept me up to date on what was happening in town. Melissa mentioned Detective Ziebold searched his house already. I wonder if they found anything. You know Melissa cleaned for him. Do you think she'll have to clean up after the police?"

"I have no idea." I looked at her more closely. "Are you going to be okay?"

"Yes, it's just such a shock. Oh, Jenny got home a half hour ago."

"Thanks. She texted me when she got here. See you later."

Entering the house, I checked to make sure the cats had food and water. A quick petting session for each, and I climbed the stairs to knock on Jenny's door. "Enter."

I leaned on the doorjamb. "How are you doing?"

"I'm fine. Everyone at school wanted to know what happened to Mr. Ford."

"How did you handle it?"

"I just told them what I knew, which isn't a lot. Have you heard any more? Do they know who did it?"

"Not yet, honey. It's probably going to take some time." I sat next to her on the bed and put my arm around her.

"It's kind of scary to think someone would do this in our town."

"You're right. It's a good reminder that we should always be careful and aware of our surroundings. I have a favor to ask: Would you help me figure out what to wear tomorrow?"

"What's tomorrow?"

"Nothing really. I'm meeting Mr. Gordan for coffee in the morning. He wants to get my thoughts on the school district."

"I told you he was hot."

"I don't think you should be calling your school superintendent hot."

"Is lukewarm better?"

"You know what I mean." I shoved her toward the edge of the bed. "Are you going to help?"

Getting up, she pulled me to my feet, and we went to my room. "Of course. Everyone knows you're wardrobe challenged!"

"What would I do without you?" I rifled through my clothes.

I was up bright and early the next morning. Having some work to catch up on, I wanted to make sure to exercise. I skipped a few days the past week because it had been so hectic. Finished, I showered, changed into the Jenny-approved clothing, and sauntered to the Morning Pastry. John was already there. Waving, I ordered a cappuccino and a blueberry scone at the counter and joined him.

"I'm not sure my waist is going to thank you for introducing me to this place."

"It's good, isn't it?" I took a sip of my cappuccino. "How are you settling in?"

"I'm getting close to a house on Willow, just a few blocks from here." He pointed out the window due north.

"Is it that Craftsman on the corner? I thought I saw it was for sale."

"Yes. I like the attention to detail and the large front porch. It's good for people watching since this town is so walkable."

I smiled.

"Might be a bad subject, but I heard you were involved in some excitement again over at the church?"

"Unfortunately, someone murdered our postman, Ben Ford. He was such a nice man."

"I think I met him when I was getting a change-of-address form. What happened?"

"The girls, Jenny and Cindy, had been assisting Father Tom at the church, and unfortunately, they ended up tripping over Ben."

He settled back in his chair. "They seem to get mixed up in a lot around here."

I gave him a look. "They can't be blamed for this. They were just in the wrong place at the wrong time." I leaned forward. "Didn't you want to talk about my thoughts on the school district?" I took a bite of my scone.

"That, plus, I wanted to get to know you better." He smiled and moved closer.

My scone went down the wrong way, and I coughed. *Nice way to impress.* I tried to catch my breath.

"Are you all right? Would you like some water?"

"Yes, please," I squeaked.

He went to the counter for water and brought it back. I took a deep drink. "That's better. Sorry."

"I'm just glad you're no longer choking." He patted my shoulder.

"You said you want to get to know me better?"

"Yes, I'd like to be friends."

Friends. That's kind of middle of the road and noncommittal. I can do friends. "Sounds good. Why don't you start? Did you always want to be a superintendent of schools?"

He smiled and said in a confidential tone, "I don't think anyone aspires to be superintendent of schools when they are growing up. I wanted to be a teacher."

"Then why the change?"

"I realized I could have more control over the overall educational process."

"Do you like it?"

"I like parts of it. I miss being a teacher. I miss the day-to-day interaction with the kids. And sometimes the bureaucracy drives me nuts. What about you?" He encouraged me with his eyes.

"I have my own insurance agency in town. So when you close on your house, you may want to think about me."

"I will." He smiled. "Did you grow up wanting to be an insurance agent?"

I grinned. "Yes, I did. My dad was an agent. When I was young, I used to go with him on calls, and I saw how well respected he was in town. He helped people when they needed him most. That's what I try to do for my clients."

He took a sip of his coffee. "Sounds like a calling."

"In a way, maybe it is." I smiled. "Do you have any kids?"

"No. I just haven't found the right woman."

Someone hovered just on the edge of my vision. I looked up straight into Rob Jenson's sea-green eyes. I jumped. "Rob, I didn't see you come in." John stood. "Rob, I don't know if you've met John Gordan?"

"Actually, I have a call in to his office." Rob extended his hand. "John, I'm Rob Jenson, the new owner of the local newspaper, and I was thinking of doing a piece to introduce you to the community. Would you be interested?"

John shook Rob's hand. "Sounds great. Please let my assistant know where and when, and I'll make sure we get some time together."

"Merry, I was going to give you a call as well. I was wondering if you had heard any more about the postman's death?"

"I would think the police would know more than I."

Rob smiled. "Yes, but they aren't as cute as you."

Heat filled my face as Rob and John exchanged looks and stared down at me.

"She is pretty cute," John said. "I have to agree with you there."

Becoming even more flustered, I said, "Thank you both, but I need to be getting back home." Sliding out of my seat, I squeezed past Rob and tried to glide nonchalantly toward the door. "John, it was nice to get to know you better." *That went well. Not!*

CHAPTER 6

Waking up, I was concerned that Patty hadn't called or texted. I made a mental note to call her once it got to a decent hour. The cats were quite vocal this morning, letting me know I had been neglecting them. Tossing them a few treats, I stroked their fur as they inhaled them. Satisfied my pet owner's duty was finished for the moment, I decided to make my daughter happy with some cinnamon buns. I popped them in the oven and set the timer. Pulling over the paper, I sipped my coffee. The headline read, "Local teen person of interest in popular postman's demise."

I grabbed my phone and nearly knocked my coffee over. "Siri, call Patty."

"Hello."

"What happened? Why didn't you call me? What can I do to help?"

"There was no time to call you. Detective Ziebold questioned Cindy for four hours the other day. That's when Patrick and I decided it was time for a lawyer."

"A lawyer? They can't be serious. Who would suspect Cindy?"

"Apparently, the police do. Cindy didn't help her cause either."

"What do you mean?"

"Remember how you told me Jenny said Cindy had a stomachache and had disappeared?"

"Yes."

"Well, Cindy didn't tell the police that. She stuck to her story that she had been there the whole time. It was only after the lawyer got involved that she confessed she snuck away with Michael."

"Did Jenny know?"

"No. Cindy didn't want to tell her because she didn't want her to get into trouble. That's why she made up the story about her stomachache."

"Now that the police know the true story, she should be in the clear, right?"

"One would think so, but they also were very suspicious about how she got the cut on her hand. And now they have Michael in for questioning. It's such a mess."

"What a nightmare! What can I do?"

"Find the real killer!" Patty started crying. "I need to go. I have to get the other kids to school."

Hanging up the phone, I began to pace. Patty's request was a big one. My life had finally settled down to a comfortable existence. I was respected again in town. If I got involved, I might threaten that. But I couldn't let Cindy continue to be suspected. It was tearing Patty apart. I remembered writing a paper my senior year of college on the number of wrongful convictions each year in the United States. It stunned me and hasn't much changed today. The police do an admirable job, but sometimes people slip through the cracks. I couldn't let that happen to Cindy, no matter what the cost. She was like another daughter to me.

Resolved, I made a list of people to talk with. First was Barbara Ziebold. Maybe she'd be able to give me some information on what was happening. Second was Father Tom. It would be good to find out what he had told the detective. And third—deep sigh—was Rob Jenson. He certainly had been trying to get information from me. Turnabout is only fair play. The clock chimed. Barbara's kids should be in school by now.

Barbara lived only a few blocks away, and she had a famous sweet tooth. Deciding to take a quick detour to the Morning Pastry, I examined the shelves to see what looked appetizing. Suzie Krump, the owner, was behind the counter. "Hi, Suzie, how's the morning been?"

She smiled. "Busy—just the way I like it. What can I interest you in?"

"I was thinking about a coffee cake. What kind do you have?"

"I just pulled an apple-and-cinnamon swirl out of the oven. It's got a drizzle of vanilla icing on it and some toasted almond slivers."

My mouth watering, I nodded. "That will work."

After paying, I strolled the two blocks to Barbara's house. As I stood admiring the fall wreath on her door, I rang the doorbell.

Barbara opened it. "Merry, what a pleasant surprise. Come in."

I held the box in front of me. "I come bearing gifts."

"Mmm. I smell cinnamon."

"It's a coffee cake from the Morning Pastry."

"That will hit the spot! I just made some coffee. Let's go in the kitchen."

Sitting at her counter, we savored our first bites of the coffee cake. Barbara's eyes closed, and she had a slight smile on her face. "Not that I'm complaining, but what brings you by today?"

"Ben Ford's murder. I spoke with Patty Twilliger last night, and she said they've been questioning her daughter, Cindy."

She shifted in her seat, and her face became flushed. "You should leave this in my husband's capable hands."

"I know that, but there is no way Cindy was involved in this."

"All I can say is I've known Cindy all of her life, and it would be difficult for me to believe as well. However, Jay has to go where the evidence leads him, and right now there's not a lot, and what there is raises questions. I shouldn't say, but after everyone left the rectory the other night, he confiscated the paper towels from the trash. The techs were able to match the blood on the towels to some of the blood on the knife. That means Cindy was in contact with the knife."

"Her hand must have hit the knife when she fell over him. That must be how she cut her hand."

"That's not all. Jay searched Ben's house the other day. He mentioned that Ben seemed to be making large, regular deposits to his money market account."

"Why would that be suspicious? He was getting paid for his work as a postman, right?"

"Of course, but his paycheck was direct deposit. This was a set amount of $15,000 per month in cash. Jane Wilcox at the bank said he came in like clockwork on the third of the month for the past few months. They don't get many nonbusiness people with large cash deposits anymore." She took another bite of the coffee cake and stood. "I'm sure Jay will work it out. I hate to cut this short, but I have about fifteen loads of laundry to get to. I love all my boys, but they do generate a lot of mess."

I rose. "Thanks for being so straight with me. I appreciate it."

"You're a good friend." Holding my shoulders, she stared into my eyes. "I trust my conversation with you will not go any further."

"You can count on me."

I trudged out the door. Cindy was the only person they were looking at. Taking a deep breath, I squared my shoulders and headed for the rectory. Father Tom's assistant answered the door.

"Good morning, Belinda. Is Father Tom in?"

"Yes, he's in his study. Come in and give me a moment to see if he can take a break."

The entryway had such beautiful wood molding that always seemed polished to a high sheen. I reached out and sketched one of the curves with my finger.

"The father will see you now."

I jumped. "Thanks, Belinda. I appreciate it." She led me to his study.

I shook his hand. "Good morning, Father."

"Good morning, Merry. To what do I owe this pleasure?" We both sat.

"I'm worried about Cindy Twilliger and the murder of Ben Ford."

"The police will catch the guilty party, I'm sure. There's no need to worry."

"Patty's really worried, and when Patty's worried, I'm worried. What do you think happened?"

"I don't know. However, the police mentioned the knife that was used was from my pantry."

"Your pantry? How many people would have access to that?"

"Quite a few, unfortunately. As you know, I meet with any parishioner who has need of me, and most of the people in town have been through my door."

"But don't you see most of them in your office?"

"Yes, but my office is right down the hall from the kitchen." He pointed. "You've been in my kitchen many times yourself."

"That's true. When did you discover it was missing?"

"Neither Belinda nor I noticed it until Detective Ziebold asked about it. The last time Belinda remembered using it was a few days before Ben died."

"Well, then it should be easy to figure out who was here in that small window of time."

"As I told the detective, I do know who had appointments with me. However, sometimes people come unannounced, such as your pleasant arrival this morning."

I moved forward in my chair. "Do you remember who you saw prior to Ben's death?"

"I gave the police a list as well as Belinda and I could remember."

"Would you share it with me?"

"No." He shook his head. "When people come to me, they have an expectation of privacy, and I intend to respect that." He sighed. "However, I can tell you two of the people who had access."

"Really? Who?"

He smiled and waited a beat. "Cindy and Jenny."

I sighed. "Thanks for your time, Father. I appreciate it."

This was going to be a tough slog. Picturing Cindy's lovely face, I resigned myself to soldiering on. Gritting my teeth, I punched in Rob Jenson's number on my way back to the office. "Hi, Rob. It's Merry March. How are you today?"

"Merry, it's good to hear from you."

"I wondered if you'd be free for a drink this evening, say around five thirty?"

"That would be great. Where would you like to meet?"

"How about the Pickled Herring?"

"I'll see you there. I'm looking forward to getting to know you better."

I grimaced. "Me too."

CHAPTER 7

My afternoon was productive. At four thirty, I ducked out so I could prepare for my meeting with Rob. Letting the cats out for a few minutes, I touched up my makeup and ran a brush through my hair. Texting Jenny I was going out, I brought the cats in by tempting them with treats. That done, I went to the Pickled Herring. A few minutes early, I grabbed a table and asked for a glass of water. At five thirty exactly, Rob came in the door. *I like a man who is punctual.* We shook hands and sat.

"I'm glad you suggested this, yet somewhat surprised." Rob said.

"What do you mean?" I asked, my eyes wide. "I told you I'd get back to you in a few weeks."

He grinned at me. "I know, but I thought you were just letting me down easy."

Darn. What a great smile. I smiled back. "Not at all. How are you finding the newspaper business?"

"For a small town, there's a lot going on."

"What do you mean?"

Leaning forward, his eyes narrowed. "The murder was a biggie."

Shifting in my seat, I came to attention. "What have you found out?" Just then, the waiter approached.

"Let's order first. What would you like?"

"I'll have a glass of the Cabernet. Would you like to share an order of the calamari?"

"That would be great." Rob turned to the waiter. "The calamari and I'll have a pint of your house ale." After the waiter left, Rob smiled at me. "Now, where were we?"

"You were going to share what you found out."

"That's right. To be honest, I haven't gotten very far. I'm the new kid in town, and people are reluctant to talk to me." Rob rolled his cocktail napkin and then unrolled it. He fixed me with his brilliant green eyes. "I do know that the knife came from the priest's house and that the police believe the prime suspect is Patrick and Patty's daughter."

"It can't be Cindy. Have you heard anything else from the police?"

"Apparently, the priest—"

"Father Tom."

"Yes, Father Tom gave the police a list of people who had access to the rectory during the time frame in question."

"Were you able to get a copy of it?"

"No. They are playing it very close to the vest."

Our drinks and calamari arrived. Sighing, I bit into one. "I love the fried calamari here. It's nice and crispy, and it comes with a very tasty marinara sauce."

Rob ate a piece and smiled. "I agree. Some places don't cook it enough, and others overcook it so it tastes like rubber. If the rest of the food is as good, I'm going to come here more often."

"It is. I can attest to that."

Rob lowered his voice and moved closer. "I do know one person who was at the rectory."

"If you say Cindy Twilliger, I'm going to scream."

Sitting back in his chair, Rob gave me a strange look. "Why would I say that? You already know Cindy and your daughter were there."

"Never mind. I had a run-in with someone who thought he was being funny earlier. Who was there?"

Rob moved even closer and again lowered his voice. "John Gordan. He mentioned it when I ran into him after you left the Morning Pastry the other day."

"How did that come up?"

"We were commiserating about all of the things you have to do when you move. He talked about meeting with Father Tom to join the parish and the fact that they had coffee in the kitchen. He remarked on it because he said it was a departure from the larger parishes he had been a part of."

"Well, I can't see the superintendent of schools being a murderer."

"You never know. Stranger things have happened."

I swirled the wine in my glass. "What would you think about working together on this?"

"What do you mean?"

"I'm concerned about Cindy, and I know everyone in town. They're more likely to talk to me than to you."

"What about your feelings on reporters?"

"I'm willing to set them aside to tackle this issue."

Rob smiled. "Deal."

I clinked his glass. "So what's next?"

"I have a request in to see the autopsy report. Luckily this is an open-records state."

"When do you think you'll get it?"

"In the next day or so. I'll call you when it comes in."

The check came, and Rob moved to cover it with his hand. I snatched it up. "My treat. I invited you."

"Okay, but the next one is on me."

We both grinned and shook hands. "Do you need a lift?" he asked.

"No." I laughed. "Don't read into this, but I'd rather walk. Thanks for the offer."

Stretching my legs on the way home, I replayed our discussion. I was still concerned about working with him, but I was hopeful that between the two of us we would figure out who the killer was. When I opened my garden gate, Nancy waved to me from her porch. I joined her."Good evening, Merry. Coming home a bit late, aren't you?"

"No, not really. Just met a friend for a quick drink." I reached into one of her container mums and touched the soil, my hand coming away dry. "Do you want me to water this?"

"I'd appreciate it. It's difficult for me to reach up like that."

Retrieving the watering can, I poured a steady stream onto the plant. "I have a question for you."

"What is it?"

"You mentioned you and Ben Ford were friends the other day. I was just wondering if he seemed different or more worried in the last few weeks?"

"No, not especially. Though now that you mention it, he was kind of quiet the last time I saw him. He also said he might be planning a trip, and that was really odd."

I put the watering can next to the porch swing and sat. "Why?"

"He was a real skinflint. He hated to spend money, and he told me on more than one occasion that he never took vacations because they were just a waste of money. He'd say, 'Why go on vacation when you have a perfectly good roof over your head right here?'"

"That doesn't sound like someone who would be planning a trip."

"That's why I thought it was strange." Nancy sat back in her chair. "But we just had a quick conversation. I wish I had had more time to talk with him."

"If you think of anything else, please let me know."

"I will. I know you are concerned about Patty Twilliger's daughter."

"I am. Thanks."

Waving one last time, I let myself in the house. There was a note from Jenny that she was at the library studying, so I took a pad out and wrote down everything I had learned so far. Quickly heating up some soup and eating it, I headed upstairs for a long bath.

CHAPTER 8

Meetings all day helped keep my mind off the murder. There was a message from John Gordan on my desk when I returned. Smiling, I punched in his number.

"Hello?"

"Hi, John, it's Merry. I'm returning your call."

"Merry, it's good to hear from you. I wanted to follow up after you ran off the other morning."

I laughed. "I did not run off. It was just time to leave."

"Regardless, I wanted to see if you were free for dinner on Saturday?"

"That would be great. What time?"

"How about if I pick you up at six thirty?"

"I look forward to it."

Smiling like a girl about to go on her first date, I stuffed some things in my briefcase and walked out the door. The last one in the office, I locked the outer door. As I turned, Belinda Harper, Father Tom's assistant, scooted by. "Belinda."

"Hi, Merry. How are you?"

"Glad this busy day is over."

She looked at her watch. "You and me both! Father Tom has been having so many visitors it's hard to keep up."

"I'm sure it is." I tried to keep her talking. "That reminds me. Belinda, do you remember who visited the rectory the day Ben Ford died?"

She shifted her packages from one hand to the other. "I wasn't there the whole day, but let me think. You, of course, and Jenny, Patty and Cindy, that reporter fellow—"

"Rob Jenson?"

"Yes, that's him. Let's see, who else? Oh, that's right—the new superintendent, John Gordan. And, of course, poor Ben Ford came by late with the mail, God rest his soul. I think that's everyone. Oh, and Gloria Krump came by from the Morning Pastry. She brought a coffee ring for the evening Bible study group. I love their food, don't you?"

"Yes. It is tasty."

Belinda stopped fidgeting. "Why are you so interested in who came by the rectory?"

"I'm trying to see if I can help Patty with Cindy."

"I'm sure she had nothing to do with it. She's just a child."

"Belinda, would it be okay if I called you if I have other questions?"

"If I can help, I will, but I need to be getting home now."

"Thanks."

After stopping to pick up a few things for dinner, I rounded the corner to my house. Patty Twilliger sat on my front porch. Quickening my steps, I gave her a big hug before sitting beside her. "How are you?"

"Exhausted. And Patrick isn't much better."

"Are you running away from home?"

"Thinking about it. They've asked Jenny and Michael not to leave town. Needless to say, they weren't planning on it, but the fact that the police told them not to is really troubling."

I rubbed her shoulder. "I've started investigating, but it's been slow going. I've even teamed up with Rob Jenson."

Patty slowly raised her left eyebrow. "Isn't that interesting?"

"Nothing more to it than that, no matter what you are implying. In fact, I have a date with John Gordan on Saturday night."

She smiled. "You're becoming quite the popular lady."

"As I remember, you're the one who set me up." I leaned into her shoulder.

"I wasn't thinking you were going to go out with both of them. Plus, I thought you had sworn off men."

"Just weighing my options. It's early days yet. I may end up being just friends with one or both of them."

"Friends." She laughed and completed it with air quotes. "I need to get back."

"Let me know if there is anything you need me to do." I gave her a quick hug.

Finally opening the door, I put down my briefcase. Jenny sat at the kitchen table with four books open. Her elbow marked her place in one, a coffee mug another, and her hands the last two. I gave her a quick squeeze. "What would you do if you had another book?"

Without looking up, she quipped, "I still have my feet."

I laughed. "Are scallops okay for dinner?"

"Always!"

"I'm going to run up and change."

Coming back down in my sweatpants and T-shirt, I grabbed a glass of wine. I asked Jenny, "Have you talked to Cindy?"

"We've texted a few times, but she really hasn't had a lot of time to talk."

"Did she explain why she left with Michael the day you were helping Father Tom?"

"She said they needed to talk."

"About what?"

"She didn't tell me." Jenny returned to her book and made a quick note.

From her rigid body language, I could tell it was time to change the subject. "I have a date again on Saturday, so I'll need some wardrobe consultation."

"I'm always happy to help, but I need to finish this term paper now."

"I'll let you know when dinner's getting close."

"Thanks, Mom."

Chopping vegetables for a salad and mixing up some Italian dressing, I ran through the list of people who had visited Father Tom the day of the murder. I knew Patty, Cindy, Jenny, and I hadn't been involved. So that left Rob Jenson, John Gordan, Michael Kinsley—Cindy's boyfriend—Gloria Krump, and potential stragglers from the Elderflower funeral as well as Belinda and Father Tom. I really had to rule out Father Tom, and my heart told me that Belinda couldn't have done it. What about Rob and John? I really didn't know them that well, but they seemed like nice men. And Gloria had just been dropping off a coffee cake.

Feeling I was back to square one, I pulled out the frying pan to get it hot for the scallops. Some salt and pepper, a quick sear on both sides, and a quick toss of the salad meant it was dinnertime. Setting some places on the island, I bent over Jenny with a kiss. "Dinner's ready."

"Thanks. I'll wash my hands and be right with you."

I sat at the island. "What do you know about Michael Kinsley?"

"He seems to be a nice guy. He's in some of my classes at school, and he really likes Cindy."

"How long have they been dating?"

"I don't know—five or six months? Why all of the questions? Don't tell me you're into younger men now."

I rolled my eyes. "I'm just trying to learn more about him, especially since it seems he was in your vicinity the night Mr. Ford was killed."

"Mom, you can't think that a seventeen-year-old killed Mr. Ford!"

"Worse things have happened."

"Well, I can't believe it. What would make him do it?"

I speared a mushroom. "He could be hiding something."

"I've known him since freshman year. He's on Instagram and Snapchat. What could he be hiding that we wouldn't know about?"

"People aren't always what they seem, but I guess it is a long shot."

"It is a really long shot, and it didn't happen."

I rubbed Jenny's shoulder. "I just want to help Cindy."

"I want you to as well. But I don't think she'd appreciate you throwing her boyfriend under the bus."

I stood. "Message received. I'll clean up since you need to finish your paper."

After loading the dishwasher, I curled up in the living room with my book. Staring at the same paragraph for five minutes, I tossed the book aside and called Rob. He picked up on the third ring.

"Hi, Merry."

"Hi, Rob. I was wondering if you had heard back on the autopsy results."

"I just got them emailed to me and was planning on reviewing them. Do you have time for coffee tomorrow? I could meet at eight?"

I checked my phone. "That should work. I have a meeting at nine fifteen I need to leave for."

"I have some things to do too, but eight should give us enough time. The Morning Pastry?"

"I'll see you there tomorrow. Thanks."

"Looking forward to it."

Feeling like I had made some minimal progress, I was able to read my book until it was time for bed.

CHAPTER 9

At 7:55 a.m., I stood in front of the pastry shelves, narrowing down my selection. It was a tough choice between my usual blueberry scone and something more exotic like an apple fritter that looked bigger than my head. Since I was meeting Rob, I decided to go with the more diminutive scone. That and a skim milk latte ordered, I sat down to wait for him. At eight on the dot, he entered.

As he ordered, I took advantage of my chance to study him further. He had really good hair. I bet it's soft, and it looked thick. *It would be nice to run my fingers through it.* And his eyes were green, like mine, but with better hazel accents. It was also obvious he worked out. Too bad he was a reporter. Even worse, too bad he was a reporter who wrote well. He came over to join me at the table. Time for woolgathering ended, I looked up at him with a smile.

"You beat me here," he said.

"The siren call of the scone was too much for me."

"Did you see the apple fritter? I was really tempted."

"No. I didn't notice it." I winked. "Do you mind talking about the autopsy report while we eat?"

"No problem. There wasn't a lot there we didn't know." Rob handed me a copy of the report. "He died from blood loss resulting from the stab wound in his back. Plus, it looked like the knife was moved after he was killed."

"How powerful of a blow was it?"

He pointed to one of the sections. "It indicates the first blow was pretty powerful and was the cause of death. There was a contusion where the hilt of the knife hit. And it states that the person who did it had to have been relatively tall. The second blow was incidental."

I turned the page. "The second blow was probably caused by Cindy when she tripped over him and cut her hand. She couldn't have caused the first, though. Cindy's a small girl. She's only five-two. There's no way she could have done that."

"She might have been able to if she was standing above him on the steps."

"Whose side are you on?"

"Yours. I'm just trying to point out some of the troublesome areas in your story. However, I agree. It's a stretch to think someone that small would be able to commit this crime. But her boyfriend could have." He sipped his coffee.

"Wouldn't he have to have a motive? I just can't see it. What would make two seventeen-year-olds want to kill someone?"

"Unfortunately, it's happened before."

I inched forward and made sure I had full eye contact with him. "Yes, but not this time."

"Have you talked to Cindy?"

I sat back in my chair. "No. But I get your point. I should do that sooner rather than later. Do you think I should talk to her and Michael together?"

"It's probably best to see them separately. Who knows, maybe they saw something that would incriminate someone else. Do you want me to join you?"

"No. I think they'll give me more information if I'm alone."

"Your call. Would you like to have dinner tomorrow so we can continue this conversation?"

"Yes. I'll try to talk with both of them before we meet. Where would you like to go?"

"I've heard the Iron Skillet is good. Should we meet there at six thirty?"

I checked my calendar. "That would work. I need to run now or I'll be late for my staff meeting. See you tomorrow." I left the table and hurried to the office.

On my way, I juggled my phone and texted my daughter: "Would you see if Cindy would meet me at four at the house and if Michael would be willing to meet with me at four thirty?"

"Sure, if you promise to be nice."

I sent her back a smiley face and picked up the pace. Striding into the conference room, I took my seat just in time. There were some price changes coming from some of our insurance companies, and I wanted to make sure everyone knew the reasons for the changes. It was important that we be able to talk about them in the same way to our clients. Role-playing accomplished, we moved on to other matters and finished early. The day flew by, and before I knew it, I was going to have to hoof it to beat Jenny and Cindy to the house.

I unlocked the door. "Anyone home?"

Jenny answered, "We're in the kitchen."

Dropping my briefcase by the sofa, I joined them. I gave Jenny a quick hug and then gave Cindy a tighter one. "Thanks for coming to meet me, Cindy."

Cindy eyed the door. "I guess you want to talk about Mr. Ford's death."

"Yes, honey. I know you're probably tired of talking about it, but your mom asked me to see what I can do to help."

"It's just so frustrating. And it's hard to believe anyone would think Michael or I had anything to do with this. We're just kids."

"Would you take me through that day?"

"If you think it will help."

"It might."

"My mom took me to the church for Mrs. Elderflower's service. Jenny was waiting for me on the stairs. After that, Jenny and I helped out in the kitchen setting up the buffet and then serving the people who attended. I was there about twenty minutes when I remembered I told Michael I would try and sneak out so we could spend some time together to talk."

"Where did you meet Michael?"

"We met in the cemetery, behind the mausoleum with the angel on it. There's a bench back there under the big oak."

"What was so special you needed to sneak out?"

Jenny protested, "Mom, that's none of your business."

"Let me ask the questions," I said. "I'm not sure what's going to end up being important, and it's best to get as clear a picture as possible."

"You promise you won't tell anyone?" Cindy asked.

"I'll try not to, but if it ends up giving you an alibi, I'm not making any promises."

Cindy didn't look too happy, but she nodded. "We were talking about where to apply to college. My parents have been pretty vocal that my decision should be totally separate from Michael's, but I just know he's the one for me. I love him, and I can't stand the thought of being separated. We were trying to figure out how we could make it look like a coincidence that we ended up at the same school. It would be a lot easier if we were going to major in the same thing, but right now he's interested in writing, and I want to be an engineer."

"What did you decide?"

"We didn't come to a decision. We're still looking for schools that offer a good curriculum for both. That means we may have to go to a larger school, and we both wanted a smaller one." She started to cry. "It's tough."

"That's unfortunate." Rubbing her back, I handed her a tissue. "It's going to make your school decision harder than normal. But let's get back to that day now. When you and Michael were having your discussion, did you see anyone else?"

She blew her nose. "I saw some of the people who had been at Mrs. Elderflower's service returning to their cars, and I saw Miss Belinda going over to the rectory. That's about it."

"What happened next?"

"It was starting to get dark, so I kissed Michael goodbye and ran back to the church. Jenny and I finished cleaning up, and the rest you know."

I hugged her. "Don't worry. Everything has a way of working out for the best."

"I know you're just trying to help. Thank you. Michael's going to be here in a few minutes. May I stay while you speak with him?"

"No, I really think it's best I talk with you separately."

As Cindy was leaving, Michael ambled up the path. She gave him a quick kiss. "Tell her everything." His eyes widened, but he continued on to where we stood by the door.

I shook his hand. "Come in. I have some lemonade in the kitchen." I poured him a glass. "Mrs. Twilliger asked me to see if I can try to figure out what happened to Mr. Ford."

"I know. Cindy told me."

"Have a seat." I gestured to the chair next to me. He slid into it and put down his lemonade. It spilled a little on the table. "Don't be nervous. I just want you to tell me in your own words what happened that day."

He wiped the spill up with his napkin. "Cindy and I decided to meet in the cemetery. Do you know the big mausoleum with the angel on it?"

I nodded, and he continued, "We sat on the bench behind it. We were talking about which colleges we should apply to."

"What time did you leave?"

"I'm not sure. It started to get dark, and Cindy was worried someone would notice she wasn't there."

"Did you see anyone while you were talking?"

He took a sip of the lemonade. "There were some people leaving the funeral and Miss Belinda strolling toward the rectory. Mr. Gordan hurried by, going toward the rectory as well. He looked pretty angry."

"Mr. Gordan?"

"Yes, you know, the new school superintendent."

"Anyone else?"

"Not sure of his name, but the new guy at the paper. He rushed by, going away from the church. Those are the only people I remember." He paused, looking thoughtful. "Oh, wait. I saw that woman who works in the bakery. She was in a hurry too. I love their stuff, especially their donuts. And their apple fritters..."

I put my hand on his arm. "I agree. It's a great place, but you're making me hungry. Let's get back to that day. Where did you go after Cindy left?"

"I sat there for a few minutes, and then I went to the library to study. I'm still working on one of my papers, so if you don't mind, I really need to leave."

"No problem, but please call me if you remember anything else. And thank you, Michael, for your time. Jenny, would you please see Michael out?"

Jenny scrambled out of her seat. "Will do."

CHAPTER 10

The next day dawned bright and crisp with a hint of leaves burning in the air. I threw a load of wash in before preparing breakfast.

Jenny sprinted past me as she gathered her books. "I'm late. Love you!" I barely had time to shove a Pop Tart in her hand before she ran out the door.

I thought about my conversations with the kids the day before. Why was Rob Jenson hurrying away from the church? Why was John Gordan going toward the rectory? And why had John looked angry? I stuck two frozen blueberry muffins in the microwave to defrost, then wrapped them in a towel and grabbed my tea. Crossing the garden, I popped next door to see what Nancy knew about John. Elbowing the gate open, I managed not to spill anything. As usual, she sat there drinking her coffee.

"Good morning, Nancy. I thought you might enjoy a blueberry muffin and some company with your coffee."

"Don't mind if I do. It's a beautiful morning. We may only get another few weeks of this before winter sets in."

"We should have a little time before the snow. I'm not ready to start shoveling yet." I sat next to her and handed her a muffin.

She took a bite. "I love your muffins. I've just been sitting here looking at seeds. Never too early to start planning for next year." Her gaze sized me up. "I guess you didn't come over here to talk about gardening. What's up?"

"I was wondering what you knew about John Gordan."

"That's one good-looking fellow." She sipped her coffee. "I haven't met him yet, but I've seen him around. I believe he's from Clear Creek originally."

"Isn't that an old coal town?"

"Yes. It's pretty much a ghost town now."

I bit into my muffin. "It's so sad to see once vibrant towns die."

"It is, but I guess that's the way of things. I also seem to remember hearing something about an ex-wife and a messy divorce. Apparently, it wasn't amicable. Thank goodness there weren't any children."

I raised my eyebrows. "Ex-wife? I was under the impression he never married."

"He was married. Her maiden name was Sanders, Paula Sanders. She went back to it after the divorce. I think she moved away as well."

I nodded. "Interesting. Thanks for the intel. I guess I should get moving—work is calling." I turned to go. "Oh, by the way, is Melissa going to clean out Ben's house?"

"Yes. She spoke to Ben's heir, his nephew. He lives out of town, so he asked her to get things organized to prepare it for sale."

"Have the police released the house yet?"

"Yesterday, so she's planning on going over there early next week. Apparently, it's a big job."

"Would she be interested in any free help?"

"She's always interested in free." Her eyes narrowed. "Meredith March, what are you up to?"

"I was just thinking it might be beneficial to be there. I might find something that would tell us why this happened."

"The police didn't find anything. What makes you think you can?"

"Just a hunch. The worst that could happen is your cousin gets some free labor."

She sighed. "I'll give her a call. Thanks for the muffin. I'll let you know."

Why hadn't John mentioned he'd been married before? I grabbed my briefcase and headed out for work.

My assistant quickly followed me into my office to discuss urgent business. Next, I turned to my emails. I texted Patty: "My house eight forty-five tonight?"

"Can do. Have wine uncorked, rested, and poured."

"Really? Rested?"

"Okay, lowering standards. Just uncorked and poured."

"See you then."

The brisk breeze felt good on my face as I strode home after such a hectic day. I opened my front door. "Anyone here?"

Jenny's voice answered from the living room. "In here." She lay sprawled on the couch.

"Tough day?" I asked.

She held up her phone. "Not too bad. Just making sure I didn't miss anything."

I rolled my eyes. "Heaven forbid. Is this outfit good enough for the Iron Skillet?"

"Should be. Who are you meeting?"

"The reporter."

"Again? Is that a good idea? Isn't he one of our suspects?"

"I'm sure he has a good explanation. I plan to ask him about it tonight."

"I guess mothers know best." I started to smile, and then she continued, "Or at least some mothers, not necessarily you." She smirked.

I threw a pillow at her and climbed the stairs. "Not that you deserve it, but I defrosted some shepherd's pie for you—it's in the fridge. All you need to do is nuke it."

Quickly freshening up, I made my way back downstairs. "Love you." I left.

Back in the fresh air, I debated taking the car versus walking, and walking won. That decided, I turned right and headed toward town. The ornate streetlights, beautiful trees, and graceful, large homes with wide front porches accentuated the look of an old-fashioned village, which it was. I passed my brick storefront office and continued on for another ten minutes before reaching the Iron Skillet. A minute or two late, I was escorted to the table. "You beat me this time. I'm going to blame it on this beautiful fall weather."

"I haven't been waiting long. Plus, it gave me a chance to take a look at the menu. This is my first time eating in the dining room. I did sample a few items when I interviewed the chef for my 'Eat the Town' article."

"I'm not sure what she cooked that day, but you're in for a treat. This is my go-to place for true comfort food." I pointed at the menu. "My favorite is 'Grandma Pam's Meatloaf Extraordinaire,' but everything else I've tried is great too."

"I'm a meatloaf fan, so I'll take you up on your suggestion."

The waitress came and took our order. Rob asked, "Were you able to talk with Cindy and Michael?"

I sighed. "Yes. They're sweet kids but infuriating. The big secret reason they had to meet was to conspire on colleges."

"Colleges?"

"Yes. Apparently, it's true love, and they don't want to be separated."

"Ah, to be young again."

I took a sip of my wine. "When I was young, everything seemed so urgent, so vital."

"And today?"

"I think age gives perspective." I smiled ruefully. "Or maybe it's just the waning hormones."

He raised an eyebrow. "We're not that old yet."

Blushing, I hurried to change the subject. "Both of them said they saw John Gordan hurrying to the rectory. I wonder what was so urgent."

"Why don't you ask him?"

"I will. I'm having dinner with him on Saturday."

Rob's eyes widened. "You just had breakfast with him."

"That was a week or so ago."

He leaned forward. "I think you should be careful."

"Of John? He seems like a nice guy."

"He's a nice guy who was seen hurrying to where a murder took place. I care about you and think you should be wary."

My mouth dropped open. Luckily the server interrupted with our meals.

After a few minutes, Rob said, "You're right. This meatloaf is terrific!"

"Michael told me one other thing."

"Really? What?"

"He said he saw you hurrying away from the church."

Frowning, Rob examined the silverware. "That must have been around four. Mary Lou Turner called to tell me Sam Tuttle had hooked a whopper of a catfish over at the lake. I ran over to get a picture for the paper." He scrolled through his phone and pulled up the photo from the Facebook page. "Here it is. I didn't end up running it that day because Ben's death took precedence."

"Then how did you end up back at the church? Jenny and I saw you there when we were leaving."

Sitting back, Rob put his hands up. "I'm starting to feel like I'm being cross-examined."

"You want me to ask John the same questions. It's only fair you answer them too."

He rested his elbows on the table. "Okay. I have nothing to hide. Beth Humphreys, the woman who lives next to the church, called me to say the ambulance and police were there in force. Being the newsman I am, I rushed back in time to catch you and Jenny leaving." Satisfied, he crossed his arms, leaned back in his chair, and smiled. "Any more questions?"

"No, but I reserve the right to ask others if they come up." I smiled back. "I think we're done here."

"Want a ride?"

"No. The night is too beautiful and I ate far too many calories to ride."

"You're right. I did too, so I'll go you one better. I'll walk you home and then come back for the car."

We strolled silently for a few minutes, and then I asked, "Do you really think I should be concerned about John?"

"I don't know, but I think it would be good to err on the side of safety. There seems to be something a bit off about him."

I jostled him with my elbow. "Sure you're not jealous?"

"That could contribute to it. But seriously, think about it." We arrived at my garden gate.

"I will. Thanks for dinner. I enjoyed it." I gave him a quick kiss on his cheek.

"Me too." He turned back to the restaurant. "Talk to you tomorrow."

Heading into the house, I waved at his retreating back. I took out a wine bottle, uncorked it, and pulled out two glasses. *He said he cares about me.* I shook my head. *Don't read more into it than what's there.* I smiled.

"What's the smile about?" Patty came into the kitchen.

I jumped. "Crap, you scared me. I almost dropped the glasses!"

"Good thing you weren't holding the wine. Speaking of which, make yourself useful and pour me a glass."

Giving her a stern look, I complied. "Living room?"

"Yes, I'm in the mood to sprawl. Where's Jenny?"

"Upstairs studying. More importantly, how are you doing? What have you heard from the police? You seem a lot more relaxed. "

"I am. Good news—both Michael and Cindy were cleared. Apparently, two people who were at Mrs. Elderflower's funeral saw Cindy and Michael on the bench in the cemetery during the time the coroner believes Ben Ford was attacked. That, plus the fact no one saw Cindy with a cut on her hand at the church before she left meant she was telling the truth when she said she tripped over him."

"That's great news! I'm so relieved. This calls for a toast. To the police finding the real killer and to Cindy and Michael being cleared." We clinked glasses.

Patty sank back deep in the sofa and put her feet up on the coffee table. "This wine really hits the spot. Let's talk about something other than the murder. Which reminds me, did I just see Rob Jenson leaving here? Catch me up on your love life."

"There is no love life. However, I did meet with Rob a few times to compare notes on the murder we are no longer discussing." Courvoisier jumped up on my lap and head butted my hand. I petted her.

Patty smiled. "I'm sure that was the only reason."

"We're just friends."

"I thought you weren't friends with reporters."

"There's an exception to every rule."

She rolled her eyes. "Moving on. What's going on with John Gordan? Don't you have a date with him Saturday?"

"I do. And I just learned something very interesting from Nancy Piedmont. She said John was married before and went through a messy divorce."

"I thought he told you he hadn't been married."

"That was the impression he gave me. I'm going to ask him about it when I see him on Saturday."

"That's nice." She snuggled deeper into the couch. "Before I fall asleep, remind me to thank you for investigating for us. Now that Cindy and Michael have been cleared, you can stop and leave it to the police."

"It's not that easy. Both Cindy and Michael saw John Gordan hurrying to the rectory that day."

She laughed. "So? Maybe he was in a rush to talk to Father Tom about an annulment."

"Not funny. Rob told me to be careful on Saturday. What if the police think John did it? What if he did do it? I'm dating him. Am I setting myself up for failure again?"

Patty sat up and put her hand on my shoulder. "You told Rob you were going on a date with John?"

"Way to focus in on the important stuff. Yes, I told him. I have nothing to hide, and we're just friends."

Patty raised her glass and laughed. "First, you need to trust yourself more, and second, I think you're fonder of the luscious Mr. Jenson than you're letting on."

CHAPTER 11

While I hurried to put the finishing touches on my makeup, the clock chimed. I wasn't sure why I even bothered, but I didn't think Jenny would let me out of the house without it. She had checked in twice already to see how the outfit-picking was going. She also told me she planned on a full inspection before I left. Putting on a quick spritz of perfume, I came out of the bedroom just as the doorbell rang. Jenny answered the door as I strode down the steps.

"Hi, John, I'll be with you in just a minute." I ducked into the kitchen to grab my purse and phone. When I joined them, Jenny and John were chatting about how the school year progressed. "Ready to go?"

"Yes. Good speaking with you, Jenny."

When we got into the car, I asked, "Where are we going?"

"I thought we'd try the new pub, the Screaming Pigeon. It's not a very appealing name, but I've heard the food is good."

"I think you're right on the name. It's not very appetizing."

"True, but we only live once."

"What's new on the house front?"

"The good news is my offer was accepted and the inspection turned out okay. The closing is scheduled for next week."

"That's great! From the outside, the house looks like it has good bones."

"I think it does. I'll have you over after I close so you can take a look at the inside."

"I'd enjoy that."

Almost all of the parking spots were taken at the restaurant, but John found one toward the back by the dumpsters. "Wow. The food must be good," he said as we entered. "Reservation for Gordan."

"Follow me." The hostess took us to a secluded booth.

"Good spot." I surveyed the wood-heavy, rich, dark décor.

After taking a few moments to look over the menu, we ordered. The waitress brought our wine, and I toasted, "To your new house."

"It will be nice to get out of temporary housing and get my things out of storage."

I put my napkin in my lap. "It's been so long since I've moved, yet I still remember the hassle. Plus, it seemed like my possessions grew."

"They do. I found myself buying things I already had just because I needed them and my stuff was in storage."

"That's true. It's hard to get by without a potato peeler."

He gave me a strange look.

"If you were Irish, you'd know you can't go more than two weeks without one." I smiled. "Or at least I can't."

"I'm going to enjoy cooking again versus going out all the time."

My eyes widened. "You cook?"

"Why the surprise? Men cook."

"I know that. Some do it quite well. You just didn't seem the cooking kind."

"Ah, like Blanche DuBois you thought I got by on the kindness of strangers?" He gestured as if to twirl the mustache ends he did not have.

"No. Actually, I don't know what I mean." I took a sip of my wine to regroup. "What's your favorite thing to cook?"

"It's a cliché but steak on the grill. I'll have to make it for you once I'm set up." He rubbed my arm, his eyes issuing a different type of invitation.

"Works for me. I like to cook, but being cooked for is even better!" I raised my glass to him, and we toasted.

Our meals arrived, and we spent a few moments concentrating on eating.

"My stroganoff is terrific," I said.

"This corned beef is one of the best I've ever tasted."

"I'll be putting this restaurant on my 'visit again' list."

"Me too."

"Speaking of revisiting, John, tell me more about yourself. Where did you grow up, first have your heart broken, that kind of thing.

"I grew up in a small coal-mining town called Clear Creek. Have you heard of it?"

I smiled. "I think I may have heard of it once."

"It's one of those 'don't blink or you'll miss it' kind of places."

"Everyone must know everyone, kind of like here."

He grimaced. "True, and that can be both good and bad."

"How so?" I searched his eyes, sensing the undercurrent of emotion.

"It's tough to reinvent yourself when the collective town memory is so long."

I laughed. "It sounds like you may have been a troublemaker when you were younger."

"Nothing major, just kid stuff. It was more lowered expectations of me based on genetics. Even in small coal towns there is a class system."

"Where were you on that spectrum?"

"Dead last. Or so it felt to me. I look at how much kids have today, and I remember my childhood where the little we had was from church donations or Goodwill. My dad only worked sporadically. He was a drunk, and my mom ran away to find herself when I was five."

I rubbed his shoulder. "Was it just you and your dad?"

"Yes. But it's just me now. His liver finally gave out ten years ago."

"That's rough. You've done well for yourself. How did you get here?"

"Holing up in the public library for as many hours as it was open, scholarships, and leaving that town for good when I turned eighteen."

"I'm sorry." I put my hand back on the table and fidgeted with my water glass.

"Don't be. My upbringing made me stronger and more resilient. It made me want more for myself and taught me never to settle for less than what I want, no matter what stands in my way." John stabbed his index finger into the table to emphasize the end of his statement.

I unconsciously shifted back from the table. "Strong words."

"They're true, at least for me they are."

"But you've accomplished so much."

"There's more to come. I still have goals I'm working on." He drew back and sipped some water. "That's my start in life. Now let's talk about you. Is this the town where you grew up?"

I took a breath to steady myself after such vehemence. "No, I grew up in the town next door. It was more blue-collar then, and even though we didn't have a lot of money, we were comfortable. As I mentioned before, my dad was the local property and casualty insurance representative, and a lot of people looked up to him. My mom was a travel agent, back when you could do that and make some money. She had an inquisitive, adventurous spirit, and that job meant she could go on lots of great trips for very little money. They're both gone now, and I miss them tremendously."

"I envy you your childhood."

I looked him straight in the eye. "I've always felt I was lucky to be so loved. Similar to you, I worked hard for scholarship money so I could go to a good school. I majored in business and psychology, a perfect fit for the business I run now."

The waiter came back, and we debated ordering desserts. I opted for a decaf cappuccino and John went for the "Heavenly Chocolate Cake." A smart man, John asked the waiter to bring two forks.

"Where were we?" I asked.

"We were discussing how our schooling matched our career aspirations."

I smiled. "I guess we really knew what we were doing back when we were sure we didn't."

"I wouldn't say that. I'm pretty driven, and I always have a plan."

"Good for you. I would refer to my life as part serendipity, part plan, and part genetics."

"Genetics would have argued against me, which was why I needed to plan."

I nodded slowly. "What about fun?"

"I do have fun. That can be planned too."

I barely restrained myself from rolling my eyes. "Let's agree to disagree on the need for fun to necessarily be a planned activity."

My coffee and John's dessert arrived. My willpower was sorely tempted, but I did not immediately go for a fork. After noting my intense stare, he kindly invited me to dig in. Holding myself to a few modest bites, I showed great restraint by putting my fork down. "What about your love life?"

"Well, there's a certain lovely lady with auburn hair and green eyes I'm interested in right now." He reached his hand across the table to hold mine.

My stomach gave a pleasant tumble. "That's flattering, but I was referring to previous entanglements."

"Entanglements? Is that where we're headed?"

I blushed and carefully withdrew my hand. "To be determined. It's been terrific getting to know you better, but it's getting late."

John asked for the bill and winked. "Next time I'll cook for you at my new house."

"Can't wait to see it."

CHAPTER 12

Lying in bed the next morning, I nudged Drambuie from my arm so I could reach my phone. I texted Patty. "Weird night. Time to chat?"

"Later this afternoon?"

"Works. I'll call you."

A few moments later, my phone dinged again. Thinking it was Patty, I was surprised to see it was from Rob. I did a double take.

"You home?"

"Yep."

"Going to church?"

"Thinking ten-thirty service."

"Mind if I join you? Breakfast on me after."

"Okay. Meet you out front of the church."

"See you there."

What was that all about? I went to Jenny's room and knocked on the door. "Time to get up sleepyhead."

"Sleepyhead yourself. I've been up for an hour."

I peeked in. "You win. Leaving for church in forty-five minutes."

She looked at me in exasperation. "Mom, Cindy and I went to the five-thirty Saturday service so we could study together today. You and I talked about it at lunch yesterday. Don't you remember?"

I looked down. "Now I do. One day you'll be as old as me and will have difficulty remembering everything too."

"Doubtful."

"Regardless. I'm going to meet Rob at church, and we're having breakfast afterward, so I probably won't be home till one."

She gave me a teasing smile. "I thought we didn't like reporters."

I gave her a dirty look. Forty-five minutes later, I left and headed for the church. I waved at Nancy, who sat on her porch, the vibrant reds and oranges of her trees and mums glowing around her. Rob waited for me at the front of the church, and I grinned as we strolled in together. That smile was quickly wiped from my face as I saw Patty raise her eyebrows. Rob and I sat a few rows behind her.

I smiled at Rob. "I'm happy you suggested getting together. Was there a special reason?"

He nodded. "I wanted to bring you up to date on a few things." He picked up the hymnal and thumbed through it. "I also wanted to make sure you made it home safe last night."

"Of course I did."

The Mass began, so we stopped talking, but I gave him a sidelong glance.

At the end of the service, we left the church and chatted on the front steps with Father Tom about how much we enjoyed his homily. Patrick and Patty stalked us at the bottom of the steps. Rob and I joined them.

"Beautiful day." Patty gave me a meaningful look.

"Yes, it is," I replied in an even tone.

Patty said, "Rob, I don't think I've seen you at this service before."

"I've been trying different times to see which one I like best."

"Have you decided?"

Rob looked down at me and smiled. "This one was best."

I blushed. "Well, we should be going now."

Patty grinned. "I'll see you later."

"What was all that about?" Rob asked.

"Nothing. Patty just has my best interests at heart."

"And she thinks I don't?"

"We only met a few weeks ago. The jury's still out."

"Cut me to the quick!" He pantomimed a knife stabbing him in the chest and staggering. He then extended his arm forward. "The Iron Skillet awaits."

"I love their blueberry pancakes."

Ambling to the restaurant, we chatted about his action-packed Sundays when he was reporting abroad. After getting settled into our booth and ordering, I said, "I've been wondering why you texted this morning. What did you want to bring me up to date on?"

"I've been doing some research on your friend John Gordan."

I took a sip of my tea. "It sounds like you are obsessing."

"You have to admit, he was near the church when the postman was killed."

"But we were too."

"Yes, but we know we didn't do it."

"I know I didn't do it."

"You can't believe I did." He covered my hand with his.

"I'm just saying you're new to town and had the opportunity." I pulled my hand back, and his face fell. "That said, however, I don't think you did it." I waited a beat. "Mostly because I checked out your alibi: Mary Lou, Sam, and Beth backed you up." I sat back with a self-satisfied smile.

"You checked out my alibi?"

"Sure did."

He grinned. "That was smart of you. Now, let's get back to John. Are you interested in what I found out about him?"

"Yes."

"Did you know he was married before?"

"I had heard that."

"You knew he grew up in Clear Creek?"

"Yes, my neighbor told me that and John did last night as well." I motioned for him to continue.

"There was a man named Hugh Sanders in Clear Creek who owned the coal mine. His daughter's name was Paula."

"That was the name of John's wife."

"Yes. Apparently, they hooked up in college and married not too long after graduation. They moved back to Clear Creek, and John started working for Hugh while he studied for his master's in education. Hugh gave them a very handsome down payment on their house, and his company paid for John's continuing education."

"So?" I picked up my napkin and blotted my lips. "Many parents help their kids out with their first home. And many companies defray the cost of advanced education for their employees."

"Maybe with some financing but both? That's really generous."

"They were lucky."

"They sure were. Unfortunately for Paula, her luck ran out."

"What do you mean?"

"Just as John finished his studies, the mine started to fail and Hugh went belly-up. Paula moved her father in with them, and within weeks, John filed for divorce. Since the house was in both of their names, he forced her to sell it so he could get his cash. That left both Paula and her father without a house and without much money. Hugh died shortly after, and Paula was left to deal with her father's creditors. To say it was a bitter divorce is an understatement." Rob leaned back in his chair and took a bite of his pancake.

My mouth hung open. "How did you find all this out?"

"I have my sources, and some of it was public record."

"I admit it doesn't sound like a ringing character endorsement, but there are two sides to every story."

"What has he told you about his marriage?"

"Actually, that hasn't come up yet."

69

Rob looked down at the table and examined his spoon. "He hasn't mentioned it yet?"

"No. I tried to bring it up last night, but it was getting late." I picked up the syrup pitcher, turned it, and put it back down. I met Rob's gaze. "He kind of sidestepped the subject. But what does this have to do with Ben Ford's death?"

"Nothing that I know of, but I think it's important to find out more about people who had opportunity."

"One other thing doesn't mesh between your story and what John told me. John said he left at eighteen and never went back. If your source is correct, he did go back."

"That part is public record. He was listed as one of the officers of the company."

"Maybe he just didn't want to talk about it." My stomach started to churn. Could John have done it? I didn't do credit to the delicious pancakes on my plate.

Rob frowned. "What did you talk about last night?"

"That's really none of your business." I rose. "I need to powder my nose. I'll be back in a minute."

Why is this bothering me so much? I'm not seriously dating John. I carefully patted my face with cold water, checked my makeup, and took a few deep breaths. Feeling better, I returned to the table.

Rob rose to greet me. "Are you okay?"

"Yes. It's just a lot to take in."

He gave me a worried look. "I'm ready to go if you are."

We sauntered back to my house. He faced me. "We're still partners in this investigation, aren't we?"

"Yes. Although it seems strange now that Cindy and Michael are no longer suspects. I don't have a horse in this race."

"From what I know of you, you want to know the truth. This happened in our town. How can people feel safe with the killer still on the loose?"

"You're right, but that's Detective Ziebold's job, not ours."

"He won't mind a little help."

"I'm not sure he would echo that." I opened my door. "Thanks for breakfast and for coming with me to church. I'll see you soon."

Softly closing the door, I crept over to peek out the front window. Rob stood there for a few moments staring at the house and then left.

"What are you staring at?" Jenny asked.

I jumped. "Don't do that!"

"Sorry. I thought you heard me."

"Well, I didn't!"

She peered around me. "Anyhow, what were you looking at?"

"Rob Jenson. We just got back from brunch."

"Starting to be a thing, Mom."

"Just friends. Didn't you say you were going to study with Cindy?"

"I'm leaving now. Love you." She followed up with a quick kiss on my cheek and hopped out the door.

Sitting at my desk, I worked on my bills. Most were on autopay, but there were a few I needed to take a look at. Just as I felt like I could concentrate again, my phone dinged with a text from Patty: "Can come now. Okay?"

"Works."

After tidying up my desk, I went to the living room. A few moments later, Patty stuck her head through the front door. "Anyone home?"

"Come in. Do you want some lemonade?"

"Fresh squeezed?"

"Is there any other kind?"

"Yes, the kind that I use. It comes frozen in a can; you add water and stir." She winked. "Since you put in all that extra work, I would love a glass." She came into the kitchen. "What's up, girlfriend? What's so weird?"

"Nothing much—Rob's investigating John, John may be lying to me, and Ben Ford may have been blackmailing someone."

"Whoa. That's a lot to take in. Can we take this one thing at a time?" Patty began pacing as she listed off the topics to discuss. "Why is Rob investigating John?"

"He says we should find out more about each potential suspect."

She halted in mid-stride. "He thinks John is a suspect?"

"He was seen going toward the rectory at around the right time."

"Makes sense, but is there an element of jealousy working?" She smiled.

"I asked that. He says not."

"Next, why do you think John might be lying to you?"

"First, he was married, and every time I bring up the subject of past loves, he changes the subject." I handed her a glass of lemonade.

"That's odd."

"And second, he said he left his hometown at eighteen, but Rob says that he went back to live there after college."

Patty pointed at me. "I think you should have a discussion with John about the discrepancies."

"That's going to be tough. How would I lead off? We've been investigating you, and there are some inconsistencies in your stories? How's he going to feel about that?"

She took a sip of the lemonade and continued pacing. "We need to figure out a way to lead into it gently without being quite so forthright."

I sat, putting my head in my hands, and moaned. "My head hurts."

"Not surprising. This is a tough one." She lifted my chin. "What was the last thing? Something about Ben Ford blackmailing someone?"

"He's been making regular, large cash deposits over the past few months. Blackmail is the only reason I could come up with. Nancy is going to ask her cousin Melissa to let me come with her when she cleans out Ben's house. That will give me a chance to see if I can find any proof."

"Didn't the police search his house?"

"Yes. This may be a wild goose chase, but I need to do it."

"You worry me."

"Rob said the same thing, and he doesn't even know about this yet."

"I thought you were working together?"

"We are. I just haven't found the right time to talk to him about this with everything else that has been going on."

Patty rolled her eyes.

CHAPTER 13

As I was leaving for work the next morning, Nancy motioned to me from her porch.

"I spoke with Melissa. She said she's scheduled to begin the cleanup of Ben's place on Thursday. Will you be able to make it?"

I nodded and checked my phone. "I'll make it work. Thanks for doing this."

"Ben was a good man. I want to make sure his killer is caught."

While I walked to work, my mind raced. Patty was right. If Rob and I were working together, I should be sharing all the information I had. Why was I holding back?

Opening the door to my storefront, I was distracted by Cheryl putting up one of our new product displays. "That looks great. I know your creativity will spur questions from our clients on what we have to offer. Thanks for setting this up."

Cheryl grinned. "Thanks for the opportunity to show you what else I can do."

"That's what I like about you: your can-do spirit!"

"Oh, by the way, Rob Jensen called. He'd like you to call him back."

"Will do. Thanks."

After checking my desk for urgent items, I made a to-do list for the day. I punched in Rob's number. He picked up on the second ring.

"That was fast."

I smiled. "We aim to please."

"You seemed upset by what I told you last night, and I wanted to see if you had any other questions. I also wanted to make sure you know my motive is pure in investigating John. It isn't because I'm jealous of him."

"So you are jealous of him?"

"You know what I mean."

"I do. And I appreciate the phone call. It gives me a chance to bring you more up to date."

"Something happened overnight?"

"No. It's something I learned the other day."

"Why did you wait so long to tell me? I thought we were working together?"

"We are. I heard something, and I needed some time to mull over what it might mean."

"Well?"

"Ben had been making some large cash deposits for the past few months. I think he might have been blackmailing someone."

"That's a big leap. How did you find out about the deposits?"

I tapped my pen on the desk. "Just like you, I have my sources."

"Do you trust the person?"

"Yes."

There was a pause. "Why blackmail?"

"What else could it be? The deposits were in cash and were for the exact same amount each month."

"Maybe Ben had loaned someone some money and they were paying him back in cash."

"Maybe. Regardless, I figured out how to investigate further."

"How?"

"My source's cousin has been asked to clean Ben's place up so his nephew can sell it. She's agreed to let me help her. I'm going to use that opportunity to see if I can get any proof."

"I don't think it's safe for you to be investigating."

"Who's going to find out?"

"I don't know, but I worry about you. When are you scheduled?"

"Thursday."

"I want you to text me every hour on the hour."

"Seems excessive, but if it will make you feel better—"

"It will."

"Okay, I promise. I have to get some work done, so I need to hang up."

"Me too. Remember, every hour."

"Yes, Dad."

As soon as I hung up, Cheryl came in. "I've been trying to rearrange Thursday so you can take the day off. Do you mind staying late tonight and Wednesday so I can squeeze in some of your appointments?"

"That should be okay. Let me double-check with Jenny to make sure I don't have any commitments she hasn't shared with me."

"Is it just Thursday, or are you going to need Friday too?"

"Better clear Friday. If I get done early, I can always take Jenny to the lake."

"That sounds nice. Want to take me too?"

"Cheryl, you know you are always welcome."

"That means a lot." She smiled as she left.

I sat there for a few minutes and took a breath. Was life getting more complicated, or was I complicating it? No matter. Either way I ended up at the same place.

* * *

Thursday was one of those sunny, blue-sky days that make you feel glad to be alive. As I strolled over to Ben's house, I marveled at the reds, golds, and browns of the changing trees. The air smelled clean. I rang the doorbell, and Melissa answered.

"Thanks for coming. I wasn't sure you were going to make it."

I smiled at her as I entered. "Of course I came. I said I would." My smile drooped. Ben's living room had piles of stuff everywhere.

"I told him he needed to throw stuff out. I worked hard to make sure the place was at least somewhat clean, even with all the piles."

I took a deep breath. "Where do we start?"

"I'll start in here. Based on what Nancy told me, you may want to start in Ben's office. It's the second door on the left. The brown bin is trash, the blue recyclable, and the red is stuff that needs to be shredded. Let me know when they get full. I contracted with an organization that will take it from there and give you fresh bins."

A bit overwhelmed, I plotted my way around the stacks to the office. "Thanks." I carefully maneuvered there successfully. Luckily the door was ajar or I don't think I would have been able to get through. I edged through the piles in the office to find a relatively clear desktop and chair. I sat at the desk and got started. Three hours later, I was pleased to see I had made a small dent in the room.

Melissa poked her head through the door. "Pizza's here if you are hungry."

My stomach growled. "You bet."

When I joined her in the kitchen, my mouth dropped open. It was clean and uncluttered.

Melissa took a slice of the pizza as she gazed in satisfaction and nodded. "You seem surprised."

"I am. The difference between the kitchen and the rest of the place is night and day."

"I told Ben three years ago that there wasn't any point in me cleaning if the kitchen and bathrooms were just as clogged as the rest of the house. He must have really wanted it clean because he agreed and we spent two weeks getting rid of stuff in this room. He kept it uncluttered from that point on. Of course, the other rooms just got worse."

"I noticed."

"Find anything?"

"I found receipts for books he bought twenty years ago, tax returns since he started working at age sixteen, and what appears to be every new stamp issued since he started working at the post office. I've set the stamps aside in case the nephew wants them or wants them sold to other collectors."

"I'm putting anything that might be of value in the small back bedroom." She gestured toward the hallway. "I started there first, so it's clean. Ben's nephew is coming back in a week or so depending on when they release Ben for burial."

Finished with lunch, I took the stamps across the hall to the small bedroom. After the chaos of the office, it looked serene and neat, aside from the few piles of potential valuables on the bed. I put the stamps down. There wasn't much to see: a small twin bed, a dresser, and a tiny closet. As I opened the closet, I noticed that the wood floor looked strange. It was level, but the pattern seemed wrong. I stepped back and studied the floor in the bedroom. The wood planks were the same and they were of staggered lengths. When I checked the closet again, I realized what bothered me. The planks were cut to the same length in the corner of the closet.

I grabbed a small nail file from my purse. Kneeling in the closet, I inserted the nail file, pried a bit, and a small section of the floor lifted up. In the space between the joists was a bag. Pulling it out, I found a ledger inside. Luckily I carried a "mom" purse Jenny teased could hold a small nuclear missile. Tossing the book in my purse, I closed up the opening in the closet and returned to the office to continue clearing it out.

At four thirty, Melissa poked her head around the corner. "Quitting time."

Stretching, I looked at my watch. "Already?"

"Yes. You put in a full day." She laughed. "You could always come back tomorrow."

"No. I'm sorry, but I promised my daughter I'd take her to the lake."

"I can see why you'd prefer that over this any day." She smiled. "Thanks for doing this. I don't often get free labor. Did you find anything helpful?"

Avoiding her eyes, I stared at the floor. "Oh, by the way, were all of the bedrooms cleared out when the police searched?"

"No. They wouldn't let me in till this week to start removing all this stuff."

"Wow. It must have been tough for them to find anything."

Melissa grinned. "To be honest, I think they saw the living room and just kind of gave up."

The doorbell rang, and Melissa answered it. Rob stood on the porch. "Hello?" she asked.

"Rob, what are you doing here?" I sputtered, as I realized I had completely forgotten to text him the last two hours.

He smiled. "Looking to see if you were done for the day." He held his hand out to Melissa. "I'm Rob Jensen."

She shook his hand. "Melissa Stone. Pleased to meet you."

I moved out the door to join Rob. "Thanks again, Melissa. I'll see you around."

She waved and shut the door.

Rob frowned. "I thought we had an agreement?"

"We did. I'm sorry. I got focused on the task at hand and forgot."

"Did you find anything?"

"Let's go back to my place instead of discussing this on Ben's stoop."

We footed it back to my house, the ledger burning a hole in my purse. I unlocked the door and invited Rob in.

"Nice place."

"It suits Jenny and me."

"I like your gardens too."

"They're not half as nice as Nancy's next door, but I don't have the kind of time she does. They take some work, but I think they're worth it. You should see them in spring."

"I'll take that as an invitation."

I smiled and gestured to the sofa. "Why don't you have a seat? Would you like something to drink?"

"Water would be fine. Thanks."

Putting some ice and water into two glasses, I carried them out to the living room. The cats followed me in and were soon vying for Rob's attention. He saw some string Jenny left out and soon dangled it to play with them. "Who are these beauties?"

"The brown-and-gold one is Drambuie and the black-and-white one is Courvoisier."

He smiled. "Do you have a drinking problem I missed?"

I laughed. "The names just seemed to fit."

Drambuie jumped up on his lap and head butted his hand. He petted her and then fixed me with his gaze. "Are you going to keep me in suspense, or are you going to tell me if you found anything?"

"I found something, but I am going to continue to keep you in suspense. I don't want to sit down on the couch in these clothes. I'm filthy, so I'm going to take a shower, change, and then we'll talk." Grabbing my purse, I headed upstairs.

"Do you always bring your purse when you take a shower?"

"Only when there is a reporter in the living room."

Closing the door to the master bedroom, I quickly stripped out of my filthy clothes. The shower was welcome, and it felt great to wash off all of the dust and grime. Throwing on some jeans and a shirt, I made quick work of a minimal amount of makeup and rejoined Rob downstairs. Jenny was home from school and sat next to him playing with the cats.

She gave me a funny look. "Showering in the middle of the day?"

"Don't be fresh. I was helping Melissa clean out Mr. Ford's house, and I really needed that shower."

She frowned. "Why were you helping Melissa?"

"Because she needed it and she asked me."

"That's weird. I didn't know you were friends."

I crossed my fingers behind my back. "You don't know all of my friends."

"You're doing that finger-crossing thing again. Whatever. I need to do my homework. I'll be in my room if you need me."

Rob smiled. "That finger-crossing thing?"

My face burned. "Okay, I know it isn't very adult, but I do it occasionally."

"When you lie?"

"Whatever." I opened my purse and removed the ledger.

Sitting next to Rob, I flipped it open. There were thirty pages with writing on them. It was in some type of code.

Rob sighed. "This is going to take a while."

"I need to get dinner started. Do you want to stay?"

"If you think you have enough. That way we can work on this."

"Agreed, but before I call Jenny down, we need to put the ledger away. I don't want her involved in this. It may be dangerous. Why don't you bring it in the kitchen so we can talk while I throw something together?"

I walked into the kitchen. "Leftover chili and corn bread work for you?"

"Love it." He sat at the counter, his head bent over the ledger.

I took the chili out of the freezer and the corn bread carton out of the cupboard. Putting the chili into the microwave to reheat, I made the corn bread. It went into the oven, and I set the table for three. "A beer sound good?"

"Sounds great."

Twisting off two beer caps with a towel, I poured the beer into glasses and put one at Rob's elbow.

He didn't look up. "Thanks."

Sitting next to him at the counter, I looked over his shoulder. "Anything?"

"Yes. Most of the recent ones seem to be repeating."

"What do you mean?"

"Look here. See this one?" He pointed midway down the page. "It has the same symbols, letters, and amounts as this one two pages later. The next three repeat as well. And they seem to be divided by months. Either Ben was making some off-book loans, or you're right—he was blackmailing people."

"People?"

"It would appear so, since there are recurring different entries."

"So it's possible more than one person had a motive to kill him."

"Yes."

Worried, I took the book and put it down. "We need to give this book to Detective Ziebold."

"How are you going to explain finding it?"

"Just the way I explained it to Jenny."

"Including the finger-crossing thing?"

I gave him a dirty look. "You are too funny."

"Mind if I take this over to the office to photocopy it before you turn it in?"

I smiled and handed it to him. "I thought you'd never ask."

CHAPTER 14

The next day, I explained how I unearthed the ledger to Detective Ziebold. His eyebrows rose several times, but at the end he thanked me for bringing it by. Writing out a statement, I signed it. Then he drove me to Ben's house.

Melissa answered the door. Detective Ziebold said, "Ms. Stone, I understand Ms. March was helping you clean out this place yesterday. Is that correct?"

Melissa caught my eye over his shoulder. I nodded slightly. "Yes, yes, she did." She gave me a pointed look. "I thought you weren't going to be able to help today, Merry."

"That's right, but the detective wanted me to stop by with him this morning, so here I am."

Detective Ziebold entered the house. "I want Ms. March to show me where she found something yesterday."

Melissa gave a visible start. "Found something? What did you find?"

I jumped in. "I didn't mention finding anything to Melissa yesterday. Sorry, Melissa."

"It's better you didn't," he said. "The less people who know, the better."

Melissa frowned. "Know what?"

"Never mind. Ms. March, please show me where you found it. Ms. Stone, I'd appreciate it if you would remain here until we come back."

"I'm responsible for this house right now."

"Regardless, this is police business, so please stay here."

Melissa gave me a dirty look as Detective Ziebold followed me to the small bedroom. I opened the door and marched over to the closet. Pointing at the difference in the flooring, I stood aside. Detective Ziebold put gloves on and used his pocket knife to pry up the loose boards. He saw the bag in the open space and arched an eyebrow at me.

"The ledger was in that bag."

"I still don't understand how you found this when you were working in the other room."

"As I explained, Melissa told me to put anything valuable on the bed in this room." I pointed. "Those are the stamps I found."

"Why did you look in the closet?"

"The door was open, and I just happened to see the difference in flooring."

"Must have good eyes."

"I do. Do you need anything else, or can I go now? I promised to take my daughter to the lake this weekend, and I still have a few things to do to get ready."

"Yes, you can. Please stop by the police station so we can get your prints, since I'm sure you weren't wearing gloves."

"Will do. Will Monday be okay?"

He put the floorboard back. "Yes, that's fine. Have a nice weekend."

I quickly left the room and was trying to make a graceful exit when Melissa stopped me. "Why didn't you tell me? I specifically asked if you found anything, and you said you didn't."

"I know. But I felt the police would be even madder at me for meddling if I did tell you." I paused. "I'm sorry. Thanks for sticking your neck out for me."

"That's okay. I don't think I want to know what you found anyway."

I returned to my house. As I opened my garden gate, Nancy called over, "I heard you found something at Ben's house. What was it? Does it explain why he was killed?"

Pivoting, I joined her on the porch. "Nancy, this is dangerous. Someone was killed, and we don't know who did it. We need to be quiet about this. We don't want to turn ourselves into targets."

She lowered her voice. "Huh. I hadn't thought about that. What did you find?"

I took both of her hands in mine and gazed into her eyes. "Because I like you, I'm not going to tell you. I'm also going to ask you not to tell anyone else I found something."

"Don't worry. I only had time to call two people, and I swore them both to secrecy."

I sighed. "No one else. Promise me."

"My lips are sealed!" To show she meant it, she pantomimed locking her lips with a key and throwing it over her shoulder.

"Jenny and I are going to the lake this weekend. Will you check on the cats for me?"

"Of course."

"You still have my cell phone number, right?"

"Yes. You programmed it in for me. Have a good weekend."

"Thanks. I'll see you late Sunday. I'll make sure to bring back some of those apples you love. You have a good weekend too."

Scooting over to the house, I made sure the cats had extra food and water and put a few things in my overnight suitcase. Next, I grabbed Jenny's bag from her room, snatched some food from the kitchen for the weekend, and packed the car. Locking the house up, I drove over to the school to pick her up. By a few minutes past three, we were on the road to the lake.

"Not as much traffic as there is in the summer," Jenny said.

"Thank goodness. How was school?"

"Busy, as usual. Mind if I listen to my tunes on the way?"

"No problem."

Putting in her earbuds, she was lost to the world. An hour later, we unpacked the car. Entering the small A-frame house, my shoulders loosened. The wall of windows on the back showcased the sun dancing on the lake's surface. "Why is it we don't get here more often?"

She stowed the milk in the refrigerator. "We're busy."

"But still. It's so serene, and the colors of the trees are brilliant this fall." I hugged her and stepped back. "We're lucky to have this place."

Jenny smiled. "Luck had nothing to do with it. You work really hard! When's dinner?"

"An hour or so."

"Call me and I'll set the table."

Pouring myself a glass of wine, I pushed the French doors open. I ambled across the flagstone terrace and sat in one of the Adirondack chairs. As I sank into it and shut my eyes, the bird calls and the lake lapping against the shore gave me a feeling of peace. My troubles slipped away. Then it occurred to me that I hadn't gotten a copy of the ledger before I left. Darn! I wondered if Rob had worked out the code yet. My mind wandered to his green eyes and chiseled features. *I could get lost in that face and, oh my, that body.*

I mentally slapped myself. I was not ready for another relationship. Or maybe I was. Then my mind flitted to John. I hadn't heard from him lately. Probably because he was busy closing on his house. Feeling faintly guilty for not having offered to help, I made a mental note to call him on Monday. Why was he being less than truthful with me? Blue eyes or no, caution was advised when it came to Mr. John Gordan.

The next morning dawned cold. Sipping our cocoa, Jenny and I planned a canoe ride. Interrupted by the phone ringing, I pressed speaker. "Good morning, Nancy. How are you?"

"Well. But you're not going to like what I have to tell you. Your house was broken into last night. I came over to check on the cats this morning, and it's all topsy-turvy."

"What?"

"I called the police, and they're on their way, but I think you should get back here."

"Are the cats okay?"

"Yes, they were hiding in the basement. They're fine, and I've shut them in the upstairs bath with their food and litter box so they don't wander off."

"We're leaving right now."

Jenny and I raced around the house throwing the things we had unpacked the night before back into our bags. Just as we were putting them into the car, I received a text from Rob. "Are you okay? Just heard about break-in on police scanner."

"Yes, getting into car now."

"I'll meet you at your house."

I glanced at Jenny. "Rob's going to meet us at our house."

"Why?"

"He's concerned."

"No, why would someone break into our house? Is it because you found something at Mr. Ford's?"

I sighed. "How did you know I found something at Mr. Ford's?"

"Cindy, who found out from Michael, who found out from Bobby Ziebold. You know there aren't any secrets in this town. And why wasn't the alarm on?"

"I must have forgotten to set it. That won't happen again."

"What did they take?"

"I have no idea. You heard as much as I did from Nancy."

"Mom, I'm scared. What if we had been there?"

I came around the car and hugged her. "It will be okay. I'm sure it's not that bad, and as soon as we can get there, we can see for ourselves."

"Drive fast."

"I'll get us there safely as expeditiously as possible."

We both hopped in the car and raced home.

When we came down our street, the sun glinted off the patrol car's red-and-blue lights twirling silently in their compartments. Rob, Nancy, and the patrol officer talked on the sidewalk. As we pulled up, Rob broke away from the group and hugged me as I got out of the car.

"Thanks. How bad is it?"

"It's pretty messed up, but it doesn't look like much was taken."

The patrol officer stepped forward. "Ms. March, we'll need you to go through the house and identify anything that's missing."

"Did you find out how the person got in?"

"The laundry room window was smashed."

Hurrying to the front door, I gasped as I opened it. My sofa cushions were tossed, all of the drawers to the built-ins were out on the floor, and the chairs were overturned. Jenny started to cry.

I put my arms around her. "Maybe you should wait in the car or go over to Mrs. Piedmont's until I take a look in here."

"That would be worse—not knowing how bad it is. Can we go up to my room next?"

"Yes, of course, honey."

She ran up the stairs with me trailing on her heels. As she rounded the corner, she saw her door was open and came to a dead stop. Almost running into her, I put my hands on her shoulders. "I'm here, honey." Everything from her drawers seemed to be on the floor or bed. It looked like someone had been searching pretty thoroughly.

"Mom, all of my stuff is still here: my flat screen, my iPad, everything. But some stranger touched my things! Why would someone do that?"

Rob and I exchanged a quick glance. I asked the patrol officer, "Would it be okay if she straightened up her room?"

"Yes, we've already fingerprinted everything."

I squeezed Jenny's shoulders. "Would you feel better if you cleaned up?"

"I'd feel better if this hadn't happened. But I do want to clean up my room."

"Anyone home?" Patty called from downstairs. "Wow. What a mess."

"We're up here."

Patty ran up the stairs with Cindy right behind her. "What happened? I heard your house was robbed."

Cindy hugged Jenny. "Let's get busy and get this cleaned up."

Giving her a smile, I hugged Patty. "Thanks for coming."

"You bet. What does your room look like?"

"I'm sure it's more of the same."

"Let's go rip the bandage off."

Everyone followed me to my room. I gasped. It looked like a tornado roared through. But again, nothing valuable seemed to have been taken. I suddenly realized far too many people were seeing my underwear up close and personal. "Let's go down to the kitchen and see how bad that is."

We trooped down the stairs and took a right into the kitchen. Cookbooks were on the floor, appliances had been moved, and things had been swept from the pantry shelf. As I looked around in despair, Detective Ziebold came in. "Quite a mess."

I said, "The understatement of the century."

"Let's talk outside."

I joined him, and he said, "I think whoever did this was looking for the ledger."

"Based on what I saw inside, I'd have to agree with you."

"How many people knew you found it?"

I shrugged. "I don't think many people knew it was a ledger. As far as I know, that was limited to you, me, and Rob."

"Rob? You shared it with a reporter?"

"He's a friend."

"Can reporters be friends?"

"Maybe not all of them, but he certainly is."

He gave me a look. "I think you are being naïve."

"Let's get back on subject. So the people who knew about the ledger are a handful. The people who knew I found *something* are a legion."

"How so?"

"You told Melissa, and she told Nancy. Nancy told two friends; you do the math."

He frowned. "Then it's a safe assumption that this is related. I want you to be very cautious. I'll be sending extra patrols past your house, and I want you to remember to set your alarm."

"You don't have to remind me of that now." I gestured toward the door. "I think we better go back in. People are straining their necks trying to read lips from the kitchen window."

When we returned to the kitchen, everyone suddenly seemed busy. I yelled, "Stop!"

All eyes swiveled toward me.

"This is really depressing, and I need some time to process. So although I'm grateful to have such good friends, I'm going to have to ask you all to leave."

"We can help," Patty said. "We can clean up."

"Thank you. Thank you all. Now, please leave. I'll call you later."

They all filed out, Detective Ziebold jockeying position so he would be last out the door. He shook his forefinger. "Don't forget, keep the alarm on and be careful."

"I will, and I have your number on speed dial."

Shutting the door, I returned a cushion to the sofa and sat. *Where to start? I could at least return the chairs to an upright position.* I did that, then I started working on putting the books and DVDs back on the bookshelves. If I could just get one room straightened out, I'd have a place where I might be able to forget. Who was I kidding? This was an assault on my safe place, my home. Depressed, I sat heavily. I wanted to cry but was afraid Jenny would come down and catch me, so I just sat and stared holes in the wall. The clock chimed four, and Jenny and Cindy came running down the stairs.

Jenny said, "We finished my room a while ago, so we started on yours. We did a pretty good job, if I do say so myself."

My eyes welled up. "That's so sweet of you both." I gathered them into a hug.

We stayed that way for a long moment. Cindy broke in, "Mom's coming over with takeout in an hour. She gave us strict instructions to clear some places in the kitchen. She also said for you to make yourself useful and uncork a bottle of wine. Her words, not mine."

"I guess we better get busy then." I tried to smile.

My phone dinged. There was a text from Rob: "Sorry about the break-in. I contacted Mirror Glass, and they'll be there in twenty minutes to repair your window. Let me know when you want to talk."

I hugged the girls. "It's good to have friends. Let's get to work."

CHAPTER 15

The alarm rang way too early on Monday, but after all of the unexpected manual labor over the weekend, I was looking forward to my desk job. The only bright spot was that the house was really clean, right down to the baseboards. It's amazing how much cleaning you could do when everything had been moved for you. Focusing on glass half full, I went to work.

I was stopped three or four times by people wishing me well and wanting to tell me how upset they were that this had happened in our town. I made the appropriate noises and continued on my way. I knew when I got to the office it would be even worse.

As soon as I opened the door, there were questions. Holding my hands up, I assured everyone that I would address them during our regularly scheduled staff meeting. Cheryl and I went over my calendar for the day, and then I went into the conference room.

"Yes, my home was broken into over the weekend. However, it looks like nothing of value was taken. Thank goodness neither my daughter nor myself were home, so we are both fine. Any questions?"

One of the staff members asked, "If nothing was taken, why did they break in?"

"I don't know."

"We heard you found something at Ben Ford's house," someone else asked. "Could they have been after whatever you found?"

"I can't really comment on that other than to say if I were to have found anything, it would be in the safekeeping of the police now. And with that, I think we should all return to work and concentrate on making our customers happy. Thanks."

Just as I entered my office, the phone rang, a familiar name popping onto the screen. "Good morning, John. How are you?"

"I think a better question might be how you are. I heard about the break-in. Are you and Jenny okay?"

"As okay as we can be. Thanks for asking. How's the house coming?"

"Good. I moved in last week. Listen, I had another motive in calling. I wondered if you wanted to come for dinner on Saturday at six. I'd love to show you the place."

"That sounds great."

"It will give us a chance to catch up. I'm so sorry about what you must be dealing with. Let me know if there is anything I can do to help."

"You have enough on your plate with the move. I'll see you Saturday."

"I look forward to it."

A few moments and deep breaths later, I called Rob. "I wanted to thank you for sending the window guy by. He was able to fix it quickly, and it was one more thing I didn't need to worry about."

"I was concerned and wanted to make sure it got fixed as soon as possible. How are you feeling? I got the sense you hit your limit yesterday."

"I did. I'm doing better now that we've gotten the majority of the house back in order."

"Feel like dinner tonight?"

"No. I think I'm just going to go home and crash. How about tomorrow?"

"That will work. I'll pick you up at five."

"Look forward to seeing you then."

I sat back in my chair and remembered I hadn't asked him about the code. I picked the phone back up and hit redial.

"Change your mind?"

"No. I realized with everything that's been going on I hadn't asked where you were on figuring out the code."

"I'm not sure. I think I might have some ideas. Let's discuss them tomorrow in person."

"Okay. Could you do me a favor and drop off my copy of the ledger sometime today?"

"Will do. I have an appointment up the street from you at two o'clock, so I'll drop it by then."

I hung up and started attending to my business.

Rob dropped off the ledger as promised, and at 3:10 p.m., I texted Jenny, "Are you home?"

"Yes."

"Alarm on?"

"Yes."

"I'll be home at five fifteen."

"Okay."

While going home, it felt like I trudged through deep sand. I might be able to handle a quick dinner and some relaxing time in the tub, but that was going to be about it. Unlocking the door, I shut off the alarm and reset it. I turned toward the sofa and jumped. "You scared me," I told Patty. "And what are you doing here anyway? Don't you have a family?"

"Yes, I do, and I consider you and Jenny honorary members of it. I brought dinner, which is in the oven. I thought you might not be up to cooking."

I hugged her. "You're the best friend ever!"

She gripped both my arms, pushed me away, and held me there. "Yes, I know. And since I am your best friend, I want you to listen to me."

"What?"

"Stop investigating. I know I put you on this path, but we are now no longer involved. I don't want you to be next on this guy's list."

"Don't you want to know who did it?"

"Yes. And I'll be really happy when the police catch him. Enough said?"

"Yes."

She released my arms. "Okay. I'll leave you alone now. If I know you, bath and book are on the top of your to-do list for this evening."

After my bath, I tried to settle into bed with my book. I turned the pages, but I wasn't really reading them. With a sigh, I put the book down and reached for my copy of Ben's ledger. It was clear money was involved, as the far right side showed positive cash amounts. The left side was where it got hazy. I looked at the most recent entries: FL0910, 5,000; WO0912, 5,000; NK0915, 5,000.

FL might be the initials of someone's name. I racked my brain and couldn't think of anyone in town whose first and last names started with them. *What about states?* Florida certainly seemed to fit, but WO and NK? *Nope, that didn't work. What about the first two letters of someone's first name?* Florence? Did I know anyone named Florence?

The first set of numbers looked like they might be dates. Flipping back a few pages, I saw that they were consistent, all around the middle of the month. That matched what the bank said about when the deposits were made.

The clock chimed twelve. If I wanted to be of any use to anyone at work tomorrow, I would need to find sleep soon. Maybe Rob had come up with something.

* * *

95

The next day raced along as I dealt with several mini-crises at work. I remembered to text Jenny at 3:10 p.m. and was happy to see she was home and the alarm had been set. It wasn't long before Cheryl knocked at my door to say she was leaving for the day and that Rob was there.

"Rob, come in."

"Thanks. Is the Iron Skillet good for dinner tonight? I called ahead, and they said they could get us in at five thirty."

"That would be great. I'm just finishing up two things, and then we can be on our way."

I packed up while he checked his emails, and then we strolled to the restaurant. "Did you think I needed some comfort food?"

He smiled. "I thought you might."

"You and Patty—she's been bringing food to the house. It's good to have friends who care."

He gave me a side hug, and we entered the restaurant, where we were quickly seated.

"Thanks for suggesting we go out tonight. I needed it. I don't want to be too long, though, because I don't want Jenny alone at home too late."

"Why don't we get dessert to go? That should speed things up, and we can eat them with Jenny at your house."

"That's a great idea." I texted Jenny, "Banana cream pie okay? Coming back with dessert."

"Yum."

Settling down to the tough work of figuring out what to have, Rob said, "I'm getting the meatloaf again."

"Hot pastrami on rye for me." Our orders in, I continued, "What's going on with the code?"

"I'm not sure we should chat about that here; the tables are kind of close together. I should have thought about that when I picked where to eat."

"You're right. How has your day gone otherwise?"

"Good. I've started working on a new feature that involves shadowing the mayor to see how he and the town council decide to spend the town's budget."

I laughed. "There should be quite a few people, including myself, who would be interested in learning more about that."

The food arrived, and we ordered to-go desserts so they'd be ready when we wanted to leave.

After enjoying the food and paying the bill, we returned to the house. Rob held the door as I turned off the alarm. I busied myself making coffee.

Jenny came down from her room. "Who do I thank for the pie?"

I nodded toward Rob. "Mr. Jenson."

"It's my fav! Thanks! Mind if I take it up to my room? I'm in the middle of streaming a show."

"No problem. Don't forget to bring your dish back."

"Will do."

Rob sat at the counter, and I said, "Let me go grab my copy of the ledger."

Returning, I saw he hadn't started on his dessert. I smiled. "You didn't have to wait."

He grinned. "It wouldn't taste nearly as good without you here."

Blushing, I opened the ledger. "Thanks. Likewise. Now, to work."

"Turn to the last page."

"That's what I was looking at yesterday."

"I think the first set of numbers is dates. And the second set is the amount of cash he received."

"I agree."

"The letters are the problem, so what if we work backward?"

"What do you mean?"

"One of my top suspects is John Gordan."

"He may be yours, but he's not mine. And none of these are JG."

"No, but one of the simpler ciphers, or codes, is the Caesar code. It's what Caesar supposedly used when communicating with his generals."

"How does it work?"

He pointed to the entry. "You take the real letter and then consistently shift a number of places down in the alphabet. To see if this would work, I looked at the third entry: NK0915, 5,000.

"If you consistently shift five letters, JG would become NK, so it would read JG on September 15."

"What would the other ones be?"

"FL would be BH, and WO would be SK. So this is how it would read: BH0910, 5,000; SK0912, 5,000; JG0915, 5,000.

I raised my eyebrows. "That's a whole lot of supposition, and you are starting with John Gordan. If his name is wrong, then the whole thing is wrong."

"I don't think it is. Bear with me. If it is right, who could the other people be?"

"I don't like this." I shuddered. "The only BH I can think of off the top of my head is Belinda Harper, Father Tom's assistant. And the SK that pops to mind is Suzie Krump, the owner of the Morning Pastry. It's hard to believe they could be suspects."

"We don't have enough to bring this to the police yet. But I think we should do some background investigation on Belinda and Suzie. Let's regroup tomorrow and compare notes."

CHAPTER 16

Rising early the next day, I baked some banana bread. It had just come out of the oven when the whirlwind that was my daughter came rushing through the kitchen. I wrapped a piece quickly in wax paper and was just able to complete the hand-off as the blur went out the door. "I love you."

A faint "I love you more," wafted back.

Cutting two more pieces, I put them on paper plates with napkins in between. Stacking carefully, I grabbed my tea and headed gingerly out the door. I followed along my garden to Nancy's front porch. Nancy was sitting on her swing sipping her coffee.

"Nancy, good morning!"

"Good morning to you as well. What is that wonderful smell?"

"Fresh-baked banana bread."

"I love being the recipient when you're in one of your baking moods."

"It's good having such an appreciative audience." I sat next to Nancy, carefully placing my teacup on her table and handing her one of the slices and a napkin.

She smiled and took a bite, closing her eyes. "This is great. I love that you add walnuts. That and the bananas almost make it seem healthy."

"Don't forget the eggs and sour cream! A veritable breakfast bonanza I like to think."

She smiled. "True. What's up, Merry?"

"Besides catching up with you, I'm curious about a few people and wanted to pick your brain."

"Such as?"

"Belinda Harper for one."

"What about Belinda?" She broke off a piece of the banana bread and dipped it in her coffee.

"From what I can remember, she moved to town about five years ago."

"Yes, that seems right to me."

"Do you know where she moved from?"

"Let me think." Nancy ate a piece of the bread and took a long sip of her coffee. She studied her orange mum. "I'm pretty sure she came from White Horse. I remember she worked for another parish there."

"Do you know why she moved here?"

"I think she told me she was looking for a change of scenery."

"What about Suzie Krump?"

"Is this Twenty Questions?"

"No, don't be silly."

"Sure seems that way. You aren't still investigating Ben's murder are you? I can't believe it after your house was broken into. Didn't that warning scare you? It scared me."

"It scared me too. I'm just trying to track down a few loose ends, and I'd appreciate it if you wouldn't say anything to anyone."

She paused and shook her finger. "I don't think it's wise, but I'll try to answer. Suzie Krump?"

"Yes."

"She moved here with her mother, Gloria, about three years ago and opened the Morning Pastry. Suzie came from Urbana, where she had a different restaurant. I think it was called the Purple Plum. I remember she moved here to get away from her husband."

"Anything else?"

"Yes. There was some sort of messy situation up in Urbana when she left, but for the life of me, I can't remember what it was. Does this help? Was it worth the price of the banana bread?"

"Definitely. It gives me a lot more information than I had before. Thanks." I silently toasted her with my teacup and made my way back to my house.

Wrapping the rest of the banana bread in wax paper, I went upstairs to get dressed. I texted Rob: "Belinda Harper, parish in White Horse. Suzie Krump, the Purple Plum in Urbana."

"You work fast. I haven't finished my first cup of coffee yet. Thanks for info. See you later."

Finished dressing, I took a quick look at my schedule for the day. Seeing I had lunch free, I asked Patty to meet me at the Morning Pastry at noon.

Smiling, I hurried out the door, setting the alarm as I left.

On the way to work, I stopped by one of my client's houses. A tree limb had fallen through her kitchen window the previous week, and I wanted to check she was satisfied with how her claim was being handled.

She took me into the kitchen. "I was so happy with how everything worked. The company cut me a check on the spot and recommended a great contractor. You can see it's all fixed, and they even matched where the tile had been cracked around the window."

"It looks great. You can't even tell the tree was there."

"Thanks, Merry. Situations like these are why I like doing business with you."

I grinned. "I'm happy you're happy."

Continuing on to work, the rest of the morning was uneventful. Leaving a few minutes before noon, I hurried down the block to the Morning Pastry. Patty was waiting outside, and as I approached she pantomimed looking at her watch.

"I am just in time."

"According to my watch, you are one minute late."

"What's one minute between friends?"

"True. Inside or out?"

"Out works, if you don't think it's too cold."

She smiled. "No. Plus, it means we won't have a lot of people joining us."

We went inside to order. Standing in line, we watched the staff behind the counter prepping food for other diners. Gloria glided effortlessly past, carrying what looked to be a fifty-pound bag of flour on her shoulder.

"That is one strong lady," Patty said.

I nodded. "Sure is." We took our drinks and told Suzie we'd be out on the porch.

Suzie laughed. "You are intrepid souls. I'll bring the food out when it's ready."

Patty and I sat at one of the corner tables. "How's the love life?" she asked.

"Confusing."

"How so?"

"I've been seeing a lot of Rob lately, and I have a date with John on Saturday." I twisted my napkin.

"Why is that confusing?"

"Rob is still convinced John is the prime suspect for Ben Ford's murder."

"Awkward."

"Slightly."

Concerned, she touched my shoulder. "Should you be dating a prime suspect? I hope you're meeting him where there are a lot of people around."

"Patty, he's our school superintendent. If he's the murderer, we've got a lot more to worry about."

"Where are you going on your date?"

"His house."

"His house? Will there be other people there?"

"Not that I know of."

Her eyes widened. "Is that wise?"

"I doubt I will be in any trouble. The man is hardly going to do anything in his own house. It wouldn't be very smart, and John is a smart man."

"So *nothing* will happen?" Patty wiggled her eyebrows.

I grinned. "Nothing bad at least."

Suzie shoved the door open with her hip and carried the tray over to our table. "Patty, you had the chopped salad and, Merry, the chicken salad with grapes. Both with dressing on the side, right?"

Patty said, "Right as always!"

Suzie put the plates down. "Suzie, we are so lucky you opened up here," I said. "I heard that you used to have a place in Urbana."

She gave me a strange look. "That's right."

"Not that I'm complaining, but why'd you move? Urbana's a bigger town than this. I would think you'd have a larger customer base."

"I get plenty of customers here, and I like small towns better. You can see trouble coming quicker. If you'll excuse me, I need to get back inside. This is our busy time." Suzie quickly left the table but paused by the door to give me a long look.

Patty asked, "What the heck was that all about?"

"Nothing."

"You're still investigating Ben's death, aren't you?"

"Potentially."

"Didn't you learn your lesson? Aren't you worried about Jenny? Sometimes I really wonder about you." Patty shook her head as she dug into her salad.

After lunch, I returned to the office and kept my head down the rest of the day. Rob stopped by at five, and I quickly wrapped things up.

He asked, "What do you feel like tonight?"

"I don't really want to go out tonight. I defrosted some of my Aunt Janet's macaroni and cheese this morning, if you don't mind leftovers."

"I love leftovers. Does your Aunt Janet live around here?"

"No. Aunt Janet taught my mom the recipe, and the name stuck. I can assure you, it's tasty."

I texted Jenny, "Would you set the table for three and put some rolls in the oven?"

"If I must." She softened it with a smiley face.

While walking to the house, we admired the brick storefronts and street trees, stopping occasionally to look at the window displays.

Rob glanced around. "I don't think I realized quite how many antique stores we have."

"It's a tourist draw."

"You sound a bit jaded."

"Not at all. It's great to live in a town that's growing versus being on the decline."

"I agree."

"Is small-town life what you thought it would be?"

He smiled at me and gave me a hug. "It's even better."

I grinned up at him. "Getting better all the time."

After dinner, he loaded the dishwasher. I objected, but he said, "You cooked."

"I microwaved."

He laughed. "You cooked the original dish, which you then froze, defrosted, and microwaved. Is that more exact?"

"Yep." I cleaned up the kitchen as he continued loading. *How domestic.* It felt good. "Banana bread and coffee in the living room?"

"I love banana bread!"

We settled in the living room. "Let me grab my notes." He pulled them out of his backpack and flipped through his pad. "Thanks for the text this afternoon. Knowing where Belinda and Suzie came from helped a lot."

"What did you find out?"

"Which one do you want me to start with?"

"Let's start with Belinda."

Rob scanned his notes. "She previously lived in White Horse."

"I know all that."

"Don't be impatient."

I smiled. "Patience is not one of my virtues."

"Luckily you have so many others to recommend you. Continuing on from where I was so rudely interrupted—Belinda worked for a parish in White Horse. I checked with some of my sources, and it appears there was some trouble when she was there."

"What happened?"

"Some money went missing from the rectory."

I blinked in shock. "Do they know she took it?"

"She was never charged. And, since she ended up here working for Father Tom, I would think the odds would be that she didn't steal it. I'm assuming priests talk, and Father Tom would have checked her references."

"One would think. What about Suzie?"

"I'll tell you in just a minute. This banana bread is calling my name." He broke off a piece and chewed it, an expression of bliss appearing on his face. "I told you I loved banana bread, and this is terrific." He sipped some of his coffee. "Where was I? Oh yes, Suzie is an interesting one."

"How so?"

"Trivia moment—did you know she was a college softball star and her batting average was .730? Quite impressive." He mimed tossing a ball in the air and swinging at it.

I stared at him.

Disappointment crept into his features. "Okay, back to work. You know she ran another restaurant, the Purple Plum, right?"

"Yes."

"Someone was killed there."

"What?"

"Yes. Poisoned."

"By the food?"

Rob shook his head. "Never proven. The police bagged all of the remaining food from the victim's plate and had it tested. They didn't find anything."

"What happened?"

"The case is still unsolved. But after the murder, Suzie's restaurant also died. People were nervous and stopped coming."

"I can see why she wouldn't want that known here. Patty and I had lunch there today." I shivered.

Rob eyed me. "Why did you eat there?"

"It was close, they have good food, and there's a place to sit outside."

"No other reason?"

"I thought it might be good to ask Suzie a few questions."

"And?"

"She admitted she had a restaurant in Urbana prior to this one."

Rob shifted uneasily. "I don't think quizzing her was such a great idea."

"I don't want you to do all of the heavy lifting. We're a team."

"We are. You found out where they lived previously, and I was looking into finding out why they moved. If Suzie was being blackmailed by Ben, it's safe to say she didn't want anyone here to know about her past. And she may have killed to keep people from finding out. You could be in danger, and that makes me very concerned."

"I promise I won't knowingly put myself in danger."

"No fingers crossed?"

"No fingers crossed."

He kissed me then. It was slow and sweet and made me tingle all the way to my toes. *Wow. I've missed this.* Kissing him back, I pressed him farther into the sofa.

A moment later, Jenny's voice rang out. "Get a room."

Jumping up, I patted my hair back into place. Jenny stood at the bottom of the stairs grinning at me. I blushed. "Rob was just leaving."

Jenny smiled. "Sure looked like it."

Rob put his notes into his backpack. "Good to see you, Jenny." Pulling me out onto the porch with him, he kissed me softly. "To be continued. Remember your promise."

"I will."

I went back into the house. "Could you make a little more noise coming down the stairs?"

"I didn't know I needed to. And I thought we didn't like reporters."

I smiled. "This one we definitely like."

CHAPTER 17

I woke up the following morning feeling great. Completing my exercises with the right amount of vigor, I sat down with my oatmeal breakfast feeling virtuous. As I scanned my calendar for the day, I saw lunch was free. I called Father Tom and left a voice mail asking if he'd care to have lunch with me at the Golden Skillet. I figured I wasn't breaking my promise if I talked to Father Tom.

Cheryl stuck her head in the door at ten and said Father Tom agreed to meet me at noon. Leaving a few minutes early, I strolled to the restaurant. After I was seated, I saw Father Tom's head appear over the red pleather booths, and I gave him a wave.

He shook my hand as he sat. "It's lovely to see you, Merry. Was there something in particular I can help you with?"

"I wanted to check on Jenny's penance. I know she completed it, but I wanted to make sure you felt she served in the appropriate way."

"Yes, she did. And you should know I had several conversations with both her and Cindy, and they agreed the penance fit the crime."

"I'm glad. I appreciate you taking the time to help them."

"It's part of my calling." He studied me with his kind brown eyes. "How are you doing?"

"Well."

"I haven't had a chance to talk to you since I saw you at Mass with Rob Jenson. That was a bit of a surprise."

"I know. He's kind of taken me by surprise as well."

"He seems like such a nice man. It's good to see you getting out again after all of that mess with Drew. You deserve to be happy."

"I appreciate that, Father. More than you can know."

"Just let me know if you want to start annulment proceedings. I would be glad to support you."

I blinked in shock. "I think it's a bit too soon for that."

"It's been four years, Merry."

"I know, but there's Jenny. I'm not sure how she would feel about me having my marriage annulled."

"I'm sure she wants nothing more than for you to be happy."

"She probably has a few other things on her list, but I know deep down that's true." The conversation was definitely taking a turn I did not expect. Feeling flustered, I tried to figure out the best way to bring up Belinda. I patted his hand. "Thank you, Father. You are always so kind to all of us. I hope you feel your parish is a close-knit one."

"I do, and that's why I love serving here."

"It must be nice having a good helper in Belinda."

"She does do such a good job. I'm lucky to have her."

"She's been with you for about five years now?"

He smiled. "That's right. I stole her from another parish in White Horse. I was substituting for an ill priest when I met her and saw what a great job she was doing. It was just my luck that six months later she reached out looking for a move."

"Why did she decide to leave?"

"Because of my sterling personality and wit." He laughed. "No. Actually, I think it was because she wanted to be closer to some of her relatives." He paused for a beat and then stood. "It really was great to catch up with you, Merry, but I need to get back. Remember what I said about the annulment."

I cringed. "I will. And thanks again for all of the help with Jenny."

An annulment. That was a big step and one not to be taken lightly. When I took my vows, I meant them. *But I hadn't contemplated Drew would turn out to be a crook who almost took me down with him.* Even now I could feel the steam coming out of my ears. Con men are charming! *Maybe an annulment would be an important next step to sloughing off my past.*

Cheryl was just leaving as I entered the office. "Bad lunch?"

I looked up, eyebrows raised. "No, good lunch. Why?"

"You look like a thundercloud!"

I made an effort to relax my face. "That better? I was thinking about Drew."

"That rat!"

"He's out of my life now, and that's what I'm going to concentrate on."

"Good for you. There are some messages on your desk. I'll be back in forty-five."

As I dove into work, my tension eased. At five thirty I looked up and was surprised to see Rob standing there. "Did I miss something?"

"No, I did. You."

A slow smile spread across my face. "And I missed you!"

"Let's go for a quick drink. I need some fortification before the town council meeting."

"I aim to please. Let me text Jenny I'll be a little late."

That done, we left for the Pickled Herring. I ordered a glass of Merlot and Rob ordered their special, Pastoral Pumpkin Ale.

I shook my head. "How do they come up with these names?"

"It's all in the alliteration. It sure tastes good, though." He took a long sip.

"Guess who I had lunch with today?"

"Who?"

"Guess!"

"It better not be one of our suspects."

"It wasn't. I had lunch with Father Tom."

"Close enough."

"But not enough to break my promise to you."

"True. But skating kind of close. What did the good father have to say?"

"It was more what he didn't say. I don't think he ran a background check on Belinda."

"Why?"

"Because he met her when visiting another parish and liked her work. If you had the chance to experience someone's work habits personally, would you even bother to run a check on them?" I sipped my wine.

"I might. Did you ask him?"

"No, I didn't want him to catch on to the fact that I wasn't just making conversation."

"That's smart. I was thinking about going over to Urbana tomorrow to see if I can get any more background on Suzie Krump. And now, sadly, I need to leave. Dinner on Saturday?"

I gulped. "Uh, unfortunately, I have a prior engagement."

His eyebrows slowly rose. "Church on Sunday with brunch after? Invite Jenny too."

"That sounds great."

He gave me a peck on the cheek as he put money on the bar and left. I was in big trouble.

I texted Patty as I went home, asking her to meet me later. When I entered the house, Jenny was sprawled on the sofa. All of her electronic devices surrounded her. "Sloppy Joes for supper?"

She nodded, and I started browning the beef. After a few minutes, she wandered into the kitchen and set two places at the kitchen counter. "How was school?"

"Fine."

"Classes going okay?"

"A lot of work but fine. Can I ask you a question?" She sat at the counter.

"Of course."

"I heard from one of the Ziebold boys you're still investigating Ben Ford's death. Wasn't it bad enough someone broke into our house? Why is solving this so important? Why would you put us at risk?"

I sat next to her. "Someone shouldn't be able to get away with murder."

"But why you? Why can't you let the police handle it?"

"The police are handling it. I'm just helping where I can. Mr. Jenson is helping too."

She looked down. "I just want us to be safe."

I hugged her. "I want us to be safe too. I promise I'll be even more careful."

She gave me a guarded look and finished setting the table. After dinner, Jenny went up to play an online computer game with one of her virtual friends. Kitchen clean, I put some clothes in the washer.

The back door opened. My heart pounded. The alarm beeped as it was turned off. I peered into the kitchen and breathed a sigh of relief. "Oh. It's you."

Patty said, "You were expecting someone else?"

I laughed, my heart still pounding. "No."

"What's going on? I was worried when I got your text."

"I think I'm getting in over my head."

"On something in particular or in general?"

"In particular."

"Let me get comfortable." She went into the living room and plopped down on the couch. Putting her feet up, she gave me a hard stare. "Okay, spill."

I sat opposite her. "Things have been moving pretty fast with Rob."

"And that's a bad thing?"

"I have a date with John on Saturday."

"Oh."

"Yes, oh. It seems like I've seen Rob every night for the last week or so. Tonight we met for drinks, and he asked me to dinner on Saturday. I had to tell him I had a previous engagement."

"How did he take it?"

"There was an awkward pause, and then he asked if he could take Jenny and me to church on Sunday with brunch after."

"Do you have some sort of exclusive arrangement with him? Have you agreed not to see other people?"

"No. But it still makes me feel weird. I feel like I'm doing something I shouldn't." I shrugged.

"I wouldn't worry about it until you have a more serious conversation."

"Thanks, Patty. I knew you'd make me feel better."

"I'll see you soon." She blew me a kiss.

I locked the door and reengaged the alarm. Running lightly up the steps, I knocked on Jenny's door. "Time to wrap it up—school night."

"Okay. Five more minutes."

Saturday came quickly. After running errands and doing some much needed chores, I donned one of the outfits Jenny preselected and stopped by Pick of the Vine to get a nice bottle of wine. At five forty-five, I gathered up my purse and wine and took one last glance in the mirror. Fluffing my curls, I applied a quick dab of lip gloss and left.

John greeted me with a hug. He took the wine and my coat.

I surveyed his living room. "I can't believe how much you've done. Remind me, when did you close?"

"A little over a week ago. I find I can't relax after a move until the house is about 95 percent there."

"Not to quibble, but it looks more like 100 percent to me. I'm always amazed when people can move in and it immediately looks like they've lived there forever. I'm a mull-it-over kind of person. When I was painting the inside of my house, I painted four different poster boards and stationed them around the rooms. They stayed there for six months before I got up enough nerve to pull the trigger and choose a color."

John laughed. "I plan everything out first so when I move in, I know where everything goes. Then it's just having enough time to place everything as outlined on my diagram."

"You actually diagram everything out?"

"Yes. It's much more efficient that way."

I smiled. "Impressive." Wow, seriously anal retentive.

"Would you like some wine? I have a nice Spanish Rioja I've been looking forward to trying."

"Sounds good to me."

He went to uncork the wine, and I strode to the fireplace. Admiring his ornate candleholders on the mantel, I picked one up to study it. "These are heavy. Are they silver?"

He handed me my glass and took the holder from me, putting it back. "Yes. They're quite valuable." He smiled. "You might say they're a family heirloom."

I took a sip of the wine. "Nice depth with some good fruitiness."

"Yes. It is good. Want to know what dinner I'm pairing it with?"

"Let me guess...steak."

"How did you know?"

I laughed. "You told me it was your specialty, and I hoped I was worthy."

"Ah, I'm giving all my secrets away. But I don't mind. Not with such a pretty lady."

I smiled at the compliment. "Why, thank you, kind sir."

"Would you like a tour?"

"Sure."

He guided me around the house. The kitchen was top-of-the line, like everything else, and sported an induction cooktop. I said, "I've never had one of those. Do you like it better than gas?"

"It requires different pots and pans, but I like the energy efficiency and the fact that the top remains cool to the touch."

We went up the stairs, and I traced the ornate railing. "This is beautiful. I love the detail work on the wood. It gives the house a lot of character."

He showed me the two extra bedrooms and then the master bedroom. It was dominated by a large king bed with a deep-purple coverlet. A large mirrored headboard formed the shape of a sun. The oversized bathroom included a shower that had two rain showerhead fixtures and a bench. It even had a separate sumptuous soaking tub.

I looked at him with envy. "You are so lucky to have this setup. If I lived here, I don't think I would ever leave the bathroom."

He gently reached for my hand and put it over his heart. "You can use my bathroom anytime you like."

"I'll have to remember that." Retrieving my hand, I hurried out of the bedroom and walked down the stairs.

He caught up to me. "I'm worried about you. Do you want to tell me more about what happened at your house last weekend?"

"It's just that someone broke in while we were away."

"Did they take much?"

"No. They didn't take anything."

He frowned. "That's odd. Why wouldn't they take anything? Does it have anything to do with what you found at Ben Ford's?"

I stopped dead in my tracks and stared at him. "Where did you hear I found something at Ben Ford's?

"To be honest, I'm not sure. Information travels fast here and comes at you from all sides."

I nodded. "It sure does. I did find something at Ben's, but I gave it to Detective Ziebold. The police have it." John paled. "I was helping my neighbor's cousin. She was asked to clean out his house."

"What did you find?"

Taking a slow sip of wine, I tried to figure out what to tell him. If I told him the truth, he might let something slip. But I had promised to be more careful. *Decisions, decisions.* I swirled my wine. "This is really tasty." I stared into his eyes. "The police asked me not to talk about what I found, but if you promise not to say anything…"

"You can trust me." He pulled me toward him in a hug.

Smiling up at him, I gently untangled myself from his arms. "I'm not sure exactly what it was, but it seemed like some type of ledger. I couldn't decipher the entries. The police will figure it out."

He frowned. "I better get those steaks on the grill or we'll be eating at midnight."

Over dinner, the conversation slowly grew more personal. I told him the short-story version about my ex-husband Drew. "What about you? Were you ever married?"

"Yes, once. What a mistake! We were both too young to know what we were getting ourselves into."

"I thought you always have a plan."

"I do. But sometimes it doesn't work out quite the way I want. And sometimes it does." He smiled and moved his water glass. "But enough about me. How's business?"

Even though we chatted pleasantly the rest of the evening, I couldn't help but feel a bit uneasy with him. Was he being blackmailed? And what would be damaging enough that he wouldn't want anyone to find out? I was somewhat relieved when I realized it was late enough that it wouldn't be suspicious for me to leave. I rose. "What a nice evening. Your house is beautiful, and the steaks were wonderful! I really enjoyed myself."

"Are you sure you need to leave? The night is still young."

"Yes. I don't want to leave Jenny alone too late."

"She's seventeen. I'm sure she'll be fine."

"It's evident you don't have kids." I smiled. "No, I really must go." I picked up my purse and scooted to the door.

He joined me and pulled me toward him for a hug. I let him but stepped back quickly after I gave him a peck on the cheek. Leaving, I waved. I couldn't help but notice the raw disappointment on his face.

Hurrying home, I relaxed as soon as I opened the door. Setting the alarm and double-checking the doors and windows, I started obsessing. *What if we are wrong? What if John is just an innocent superintendent?* My head spinning, I decided I'd think about that tomorrow. I hopped into bed, turned out the light, and pulled the covers over my head.

Sunday morning was rushed. I hadn't slept well, and it was a chore to get Jenny up and functioning. At a quarter past ten, the doorbell rang. I sighed. Right on time when I could have used about ten more minutes.

Running down the stairs, I pulled the door open. "Come in. I'll be ready in a few minutes." I dashed back upstairs. Two minutes later, Jenny and I ran downstairs.

Rob smiled. "And a very good morning to you both."

I laughed. "Sorry. Today my manners are not all they should be. Good morning to you as well. We need to hurry or we'll be late." We moved quickly down the sidewalk toward the church and slid into a pew just in time. Taking a deep breath, I scanned the crowd, nodding to those I knew. I started to relax and then stiffened. John Gordan sat across the aisle, two rows down. He nodded and turned away from me.

The Mass started. Rob put his arm around me and squeezed as we sang the first hymn. The homily was about the choices we make in life and the consequences that arise from them. *How apt.*

After the Mass, we exited the pew. "Did you see John?" Rob asked. "Yes."

"He seemed upset. Maybe we'll get a chance to talk to him outside."

I smiled brightly as I bit my tongue. "Wouldn't that be nice."

Quite a few people still mingled on the steps as we came out. I waved to Patrick and Patty, and Jenny made a beeline to Cindy. John strode toward us. Rob pivoted to see what I was looking at and held out his hand. "John, great to see you again."

John shook his hand, his jaw clenched. "I thought Father Tom gave a good homily today."

I nodded. "I thought it was particularly meaningful."

John clasped my elbow and looked down at me. "I had fun last night. We'll have to do it again sometime." He glanced over Rob's shoulder. "Oh, I see Hank Jefferson. I need to talk to him about the budget. Merry, I'll give you a call soon." He patted my arm.

Rob stared at me.

"It's not what you think."

"Which do you think concerns me more? That you went out with a potential murderer? Or that you went out with someone besides me? The answer, if you are interested, is both. I'll call you later." He stalked off.

Isn't that just dandy?

Jenny returned. "Where did Mr. Jenson go? I thought he was taking us out for brunch?"

"Our plans changed."

"Oh. The Twilligers are going to the Iron Skillet, and they invited us."

"Why don't you go with them? Tell Mrs. Twilliger I'll call her later."

Jenny gripped my arms and looked me in the eye. "Are you okay? Do you want me to come home with you?"

I hugged her. "I'm okay. Go ahead with them and have a good time. I love you."

I dragged my feet on the way home. *This is not shaping up to be my best day. I may as well clean.* I finished dusting and started on the second bathroom. The front door opened, and the alarm beeped. Coming out of the bathroom, I took off my rubber gloves. Cindy and

Jenny whizzed past me as they ran up the steps. Patty stared at me, both eyebrows raised.

I sat heavily. "I blew it."

She sat next to me. "How so?"

"I had dinner with John last night. He thanked me for a good time in front of Rob this morning."

"Ah, I wondered what happened. It wasn't very sportsmanlike of John."

"No, not very." I frowned. "And I think he may have done it on purpose."

"Why?"

"Rob put his arm around me at the beginning of the service, and John was behind us. He must have seen it."

"You don't think he'd be so spiteful, do you?"

"He may have murdered Ben. Spite's a definite step down from there."

"What are you going to do?"

"I'm not sure. I don't think it's up to me to apologize. I never said I wasn't going to see other people. But, to tell you the truth, it felt weird being at John's last night. I felt like I was betraying Rob. Was I?"

The doorbell rang. Patty and I exchanged glances, and she said, "Shouldn't you get that?"

I opened the door. Rob stood there looking sheepish with some red roses in his hand.

"Come in."

"These are for you." He handed me the flowers.

I took an appreciate sniff. "They smell great. I'll put them in water."

Rob sat on the sofa. "How are you, Patty?"

She jumped up. "Just leaving. Good to see you Rob." She walked out the door.

I came back with the flowers in a vase and put it on the coffee table. "They're lovely. Thank you for thinking of me."

"Where's Jenny?"

"Upstairs with Cindy." I sat. "I want to apologize."

"I think I should apologize."

"Let me go first. I'm sorry for breaking my promise to you about investigating suspects alone."

"Thank you. My turn?"

I nodded.

"I want to apologize for being mad about you seeing someone else. Although I have strong feelings for you, we haven't agreed our relationship is exclusive. I also need to apologize to Jenny for not taking you both to brunch."

"Apology accepted." We both stood and hugged. "Did you eat?"

"No. I wandered around town until I started seeing some sense. Did you?"

"I went on a cleaning jag. I have some bagels in the freezer and some cream cheese and lox in the fridge."

"Sounds great, if you're sure it's not too much trouble." He grimaced. "I'll pass on the lox, though."

"Your loss." We went into the kitchen, and I put the bagels in the microwave to defrost. A quick toast after they came out and we were enjoying our food.

"If it won't get me in trouble, can I ask if you found out anything at John's last night?"

"No, it won't get you in trouble, and the answer is not a lot. He finally admitted he was previously married. He also asked me about what I found at Ben's."

His eyes widened. "You didn't tell him anything, did you?"

"I did. I wanted to see his reaction."

"Merry! I'm not sure that was wise. How did he react?"

"He paled and then got busy putting the steaks on the grill."

Rob brightened. "So I may be right in suspecting him."

"Yes. You may be right. Do you want more coffee?"

He smiled. "No. Two high-test is my limit. By the way, I did go to Urbana the other day to see if I could get more information on Suzie Krump."

"What did you find out?"

"Not much more than what we already knew. The husband was a brute. The police were called out several times for domestic disturbances: broken arm, collarbone, etc."

"That's awful." I pressed my napkin to my lips. "He's in jail now, right?"

"No. She refused to press charges. He made himself scarce, though, after that. I guess it scared him."

"It sounds like Suzie made the right choice in leaving him."

"Absolutely. This is going to sound bad, but it's interesting she was able to. Usually abusers don't stop. I wonder how she was able to get away. I'm sorry. I hate to leave on such an ugly note, but I do need to get some writing done."

He hugged and kissed me. Then he took both of my hands in his, and stared deeply into my eyes. "We are going to have that exclusivity discussion very soon." Giving me a stern look, he left.

I watched him till he turned the corner. Shutting the door, I leaned against it and sighed. Was I ready for that conversation?

CHAPTER 18

Midway through work the next day, a text from Rob popped up on my screen: "Next steps?"

"On what?"

"Murder investigation. We need a plan."

"Okay."

"Dinner tonight? Pick you up at five thirty?"

"Great."

I texted Jenny to let her know I'd be late and outlined her frozen leftover options. At five thirty exactly, Rob came into my office. Packed up and ready to go, I asked, "Fiorella's?"

"That sounds good. Want me to drive?"

"Yes. I left my car at home."

"I thought you might have. It's been another lovely day."

Settling into the plush leather seats of his coal-black Audi, I enjoyed the quick drive. Luckily we were seated right away because I was starving. I ordered the pasta carbonara with shrimp, vowing to only eat half and to double my workout in the morning. Rob ordered chicken parmigiana.

He sipped his wine. "Have you thought about what our next steps should be?"

"Should we try to talk to John's ex-wife?"

"Together?"

"Yes, together. We've found out quite a bit separately, but it may be time to try tag-teaming."

"I'm game if you are." He moved his chair closer to mine.

"I'll try and find her contact information tomorrow and see if she is willing to speak with us."

"Afternoon on Wednesday would work for me or Thursday morning."

"I'll let you know."

In what was becoming a habit, we ordered our desserts to go and brought them home to eat with Jenny.

The next morning, I asked Cheryl to track down Paula Sanders. She was motivated by the challenge, and by ten o'clock I had Paula's phone number in hand. I punched in her number. "Paula Sanders."

"Hi, Paula. You don't know me, but my name is Merry March. I live in Hopeful."

"Yes?" she said in a cautious tone. "Why does that town's name sound familiar?"

"Your ex-husband lives here."

"That bastard! I wish I never met him!"

"A friend of mine and I were wondering if you had a few minutes to talk with us about him."

"Why? What's he done now?"

"We're not sure he's done anything. We'd just like to ask you a few questions."

"I'm off work on Wednesday at five. I guess I could meet you for a drink, if you buy."

"Yes, of course."

"Good. Money's a little tight right now."

"No problem. Where should we meet you?"

"There's a place called the Town Tavern on Main Street in Chesterville."

"I'm sure we'll be able to find it. We'll meet you there at five fifteen. My friend Rob is about six feet tall, and I'm short and have reddish-brown hair."

"I'm tall with blond hair."

"See you then." I hung up and texted Rob with the particulars.

Getting back to work, I was distracted. Paula certainly sounded bitter. And if what I heard was true, she had good reason.

The next afternoon, Rob picked me up right on time. "How do you want to handle this?"

"I think the important thing is to get her talking about John. Do you think we should tell her what happened to Ben and that John may have been blackmailed?"

"Let's play it by ear."

The bar looked like a typical dive: dark paneling, pool tables in the back, and well-used linoleum-covered card tables. It wasn't that crowded, and I spotted a pretty blond woman sitting alone. She waved hesitantly. Rob and I made our way over to her.

"Merry?"

I nodded. "And this is Rob Jenson."

He shook her hand.

She smiled. "They don't have table service here, so you'll need to get the drinks at the bar. I'll have a Bud Light in the bottle, no glass. Another tip—I wouldn't order wine here."

"Good to know." I sat across from her. I looked up at Rob. "The same for me."

"That makes three. I'll be right back."

Paula searched me with her eyes. "What's this all about?"

"We heard some things, and we were wondering if they were true."

"Like what?"

I hesitated for a moment. "My understanding is your marriage did not end well."

Paula twirled her hair with her finger. "That's the understatement of the year. Let me tell you about that jerk."

Rob rejoined us carrying two of the beers and then returned with his. "I ordered some nachos for us to share."

Paula nodded. "Good choice. Now, where was I?"

I prompted, "You were going to tell us about the end of your marriage."

She tipped the bottle up and gulped some beer. She wiped her mouth with the back of her hand. "That creep. I'm glad he's out of my life, and I pity the next sucker he's going to take for a ride."

Rob gave me a look, and I elbowed him in the ribs, hard.

"It seemed like such a fairy tale in the beginning," Paula said. "He's good looking. I'm good looking. I figured our kids would be spectacular. It's about two years in, and he tells me he never wants kids because his childhood was so bad. Boo-hoo. He had a secret vasectomy before the wedding to make sure we wouldn't have them." Taking another guzzle, she put the bottle back down. "Wouldn't you think that's something you'd tell your fiancée before you got married? He knew I wanted kids."

Rob and I nodded sympathetically.

"Then he badgered my dad to get him to pay for his master's degree. And he made me move into Dad's house so we could save on rent. My dad was terrific about it all. He set up a special program at work so John could get his advanced education funded *and* paid for all of our expenses while we lived with him. It was embarrassing. Here we were—adults, married, and living off my dad. Dad knew how uncomfortable I was, so eventually he gave John money for a down payment without telling me. I was so happy we were able to move out. It was a nice Dutch Colonial: two stories with plenty of character. I spent a lot of time remodeling and decorating." She shook her head sadly. "What a waste of my time and Dad's money. My dad ran a mine, and as soon as it closed and times got tough, that was it. John was history."

I frowned. "What happened to the house?"

"John and I owned it. It had to be sold so he could get his half of our combined assets. What a joke! John took our savings and moved it to his own separate account. I didn't miss it, since I thought the money had been used for the down payment. He also reaped the benefits of the improvements I made when we got a better price for the house at sale.

"When the mine shut down, my dad moved in with us. Selling the house meant Dad and I no longer had a place to live. John's betrayal was too much for him. He had a massive heart attack and died. I will never forgive John. Never."

Rob and I shifted uncomfortably in our seats, unsure what to say about the raw display of emotion. I finally spoke, staring deeply into her eyes. "Betrayal is awful, but your father's death is so much worse."

She responded almost under her breath. "I will get my revenge. It's all I dream about at night." Snapping out of it, she smiled. "Anyone want to get me another beer?"

I jumped up. "My turn."

When I returned to the table, the nachos had arrived and Rob was talking about his career as a journalist. I asked Paula, "So what are you doing now?"

"I was able to get a job as a teller at the local bank. Plus, I bartend on weekends. I'm still paying off my father's bills."

"That must be tough."

"It keeps me busy."

I stood, and Rob joined me. "Paula, it was good to meet you. Thank you for being so open with us."

"I'm sorry if I was too emotional. As you can tell, it's a really sore subject for me. You said you were both from Hopeful?"

"Yes," I said.

"Didn't I hear about a murder there recently? I think it was the postman?"

"You did. It was horrible and surprising that it happened in our small town."

"Lots of horrible things happen in small towns." She smiled grimly as she rose from the table. "Thanks for the drinks." She left without waiting for a reply.

"Wow," I said.

"Wow is right."

The ride home was silent as we processed what we had heard. As we got closer to my house, Rob said, "John is a piece of work."

"That's if we take Paula at her word."

"Are you defending him?"

"No. There's enough smoke to make me believe he's a slimeball. It's just a question of how big a slimeball."

Rob smiled. "Good. Then we're on the same page. You won't see him again."

"I didn't say that."

His neck flushed. "You have to admit, slimeball kind of implies it."

"True, but I may need to continue to see him to see if I can get more information."

"No. Just no. It's not safe."

"Here's a promise I'll make: I will only see him in a public place and only after telling you about it first."

"I'm still uncomfortable, but I guess I can live with that."

"You'll have to." I hopped out of the car. Moving to the driver's side, I leaned in for a quick kiss. "I'll see you soon."

The next morning, I rose with the birds and decided to go to the early Mass. Waking Jenny, I told her that her smoothie was in a to-go cup on the counter. I dashed out the door and waved to Nancy on her porch.

She called out, "Stop by tonight if you have a chance. I have something interesting to tell you!"

"Will do!"

The rhythm and tradition of the Mass, along with the well wishes of people attending, cleansed me of the negativity from the night before. Afterward, I caught up with Father Tom and accompanied him to the rectory. "Father, I've been thinking more about the possibility of an annulment. Perhaps we could discuss it?"

"I'd be happy to talk more about it with you, Merry. I do have another appointment now. Ask Belinda to set up some time; she should be in the kitchen."

I smiled, pleased to have a priest-approved excuse to talk to her. "I'll do just that."

Belinda was sitting at the table drinking tea. She started to rise, and I said, "No, don't get up. I'll join you."

"Would you like some tea?"

"No. I had coffee at the house, and I don't want to have too much caffeine."

"I know what you mean. I try to limit myself, but sometimes I just need another cup. What can I help you with?"

"Father Tom told me to speak with you about setting up an appointment."

She started to stand again. "I'll get the book."

I waved her back down and sat at the table. "No hurry. Enjoy your tea." I settled back in the chair. "We've never really had a chance to chat. How have you been enjoying your time here in Hopeful?"

"It's a great town. The people are nice, and it's such a vibrant parish."

"Weren't you in a parish in White Horse before you came here?"

She looked pained. "Where did you hear that?"

"Father Tom told me he stole you from the priest there."

She smiled. "I don't know that he stole me, but it was time for a change. I have family closer to here."

"Really? Where?"

She looked cornered. "Well, closer to here than there. Anyway, as I mentioned, it was time for a change."

I raised my eyebrows. "I can understand wanting to be near family. It will be tough when Jenny leaves for school year after next. I'm kind of hoping she picks a school that's not too far away."

"Family ties tug at you no matter where you live or how old you are," she murmured with a faraway look. Shaking her head as if to clear it, she stood. "Well, Father Tom isn't paying me to sit here and drink tea. Let's set up your appointment."

Appointment time in hand, I texted Rob, "Have time for coffee?"

"Ten fifteen; Morning Pastry."

Rob was examining the pastry case when I joined him. Ordering my latte, I considered a scone but remained virtuous. I sat outside and closed my eyes to savor that first sip. Rob joined me, holding a coffee and a pumpkin scone. I must have looked pitiful because he broke a corner off the scone and handed it to me without saying a word.

"Thanks." I scarfed it down.

He broke off another piece. "Lovely as this is, I have a busy day. Why did you want to have coffee?"

I gave him my best sad eyes. "Because I missed you." He looked ashamed, so I decided to let him off the hook. I grinned. "I have something to tell you and wanted to ask you to dig up some information."

His eyes narrowed. "What have you been doing?"

"Nothing bad. I went to morning Mass and ran into Father Tom. I wanted to talk with him, so he asked me to make an appointment with Belinda."

"And?"

"Belinda and I ended up chatting." I rolled and unrolled the paper ring that had been affixed to Rob's napkin, and he stilled my hand. I looked into his eyes. "It was a weird conversation."

"How so?"

"I asked her specifically where her family lived, and she didn't answer. She avoided the question. And I got the distinct impression there's something not quite right with her family dynamic. She spoke of them tugging on her no matter where she lived."

"That is odd. It doesn't necessarily mean there's anything there."

"We need more information. Can't you do some type of search on her relatives?"

He sat back and sighed. "Yes, I can, and I have a feeling I'd better or you won't give this up."

"You're right about that." I smiled. "Now, wasn't this a nice coffee break?"

"You didn't get a task; you delegated."

I smiled again. "Sign of a good manager. Well, I better get back." I gave him a quick kiss. After a beat, I turned back. "Dinner at my place tonight? Sixish?"

"I feel far less used now that I know you are going to feed me. You're on. Need to leave to cover the basketball team by seven thirty, though."

"Maybe I'll go with you."

"I'd like that."

I went home at lunch, threw a few things into the slow cooker, and set the table. I texted Jenny, "FYI, Rob coming for dinner tonight."

She texted a two-faces-kissing emoji.

I need to talk to that girl. I am her mother. After work, I put some rolls in the oven. Right at six, Rob rang the doorbell.

I answered it. "Want some wine?"

He grimaced. "I do, but no, not with the game tonight."

"Okay, I'll be good too then. Iced tea?"

"Yes."

Giving him a glass, I ran upstairs and knocked on Jenny's door. "Dinner in five."

Hearing a mumbled reply that sounded like a yes, I returned to the kitchen. "Did you find anything out?"

"Belinda's parents are deceased, but she has a brother who was released from prison a few months ago. He spent time in the penitentiary for armed robbery. Prior to that, he did time for assault and battery. He also had some juvenile charges, but they were blocked from view. In general, I'd say he's a pretty unsavory character."

I shuddered. "I wouldn't want him for a relation or to run into him in a dark alley."

"Me neither."

Jenny bounded down the stairs and swung into the kitchen. She plopped down next to Rob. "How's the reporting business?"

"Fine. How are your Roughriders going to do tonight?"

"They'll win, as usual."

Pulling the rolls out of the oven, I ladled the stew into bowls. We all tucked in and made appropriate enjoyment noises.

Rob said, "Wow, this is good. How did you have time to do this and work today?"

"I'm Wonder Woman! Not. The secret is a slow cooker and frozen vegetables. I ran home for lunch this afternoon and just threw them in and let the cooker do its magic."

"You can do magic like this for me anytime."

Jenny nodded. "Me too, Mom. It's really good."

After dinner, Cindy picked Jenny up for the game, and as the last dish went into the dishwasher, Rob and I left. It seemed like most of the town was there, and the game did not disappoint. It was a nail-biter, with the Roughriders winning by six. Rob dropped Jenny and me off afterward, settling for a quick kiss on the cheek. Setting the alarm, I checked the locks and went to bed. I was so tired, sleep quickly found me.

When I got up the next morning, it occurred to me that I hadn't seen Nancy the night before. Feeling uneasy, I frowned as I put the coffee on. While waiting for it, I counted on one hand the number of times she hadn't been on her porch in recent memory. And that included bad weather. It had been perfect out last night.

Opening the door, I peered at her house. Her porch was vacant, so I scurried over and knocked. After a moment, I tried the door. It opened right up.

"Nancy, are you here?"

Silence greeted me. Nothing seemed amiss in the front room, so I inched forward, calling her name again. Nothing. In the kitchen, one of her feet stuck out from behind the island. My mind went into hyperdrive. *Oh my God, she's had a heart attack. She's always using too much salt.* I rounded the island and froze. She lay there unmoving, eyes open, a boning knife in her chest.

Gagging, I clutched my chest and ran back to the front porch. I took a deep breath and dialed 911. I gave the operator the information, sank down onto the steps, and cried. *Nancy will never watch over us from this porch again.*

Sirens split the air, growing ever louder. Detective Ziebold's car screeched to a halt. He raced up the steps. "What happened?"

"Nancy was murdered."

"Where?"

I gestured toward the house. "In her kitchen."

"Wait here!" He dashed inside.

"Mom?"

Startled, I leapt up, blocking the door to Nancy's house. "Go back home, Jenny. I'll be there shortly."

"What happened to Mrs. Piedmont? I heard the sirens. Is she okay? Why are the police here? You've been crying."

"I'll explain everything in a few minutes. Please go back to the house."

Rob's car pulled up. He jumped out. "What happened? I heard the address on the police scanner and hopped in the car!"

I pulled myself together. "Rob, there's been an accident. Would you please take Jenny back to the house? I'll join you in a few minutes."

Rob glanced between my ashen face and Jenny's concerned one. "Sure." He put an arm around Jenny and walked her back to the house.

More police arrived and hurried inside. Phoning Cheryl, I told her to rearrange my appointments. Police came and went, and then the coroner's van arrived. Eventually, Detective Ziebold came out and told me to go home and that he'd come for my statement as soon as he could.

I shook as I jerked across the yard. Thinking about Nancy on her porch and our many conversations made me stop in my tracks and sob.

Before I knew it, Rob gathered me in his arms. "It'll be okay."

"No, it won't be. It won't be ever again."

"You're in shock and chilled to the bone. Come in. I called the school and told them Jenny wouldn't be in today." He gently led me toward the door.

"It was so awful."

"Try not to think about it, at least for now."

Guiding me to the kitchen, he sat me down at the counter. "Where's the strong stuff?"

"It's before noon. What do you mean?"

"You need something. You've had a shock."

"Cupboard above the fridge."

He retrieved a bottle. "I made some coffee. I'll put a bit of Irish whiskey in it."

"Whipped cream on the door of the fridge."

He mixed me an Irish coffee with two spoons of sugar and plenty of whipped cream.

Jenny ran down the stairs and rounded the corner, a concerned look on her face. "Mom, what happened? You look terrible. You're white as a sheet."

Taking a sip of the coffee, I patted the seat next to me. "Sit here, Jenny."

She sat, and I put my arm around her. "Something terrible has happened. Mrs. Piedmont is dead."

Her eyes widened. "Did she have a heart attack or something?"

"No. Someone killed her."

"What?" Rob and Jenny said simultaneously. "What happened?"

"I remembered I hadn't seen her last night, so I went over to check on her. She was stabbed."

There was a knock at the back door. Rob opened it. "Detective Ziebold."

He came in. "Is there any more of that coffee?"

Rob brought him a mug. "What happened?"

"All I can say at this point is that Nancy Piedmont was murdered in her home sometime between five last night when she spoke with her cousin and eight this morning when Merry discovered her. Merry, I need to take your statement. Is there somewhere private we can go?"

Rob frowned. "She's had a shock. Can't this wait?"

I groaned. "I want to get this over with. Let's go to my office, Detective." I saw Jenny crying silently. I hugged her. "Rob, will you make Jenny some hot chocolate?"

At his nod, Detective Ziebold and I went to my office and shut the door.

He took out his pad. "When was the last time you saw Nancy?"

"Yesterday morning. I was in a hurry to get to Mass on time. She wanted to talk to me." Tears ran down my face. "Why didn't I stop?" I grabbed a tissue and wiped my eyes.

"She asked you to stop?"

"No. She asked me to come by last night, if I had time. I forgot and went to the basketball game. She wasn't on the porch when I got home after work, nor was she there after the game. That's what disturbed me this morning. I suddenly realized I hadn't seen her." I studied the tissue. "I should have sat with her instead of going to church."

"What did she want to talk to you about?"

"I don't know. She just said she had something interesting to tell me."

"Do you have any idea what that might have been? Do you think it had anything to do with Ben's death?"

"I don't know, but I sure hope so because I'd hate to think we have two murderers in town!"

He frowned. "Are you and Rob still investigating? You need to leave it to us. Nancy's death should be a huge warning to you."

"Maybe it's time for us to compare notes."

He stood, towering over me. "If you have information you are withholding..."

"No, nothing like that. We just have some theories we're working on."

"I expect you and Rob at my office at four o'clock today with any and all information you have. This is not a game."

"I know that. We'll be there." I got up and returned to the kitchen.

He followed me. "You'll also need to sign your statement then." He inclined his head toward Nancy's house. "I need to get back over there." He sighed. "Can I have some more coffee? I'll return your mug later."

"Sure." I topped off his mug.

I found Rob and Jenny in the living room. Sighing, I dropped down next to Jenny.

"Are you okay, Mom?"

"Slightly better. This Irish coffee is great. Thanks for fixing it for me, Rob." I took another sip. "Detective Ziebold wants both of us at the station at four."

"What for?"

"He told me it's time for us to share any suspicions we have."

Rob held me with his emerald-green eyes. "Does he know we don't have any proof?"

"He's aware of that. Nancy's death scares me. I want the police to know everything we do. I want Nancy's killer caught and punished."

"How does he know Ben and Nancy's killer is the same person?"

I shrugged. "He doesn't, but it's not a wild jump. Also, yesterday morning Nancy told me she had something interesting to tell me. I'm kicking myself I didn't go over there sooner."

"Don't beat yourself up about it. It may not have been anything."

I gave him a steady look. "I think it was something. Something very specific. Something the killer didn't want us to know."

Jenny cried, "I want this killer caught! Mrs. Piedmont was a nice lady who always looked out for us, and she also looked out for our cats." She buried her face in Drambuie's fur.

I grimaced. "I have such a headache. I need a bath and a nap in that order."

"What's your network password?" Rob asked. "I'd feel better if I worked from here today. I don't want to leave you two alone right now."

I summoned a smile. "I don't want you to leave either. Have whatever you want to eat." I handed him the paper with the network code on it and went upstairs.

Jenny said, "I don't want you to leave either. I'll be up in my room catching up on schoolwork." She ran up the stairs behind me and gave me a hug before opening her door.

I soaked in the tub for quite some time. I couldn't get the sight of poor Nancy out of my head. I hoped she hadn't been in too much pain before she died. All cried out, I dried off and pulled on some sweats and a T-shirt. Sinking onto the bed, I covered myself with an afghan. I slept, amazingly enough.

At one, I woke with a start and looked warily around my bedroom. Why was I in bed so late? It all came rushing back: Nancy, dead. I rose and brushed my hair. Noises came from the kitchen. I headed down. Jenny pulled the panini press out of the cupboard, while Rob slathered slices of bread with butter. Jenny noticed me first.

"Mom." She ran over to give me a hug.

Rob was right behind her. "Group hug."

We all embraced. "What are you two doing?"

Jenny said, "We decided on grilled cheese sandwiches and tomato soup. You said when you were my age and sad, your mom used to make it for you."

"They are the true comfort food. Thank you both, but I'm not sure I can do them justice."

"Normally I'm more humble, but my grilled cheese is one of the true wonders of the world," Rob said. "I think if you try it, you'll finish it."

I smiled. "I'll certainly try."

They bustled about, finishing the sandwiches and heating the soup. It occurred to me that I should set the table, but I didn't have the energy. After a few minutes, there was a wonderful-looking grilled cheese sandwich in front of me, along with a cup of soup.

I tried the sandwich first and gestured with it to Rob. "You may have understated; this is really tasty. Nice and gooey, just the way I like it."

"The secret is equal parts Velveeta and Havarti with a sliced tomato on it to make it healthy."

"I'm not sure it's healthy, but it sure hits the spot." Looking down at my plate, I was surprised to see I had eaten the entire sandwich. "You were right. I finished it."

"You needed the energy."

Jenny and Rob finished their sandwiches and soup. "What time do we need to be at the police station?" I asked.

Rob answered, "Four." My head snapped toward Jenny, and Rob put his hand on my arm. "Patty stopped by while you were sleeping. She's going to pick Jenny up at three forty-five. She'll be staying overnight with Cindy at their house."

"Thanks for arranging everything. I seem to be stuck in molasses mode today."

"I'm going to finish up some of my homework and pack a bag," Jenny said. "I'll be down in time to leave."

Rob gave me a quick hug and started cleaning up. I shook my head. "No way, fella. You cooked. I clean up."

Acquiescing, he slid back onto one of the stools at the counter. He studied me. "How are you feeling?"

"I'm still a little numb. It's such a shock. How could this happen here?"

"How could it happen anywhere?"

"Please take the lead with Detective Ziebold. I'm not sure my brain is functioning well enough to handle it."

"No problem. We're a team."

CHAPTER 19

When we arrived at the police station, the sergeant ushered us into one of the interview rooms and said Detective Ziebold would join us. After a few minutes, the detective came in with a couple of bottles of water.

"Tough day." He handed us both a bottle and slid onto one of the rock-hard chairs.

"It's just so sad. Do they know if she was killed immediately?"

"Not yet. The autopsy is scheduled for tomorrow, so we'll know more then. Merry, you mentioned this morning that Nancy had something to tell you. Have you thought of anything more?"

"No. She was aware that Rob and I were still looking into Ben's death. I'm assuming that had something to do with it, but it could have been anything."

"Let's talk about what you and Rob found out."

Rob jumped in. "Let me give you a summary."

"Please do."

"You remember that Merry found that ledger at Ben's place. Have your people been able to figure out the code?"

"It seems really simplistic but hard to crack without having a place to start."

"Merry and I started with John Gordan."

The detective's eyes widened. "The school superintendent? Why?"

"Because he had opportunity. Plus, we felt he had something to hide." Rob explained what we knew about John and his ex-wife.

"You think that John killed Ben so he'd keep quiet about the fact that John treated his ex-wife badly? Seems a little thin to me." He shook his head.

"That's why we were reluctant to bring you this information," Rob said. "We didn't have proof. As we see it, three people were potentially being blackmailed: John Gordan, Suzie Krump, and Belinda Harper. Before you ask why the other two, it was because their initials lined up. And each of them had secrets they wanted to keep."

"Everyone has secrets they want to keep. It doesn't mean they are murderers."

I crossed my arms. "It may not mean they are murderers, but it could mean they were being blackmailed. It seems like you're belittling all the work we've done. The police haven't solved Ben's murder yet, and now Nancy is dead! This has to stop."

Rob held my hand. "Merry's right, Detective Ziebold. I'm sure you and your team are working away at this, but we're frustrated because we're not seeing any progress."

"My team is frustrated too. But you really need to leave this to us. We know what we are doing, and I don't want either of you taking unnecessary risks. There is a murderer out there, and we don't need any more bodies." The detective took a sip of his water. "That said, I do appreciate your work and the fact you are sharing it with us. And please call me Jay. There's no need to be so formal. Now, was there anything else?"

Rob said, "No, that's it."

"Thank you for coming in and sharing your ideas. We take them seriously and will be looking into them. Merry, here is your typed statement from this morning. Please read it, make any corrections necessary, sign it, and leave it with the policeman outside the door."

Jay stood and turned to leave. Pausing, he gave us a long look. "Please be careful, both of you. This is not a game."

Rob scowled. "We never thought it was."

"Well, that was depressing."

"He's going to look into what we found. We should view this as a win."

I gave him a measured look. "You must be one of those glass-100 percent-full people."

"Yep, and proud of it. We should heed Jay's warnings. I'm going to stay at your house tonight. I don't think you should be alone. Do you mind if we make a quick stop so I can pick up a change of clothes?"

"You don't have to do that. I'll make sure the locks are on and the alarm set."

Rob held my arms and looked deeply into my eyes. "If I don't stay over, I won't get any sleep. I'm grumpy without sleep, so you better say yes."

I put my arms around him. "I appreciate it. I don't know if I'll sleep tonight anyway, but at least this gives me a chance."

Rob and I made a quick pit stop at his place. I went inside with him and was surprised at the décor. He had sleek dark-gray leather sofas paired with a chevron-patterned chair in a grouping with a quarter-sawn coffee table. "This is so nice."

"Why do you sound shocked?"

I moseyed over to his bookshelves to examine some of the lovely art. "I figured you to be more minimalist—bachelor traveling the world kind of thing. But you've collected some lovely items." I bent down to caress his Persian rug. "Eclectic, I would call it, but the effect is stunning."

He smiled. "I'll be right back."

I continued to look at the photos, the paintings on the walls, and the souvenirs from his travels on the bookshelves. Rob came back in. "Where did you keep all this stuff when you were traveling?" I asked.

"Storage places mostly. Friends kept some of the more valuable pieces for me. It's really nice to be somewhere permanent so it's all in one place."

"It's lovely."

We returned to the car, and he asked, "Do you want to stop for something to eat?"

"No. Let's just call for a pizza when we get back."

I handed Rob the phone as we entered. "Would you call the pizza place? I hate to admit it, but I have their number on speed dial. I'll make up the spare bedroom."

"No need to bother. I can just sleep here on the couch."

I shot him a look. "No guest of mine is going to sleep on the sofa. The bed's way more comfortable. It'll just take me a minute."

"What do you want on your pizza?"

"Anything but anchovies."

I made up the spare bedroom and put a new toothbrush and towels in the bathroom. Changing back into my sweatpants and T-shirt, I rejoined Rob. I sat next to him on the couch. "What do you think Nancy was going to tell me? I keep going over and over it in my head."

"Don't drive yourself crazy." He put his arm around me.

"I'll try not to. Want some wine?"

"I'd love some."

I retrieved the wine and sat back down next to him. I handed him a glass. "To Nancy."

"To Nancy."

The pizza came, and Rob paid. He brought it into the kitchen, and I followed with our glasses. Topping them off, I took another sip. "Hmm. Maybe Melissa will know something."

He kissed the top of my head. "It's late now. Let's eat the pizza and figure out our plan of attack later."

* * *

Jenny bounded through the front door first thing in the morning just as Rob was coming down the stairs. She stopped in her tracks. "I, uh, forgot my math book." She sidled past him to get to her room, then she ran back down the stairs, book in hand, as I came out of the kitchen. She gave me a long look. "We need to talk when I get home."

"It's not what it looks like," I yelled after her as the door banged shut.

Rob and I looked at each other. "Why am I explaining myself to my daughter?"

"Plus, we didn't do anything wrong."

"And we're adults anyway." I smiled as I brushed past him on my way back into the kitchen. "Coffee?"

"Yes, please."

"I defrosted some muffins. I hope you like strawberry."

He nodded. "I love all muffins equally."

We sat companionably at the kitchen counter, drinking our coffee and eating. I asked, "What's the plan today?"

"I think you're right. We should try to talk to Melissa."

"Let me call her."

I punched in her number, and after a few rings, she answered. "Hello?"

"Hi, Melissa. It's Merry. I'm so sorry about Nancy."

"The police told me you found her. Would you come over today so we can talk?"

"Yes, I can. Is nine thirty too early?"

"No. I didn't get much sleep anyway, so come ahead."

I hung up. "I didn't mention you'd be with me. I'm not sure how comfortable she's going to be talking in front of a member of the press. Maybe I should go on my own."

"No more going on your own. We're a team."

"Yes, we are. I'll just have to talk fast." I took a casserole from the freezer and started for the door.

Arriving at Melissa's house, I handed Rob the casserole to hold and rang the doorbell. She answered with a tear-streaked face. I gave her an extended hug as she asked us in.

"Melissa, I'm not sure if you've met Rob Jenson?"

"Yes. I met him briefly when we were cleaning Ben's house." She eyed Rob. "You're the new newspaper guy."

"That's right."

"I don't want to talk to you."

I jumped in. "He's not here as a newspaper man, Melissa. He's here as my friend. We've both been looking into Ben Ford's death and now, unfortunately, Nancy's."

"It's just so hard," she sobbed. "I can't believe it! I spoke with her the day before yesterday about our plans for Thanksgiving. Who would do this kind of thing?"

"I'm so sorry." I patted her arm with my free hand. "Let me just stick this casserole in the fridge. I've got instructions taped to the top."

"Thanks for bringing it. You may have to rearrange some things in there. Quite a few people have been by."

I took it from Rob and walked into the kitchen.

When I returned, she said, "We may as well sit down." She sat heavily. "Did you really find her?"

"Yes, I did."

"Did she suffer?"

"I don't think so, but the medical examiner will give us a better idea after the autopsy."

"We were more than just cousins. We were best friends. Being the same age, we went through everything together. When we were young, we were hardly ever separated. My mom used to joke that there was a revolving door between Nancy's house and mine. We discovered boys, had our hearts broken more than once, and told each other everything. Neither of us kept a diary because there wasn't any point. I always thought after we got old we'd move in together and look after each other." She sighed. "That's not going to happen now."

"What can I do to help? Do you know when they'll release the body?"

"Detective Ziebold's hopeful they'll release her before the end of the week. My girls are coming in tonight, and Father Tom's already been by to discuss the wake and funeral. It would be great if you would do one of the readings at the funeral. Nancy really loved living next door to you. She always said you were so sweet to her. And she loved your morning muffins."

My eyes welled up. "I loved having her as my neighbor; she was always looking out for us. It raised my spirits just to see her waving to me from her front porch."

"She loved sitting there, looking at her garden and seeing all the hummingbirds in the summer."

"The morning before she died she told me she had something interesting to tell me. Unfortunately, I was in a hurry and didn't have time to chat. I will always regret I didn't stop and talk to her."

"Merry, don't beat yourself up. She knew how much you liked her, and she understood you have a busy life."

"Do you know what she wanted to tell me?"

"No." She paused. "Unless it was about the woman she saw. She mentioned her to me the other night."

"Can you remember what Nancy said?"

"I wasn't paying too much attention, but it seemed like she had seen a strange woman in town. When she introduced herself, the woman didn't give her real name."

"Do you know what her name was?"

"No. I can't remember. The doc gave me a sedative, and my brain is scrambled. I'll think on it, and if I remember, I'll call you."

"Melissa, please do call if there is anything you need. I'd be honored to give a reading at the funeral." I stood and hugged her again. Rob shook her hand, and we left.

He frowned. "Who do you think the woman was?"

"I don't know, but I'm going to try and find out."

"Lunch?"

"I don't know if I feel up to it. Don't you have work to do?"

"Are you trying to get rid of me?"

"No. I feel safer with you around, but I don't want to take advantage."

"Please do. And I think you should try to eat something. How would you like some soup at the Morning Pastry?"

"They do have great soup there. I could try."

We debated sitting inside or out. Outside won, as it was a lovely day. I chose the butternut squash soup, which was served with a thick slice of nine-grain bread, and Rob went with a turkey and cranberry sandwich on sourdough.

Rob said, "I think I may be jealous of your soup."

"I know I'm jealous of that sandwich. It's huge!"

He took a big bite. "And tasty."

There were a lot of people out strolling at lunch, enjoying the weather. A few came up to us and mentioned how sad they were about Nancy and inquired about the wake and funeral. It was nice to see that she had touched so many lives and that people cared. I was virtuous and refused dessert but did keep Rob company by ordering a latte.

I sighed. "Melissa didn't give us a lot to go on."

"No, but what she said was intriguing. Nancy saw someone who was not who she said she was."

"Should we tell the detective?"

"I'm not sure how he would react. We gave him three suspects yesterday who he didn't believe in, and today we're going to hand him an even more mysterious one?"

"You're right. It may be premature. What's next?"

"I have a source in the post office I could check with."

"Looking for what?"

"A change-of-address report. We could see if there was anyone new to town in the last few months. I could say I want to create a 'Welcome to Town' section on the newspaper's Facebook page."

"And then we could follow up to see if we recognized the person." I sat back. "It does seem kind of needle in the haystack. Plus, how do we know the person relocated here? She could be from a nearby town and was just stopping to try one of our great restaurants."

"The person who did this would have to have some familiarity with the town. Getting into and out of the rectory, knowing where Nancy lived, and even recognizing Nancy." He arched an eyebrow. "Do you have any other suggestions?"

"None, other than I might see if I can get into Nancy's kitchen. She had a habit of writing things she wanted to remember on sticky notes and leaving them on her fridge. I was too shocked the other day to check there. If you have to work, I could stop by and see if they have the tape down. I have a key to her house."

His eyes widened, and his mouth opened. "You are not going into a house where your friend was murdered all by yourself."

His words shocked me. I had gotten so wrapped up in the next steps that I had forgotten this was real. Nancy was my friend, and the last time I saw her she was lying dead in her kitchen. The blood drained from my face, and my eyes welled up. "You're right. I don't know that I can do this."

He took my hand. "You shouldn't have to. Let's strike a deal. If the tape is down, I'll borrow your key and check the kitchen."

Two hungry cats greeted us as we entered my house. I gave them a few treats for neglecting them and filled their food dishes. Rob leaned out the back door and peeked at Nancy's house. "It looks like the police tape is down. Are you okay with me checking it out?"

"Yes, but please go to the front and ring her doorbell. I think it's too soon for Melissa to be cleaning it out, but I would hate for you to surprise her. I'm sure she's jumpy enough as it is."

I watched out the side window as Rob cut across to Nancy's front door. It didn't appear anyone was there because he used the key to get in. It made me nervous for him to be there by himself, but I couldn't bring myself to go over there. I watched the clock and promised that if he wasn't back in ten minutes, I would steel myself and go look for him. He made it back with a minute to spare.

I exhaled loudly. "What on earth were you doing over there so long? I was worried!"

"I didn't see a sticky note on the refrigerator, so I took a few minutes to look around."

"Did you find anything?"

"No. All I found was a shopping list and this."

He held up a pink sticky note with *Tell Merry what I found out!* written on it.

I frowned. "Well, that's not very helpful."

"No, but it is worrisome."

"How so?"

"It was lying out in the open on her desk in the kitchen. Anyone could have seen it."

"And...?"

"If the killer saw it, how would they know Nancy hadn't yet talked to you?"

I dropped into a chair. "I didn't feel safe before. Now I feel a lot less safe. What about Jenny? What if something happened to her? What if she was home and I wasn't?"

"It might be best if she stayed at the Twilliger's for a few days. Hopefully this mess will be figured out by then. And you better get used to having me around because I'm not leaving this house until the killer is caught."

"I'll call Patty."

"And I'll call my source at the post office."

Phoning Patty, I explained the situation and told her I would join her at her house at three fifteen to talk to Jenny. Then I texted Jenny: "Go home with Cindy. I'll meet you at the Twilliger's."

Next, I called Cheryl, feeling bad about neglecting my business. She assured me she had everything well in hand and urged me to focus on myself. Feeling somewhat more in control, I returned to the dining room just as Rob was hanging up his phone.

"Five new people have come to town over the past few months: me, John, Candy Johnson, Beth Samuelson, and Arte Simmons. Other than John and me, do you know any of the others?"

"I've met Arte; he came in to buy some insurance. I haven't met the other two."

"I think it's time for us to see who Candy and Beth are."

CHAPTER 20

We shadowed Candy Johnson's apartment early the next day, hoping to catch a glimpse of her going to work. Just past eight, a woman left the apartment with a shawl covering her head. She slid into her car.

I said, "Darn. Can you see her face?"

"No. The shawl's in the way."

"What should we do?"

"Follow her."

Her car pulled slowly out of the lot. After a few seconds, Rob started after her. She kept to the back roads for a few miles and then got on the interstate. Twenty minutes later, she took the exit for Chesterville. Rob and I exchanged a look.

He said, "I wonder."

A few moments later, she turned into the parking lot of the United Bank and Trust. Shrugging off her shawl, she got out of the car and walked into the bank.

"Paula Sanders," I said.

"Yep. Do you think that was what Nancy was trying to tell us? That she had seen Paula in town?"

"It could be. I find it interesting Paula didn't mention she had moved to Hopeful."

"I find it even more interesting that she's using an assumed name."

Rob drove slowly back to town.

"Why do you think she moved to Hopeful and why the different name?" I asked.

"The only thing I can think of is that she wanted to keep an eye on John and she didn't want him to know she was close."

"I think we should ask Father Tom if she's been by."

"I need to pick up a few things at the office. How about I drop you by the rectory and pick you up in fifteen minutes. Text me if you're ready before then. You should be safe enough there."

I rolled my eyes. "You do know the first murder happened there?" Pulling out my cell, I called Belinda to see if Father Tom had a few minutes free. An appointment had canceled, so Rob dropped me off in front of the rectory. He watched until I went in and tooted the horn as he drove away.

Father Tom rose to give me a hug as I came into his office. "Merry, I didn't expect to see you today. I was so sorry to hear about Nancy. Did you come by to talk about the reading? I'm afraid we're not quite ready yet because they haven't released her to the funeral home."

"Thanks for being so flexible. No, I didn't come about the funeral, although Nancy's passing really depressed me. She was such a nice person." We hugged again. "I just had a quick question for you. Do you know if a woman named Candy Johnson has registered at the parish?"

"Yes, nice woman. She's tall with brown hair."

"Blond hair."

"No. I just saw her at Saturday Mass, and it was definitely brown. She joined a few months ago. We had a nice chat as I gave her a tour."

"Did that tour include the rectory kitchen?"

"I don't know for sure, but I usually offer the new members some tea after the tour. Why?"

"Just curious."

"Merry, what are you up to?"

'Nothing really. Just saw her name somewhere and hadn't met her yet. I was thinking of introducing myself. Is that the time? I really need to go; Rob's picking me up."

"It would be nice of you to meet with her. She seemed lonely and a bit high-strung."

"Great. I'll set something up. Thanks again, Father."

I rushed out the door and slid into the car. "She did join and likely saw the kitchen on the tour."

"Let's go back to your house. Do we need to stop somewhere for lunch?"

"No. I have things there. That way we can talk freely."

Rob pulled in behind my car, and we made our way to the back door. I opened the door, and the cats scrambled for freedom between our feet.

I chuckled. "I should have warned you. They get pretty demanding when they haven't had a chance to explore the backyard in a while."

Rob smiled. "I'll remember that for the future."

"Are you hungry? How does tuna on rye with some red onions and avocado sound?"

"It sounds like it would hit the spot. Want me to get the plates and glasses?"

"Yes, please."

Chopping the onion and celery, I took a can of tuna out of the cupboard. When I used the electric can opener, loud meows came from the back door. I sighed. "Let them in."

He opened the door, and I quickly had two cats dancing at my feet. Rob shook his head. "How did they know?"

"Can opener—does it every time. It's like ringing the dinner bell. I give them just a little in their special bowls. Weird family tradition, and they get very grumpy when we don't comply."

He sat on a stool by the counter. "I'm learning all your secrets."

"Iced tea okay?"

"Great. Would you like me to get it?"

"It's in the fridge."

He put some ice in glasses and filled them up just as I finished making the sandwiches. Since we had a tough morning, I gave us both chips and a few cookies for dessert.

"This looks great." He dug in.

I nodded. "I'm not sure Father Tom believed me when I told him why I was asking about Paula, aka Candy. But now we know that in addition to a false name, she disguised her appearance. He said she had brown hair."

"Maybe she dyed it."

"If she did, she's dying it back and forth. She had blond hair when we saw her this morning, and Father Tom said it was brown at Saturday evening Mass. I think it's a wig, and that's why she had the shawl on this morning. I also think you and I should attend Saturday Mass this week, since that's the one she seems to favor."

"What's the plan? We sit in the pew behind her and yank the wig off?"

"That's not a bad idea, but I was thinking of something a little more subtle."

"Such as?"

"Sitting in the back and sneaking out a bit early so we can be waiting for her on the front steps."

"Sounds like a better idea. Do you want me to go over to the Twilliger's with you?"

"It's just a few blocks. I think I can handle it in the daytime."

"If you don't mind, I'll set up my laptop on your dining room table."

"That's fine. If the cats are too bothersome, put them out back."

"Will do."

Rob set up his laptop, and I gave him a quick kiss. "Thanks for being here for me."

He smiled. "Always."

I swallowed hard. "Back soon."

Traipsing over to Patty's house, I tried to figure out what I was going to tell Jenny. I decided on an abridged version of the truth. Trotting up the back steps, I let myself in. Patty was in the kitchen giving some of the younger kids a snack.

"It's such a shame about Nancy. She was a nice lady and a good neighbor to you."

"She sure was. It's so depressing to think about."

Cindy and Jenny burst in the back door. "We're hungry. What can we eat?"

Patty rolled her eyes. "You're both old enough to get something on your own. I'm not your servant."

Cindy hugged Patty. "I don't consider you my servant, merely the fabulous person from whom all tasty things come."

"Flattery will get you everywhere. I've hidden some fresh-baked chocolate chip cookies in a jar behind the cereal on the third shelf."

"Yum! You are the best mom ever!"

She and Jenny grabbed a few cookies and milk and made for a quick exit.

"Hold on, young lady," I protested.

"Oops," Jenny said. "Hi, Mom. We're kind of in a hurry because one of our game tournaments is starting and we're playing kids in Florida."

"I think they can wait for one minute. Let's go into the living room."

We sat on Patty's sofa. "What's up, Mom? You know I love to sleep over at Cindy's, but you don't usually allow it on a school night."

"I'm nervous about what happened to Nancy, and I want to make sure you are somewhere safe."

"Why wouldn't I be safe?" She gave me a wide-eyed look. "Oh no, have you been investigating again?"

"Just a little, but I told you I'd be careful, and having you stay here is one precaution."

"But that means you'll be staying in the house on your own. Mom, don't do that!"

"Rob's going to stay with me...in the guest room, of course."

Jenny wiggled her eyebrows. "Of course, the guest room."

"Young lady!"

"Mom, promise me you'll take care of yourself."

"I will, and I'll call you tonight before bedtime."

"Love you." Jenny gave me a fierce hug before running up the stairs.

I returned to the kitchen. "Teenagers—one big bundle of energy."

"Sure are," Patty replied. "I couldn't help but overhear. Rob's moving in?"

"Just temporarily while scary things are happening."

"It's not a bad thing. I want to hear from you every day. Text me when you get up and when you go to bed. If you don't, I'll release the hounds."

"Got it. I promise." I laughed and gave her a quick hug on my way out the back door. My thoughts swirled. *Who on earth could be behind this?* Dark clouds gathered. Praying for the rain to hold off till later that evening, I didn't notice when a car pulled up next to me.

"Merry."

Stopping, I bent over to look in the car window. It was John Gordan. "John," I stammered, "what a surprise."

"A nice one I hope."

"Yes, of course." A cold shiver rolled down my spine.

"Can I give you a lift somewhere?"

"No. I need the exercise, and I'm only going as far as home."

He turned off the engine and got out of the car. "I'll join you." He tucked his hand under my elbow.

"No need. It's just a few short blocks."

"I'd feel better." His blue eyes met mine. "There's so much craziness going on lately. I want to make sure you're safe."

Not seeing any way out, I acquiesced. "Thank you for being so considerate. And thank you again for that lovely meal at your house last week. I enjoyed myself. Your house is so beautiful."

"It is, isn't it? We'll need to come up with another date that will work for both of us. I was kind of hoping you'd reciprocate."

We reached my front door. "Yes. We'll have to do that. I'll reach out when I have my calendar in front of me."

"Why don't I come in and we can settle it right now?"

I shrank back just as Rob opened the door. "John, it's nice to see you again."

Startled, John looked between Rob and me. "Is Rob living here?"

"Yes," Rob said.

"No," I protested.

"Well, glad that's cleared up," John said. "I think I'll be going now."

He walked down the steps without looking back.

Rob ushered me in and shut and locked the door. "Merry, what on earth were you thinking? What was that all about?"

"I'm not sure. He drove up next to me and wanted me to get in the car. When I wouldn't, he got out to accompany me home. It might have been all innocent, but his insistence gave me the willies."

"Come here." He wrapped his arms around me. "You're shaking. Let me get you something to drink."

"No argument here."

He handed me a glass of wine. "To figuring this out."

I sat on the sofa. "What makes us think we can do that?"

"First, we're smart, and second, I think we are getting close."

"That's what scares me. Plus, I feel bad about all the innocent people we may be maligning."

"Like who?"

"Our suspects—the ones whom we will eventually find out aren't guilty."

After dinner, I left Rob watching SportsCenter and went upstairs to read. It was so comforting to have another adult in the house with me. Especially a man. Especially this man. We seem to be so in tune together, and he is a caring person with such a nicely proportioned body. His kisses make me feel alive. It was going to be difficult to keep myself in my room tonight, knowing Jenny wasn't home. Picking up my book, I tried to read, eventually giving up and turning out the light.

Sometime later, I heard him coming up the stairs. There was a hesitation in his turn toward the guest bedroom. Unexpectedly, I heard a soft tread heading to my door. Holding my breath, I stared at the knob. The clock chimed, and he slowly walked away. I let out my breath and wondered what I would have done had he opened the door. Was I ready to take our relationship to another level?

The rest of the week went quickly enough. I threw myself back into work, and Rob was playing catch-up as well.

At four thirty on Saturday, Rob said, "Are you sure this is a good idea?"

"I don't know, but I'm anxious to see if Paula/Candy is there."

Arriving just before Mass, we followed through with our plan of sitting in the back. I was surprised by how crowded it was in the last few rows. *They're probably people hoping to make a quick exit.*

Rob elbowed me and pointed toward the front. "See the brown-haired woman in the third pew on the left about six people in?"

My eyes narrowed. "Yes, that looks like it could be her."

I started. John Gordan sat in the fifth pew on the left.

Rob frowned at me. "What?"

I pointed, and he whispered, "This is going to be interesting."

Mass ending, we exited and found Father Tom. "I liked your homily," I said.

"I'm glad you found it meaningful."

"I thought I saw Candy Johnson toward the front. Do you think you could introduce us, Father?"

Sensing someone next to me, I turned and nearly jumped.

"Hello, John," Father Tom said. "Did you enjoy the homily?"

Rob and I exchanged tight smiles with John.

Father Tom said, "Candy, Candy, come here, my dear. I have some people I'd like you to meet."

Her eyes widened when she saw me and Rob and then almost leapt off her face as she noticed John. "No time, no time." She spun around and made a hasty retreat to her car.

Father Tom shrugged. "I guess she was in a hurry."

"Yes, seemed so," I said.

John's mouth made a perfect circle as he watched Paula speed away.

I asked him, "Do you know Candy?"

"Candy?"

"Yes." I pointed to the receding car. "Candy Johnson. She's new to the parish."

"She looks exactly like someone else I know. Different hair color, though. Couldn't be." He slowly shook his head.

"Who?"

"Never mind. I'm afraid I must go. Thanks, Father." John spun on his heel and left.

"Everyone seems to be in a hurry tonight," Father Tom mused.

I said, "Must be plans for the evening."

"Yes, I suppose so." Father Tom turned to greet some other parishioners.

Rob and I moved slowly down the stairs. "Wow," he said.

"Yep. Should we be concerned about Paula?"

"I'm not sure."

"Let's go back to the house and get my car. I think we should drive past her place to make sure everything's okay."

We sped up and, as soon as we turned into the drive, hopped into my car. Driving as quickly as possible, I soon pulled into the parking lot of her building. Her car was near the door. John's car was nowhere to be found.

I said, "Maybe he didn't have enough time to follow her."

"She did leave rather quickly."

"How long did it take us to find her address earlier this week once we had her name?"

"No time at all."

I rubbed his shoulder. "I think we need to talk to Jay."

"You're right." Rob pulled out his cell phone and punched in his number.

Jay answered on the second ring. "What?"

"We need to meet," Rob said.

"I'm just sitting down to dinner with my family. Can't it wait?"

"I'm afraid not."

Jay sighed. "I'll meet you at Merry's house in fifteen."

Rob hung up. "He's not happy."

"He'd be less happy if we didn't call him."

As soon as we got home, I made coffee. "We haven't had dinner yet, and it sounds like we interrupted his. Should I defrost some dessert, and we'll eat out of order?"

"I'm all for dessert first."

Retrieving some frozen cobbler, I stuck it in the microwave to reheat. As Jay arrived, I pulled it out and reached in the freezer for ice cream. "Would you like some blueberry cobbler with ice cream?"

He shrugged out of his jacket. "Sounds great. I'll finish dinner later, hopefully."

Rob and I took him through what we found out about Candy Johnson. When we finished, Jay summed up. "So John and his wife had an ugly split, and now you think she's stalking him, but you're worried John is going to turn the tables and hurt her?"

"Good summary," Rob said.

"I'm not sure what I'm supposed to do about it. No one's been physically injured so far."

"Two people are dead," I protested.

"True, Merry, but we don't know if this is all related."

My eyes widened. "You think this is a coincidence?"

"It may be. I'll tell you what I'll do: I'll drive over there to make sure she's all right and see what I can find out."

"That would make us feel so much better," I said. "Would you call us afterward? I don't know if I can sleep not knowing."

"I guess I could." He stood and pulled on his jacket. "Thanks for the cobbler. I hope the kids haven't finished all the roast beef at my house."

"For your sake, we hope not," Rob said.

"What should we do now?" I asked as we cleaned up the table.

"We wait. Do you have any board games?"

"A few." I pointed him in the direction of the game cupboard and finished loading the dishwasher.

Holding up the backgammon box, he raised his eyebrows.

I smiled. "I'm so going to beat you."

The pace of play was fast. I forgot we were waiting for a call, and when Rob's phone rang, I started.

"Hello, Jay," he said. "She's not there? Is her car there? It's an older cherry-red Ford Corolla. Not there? Well, I guess there's not much you can do. You'll swing by her place again in the morning? Thanks. We'd appreciate that."

"She's not there," Rob told me.

"So I heard."

"What can we do? This is so frustrating."

"We could swing by John's place."

"Okay. I just need to do something."

The inside of John's house was dark with only the porch light shining. His car wasn't in the driveway.

Rob said, "It is Saturday night. Some people have dates."

"But he asked me out tonight."

Rob's eyebrows rose. "You didn't mention that."

"It was after the dinner at his house. I didn't think it was important because I obviously wasn't going to be meeting him."

Leaning over the console, he gave me a quick kiss that became a far longer one. It was broken up only by headlights flashing past us as they turned into John's driveway.

"Duck," I said.

We both scrunched down in the car, poking our heads up enough so that his car was visible. John got out and slammed his car door. Then he strode to his house and slammed the front door behind him.

I straightened. "That was close."

"It was, but I felt a bit silly."

"We didn't want him to see us."

"Why?"

I rubbed Rob's shoulder. "He seemed angry—all of that door slamming. Plus, I don't think we are two of his favorite people right now."

"Well, he's alone, and it looks like he's in for the evening. Do you want to stop somewhere for something to eat, or do you want to go back to your house?"

"Let's go back to my house."

I started to turn the key when Rob abruptly put his hand on mine. A car darted under the streetlight, coming to a halt just outside of its glare. Its headlights were off, but the streetlight had exposed a cherry-red Ford Corolla. We watched silently to see if Paula would get out. She didn't.

"Now what do we do?" Rob asked.

"What do you mean?"

"We've been sitting here long enough that if you start the car, she's going to wonder why she didn't see us get into it."

"She looks like she's settling in. I don't want to be here all night. Plus, we could be teenagers necking."

"Now, that's an idea." Rob smiled and reached for me.

I grinned at him. Her car door opened. I tensed as she crossed the street, keeping to the shadows. Tiptoeing to John's house, she peered in one of the lit windows. He moved around in his living room as she watched him.

I whispered, "This is getting bizarre."

"It sure is."

Paula crept away from the house and slid into her car. In a few minutes, it started, and she pulled away from the curb, again without headlights. The lights flicked on halfway down the block.

I released a breath I didn't know I was holding. "Do you think tonight's drama is over?"

"One can only hope. Let's go before anyone else shows up."

We covered the short distance to my house in silence. I grimaced. "Do you think she does that every night?"

"It's scary to think so. I'd hate to have someone peeping in at me."

I unlocked the door. "What do you feel like eating?" The clock chimed. "Wow. How did it get so late?"

"We've had a busy evening. How about I put together some sandwiches while you pour some wine?"

Watching Rob move around the kitchen relaxed me. "I should be tired, but I'm not. Another game?" I gestured at the backgammon board on the kitchen table.

"Absolutely."

We played two more games. I yawned. "You'll be carrying me up the stairs if we play one more time. I'm so sleepy."

"I wouldn't mind."

Smiling, I leaned over and kissed him. Before I knew it, we were making out like teenagers left alone in a den. Struggling upright on his lap, I straightened my clothes. "Much fun as this is, I'm not sure I'm ready for such a big step. We haven't really known each other that long. And I remember reading somewhere that you shouldn't make big decisions in times of stress."

Rob rubbed my back. "You're stressed?"

"Yes. Aren't you, with a murderer running around loose?"

"I wasn't stressed a moment or two ago." He gave me a wolfish grin.

"Neither was I, but you know what I mean."

"I do, and even though every fiber of my being wants you, I respect the fact that we may be moving a bit too fast for your comfort. I know what I want, and I want it long term. I can be patient."

"Thank you for understanding." I stood. "I'll see you in the morning."

As I opened the door to my room, I looked longingly at my bed. *Nope. Cold shower first.*

CHAPTER 21

"Is it just me, or is this town getting odder?" I said to Rob as we left to meet Jenny for breakfast at the Iron Skillet.

"I think strange things are happening. Hopefully we'll be able to figure out what it all means and quickly."

Jenny came in, and I gave her a big hug. "I've missed you!"

"I missed you too, Mom. I love Cindy and her family, but it's crazy there. How much longer is this going to go on?"

"Hopefully it won't be too much longer."

We chatted about schoolwork and after-school activities and ordered breakfast. The restaurant filled up fast as the churches finished their services. Enjoying my meal, I was surprised to see John Gordan. He looked distracted as he surveyed the crowd. He must have found the person he was meeting, for he waved and made his way toward the back. Five minutes later, Jay and his family came in. He stopped by our table and told his wife he'd join her shortly. Barbara waved as she shepherded the kids to their table.

Jay said, "I stopped by Candy's place this morning, and her car was there. I see your number one suspect is eating in the back."

Rob looked pained. "Maybe we should meet up later after you've had a chance to eat."

"Just get me before the game starts at two."

"Merry's at one?"

"I'll be there." Jay nodded at Jenny as he turned to join his family.

"Who's your number one suspect?" Jenny took another big bite of her pancakes.

I gulped. "Your superintendent of schools."

"Mr. Gordan? He couldn't have done it. He's nice."

"He may not have, but just in case, I want you to be careful around him."

"I will. I need to get more clothes and drop off my dirty laundry. Can I go back with you?"

"Of course. I'll take you over to the Twilliger's too."

Leaving, I craned my neck to see with whom John Gordan was eating breakfast. Unfortunately, the man had his back to me and John saw me looking. He gave me a level stare, and I made a hasty retreat.

When we returned home, Jenny pulled together another week's worth of outfits. After I loaded the washer with her dirty clothes, I ran her back over to the Twilliger's. "Tell Mrs. Twilliger I'll call her later. I love you." I gave Jenny a fierce hug. "Hopefully this will be over soon. I miss you!"

She jumped out of the car, and I watched to make sure she got safely inside. Once home, I moved the clothes from the washer to the dryer. I joined Rob at the kitchen table. "Rob, I've been thinking. Are we looking at this the wrong way?"

"How so?"

"Paula seems to be a stalker, but, for the life of me, I can't figure out why she would want to kill Ben Ford or poor Nancy."

"I agree, but we can't ignore the fact that Nancy wanted to tell you about Paula and was killed before she could."

"Was it a coincidence?"

"I don't know that I believe in coincidences."

Jay knocked on the back door. "Any coffee?"

I rose to get the pot. "I've been wondering. Do you have problems sleeping with all the caffeine you ingest?"

"Nope. Have a caffeine gene. Requirement to become a cop. That and a love of donuts." He smirked. "You'll be happy to see I brought your mug back."

I took it and put it away. "Thanks and thanks for coming. I know you want to get back in time for the game, so we should probably get started. Rob, do you want to tell Jay what we saw last night?"

Rob told him. Jay nodded. "That's interesting. Maybe we were worried about the wrong person."

"That's what I was thinking," I said. "But where I keep getting stuck is why Paula would have killed Ben and Nancy. She didn't know them and hadn't lived here very long."

Jay reminded me, "Merry, as I said last night, it could be a coincidence."

"Who here believes in coincidences?"

None of us raised our hands. "Okay, so it isn't a coincidence. What's the link?"

Jay's cell phone rang. "What? A shooting? Where? I'll be right there." He frowned. "I have to go. No game for me today."

"Who was shot?"

"Not sure yet, but it was in the parking lot of Paula's building." He rushed out the door.

Rob and I leapt up at the same time. He grabbed his keys. "My car."

Jumping in, we sped over to the apartment building. The area was cordoned off, and when we pulled up to the curb, the ambulance arrived. Rob ran forward as I tried to see what was going on. Unfortunately, my diminutive size didn't allow for much of a view. After a few minutes, Rob returned. "It's John."

"How is he? What happened?"

"Looks like some kind of shoulder or arm wound. He was talking to the EMTs, so maybe it isn't as bad as it looks. Jay has Paula in the back of his car. I'm going to follow him to the station and see if I can find out what's going on and get a statement for the paper. I'll drop you off at home. Or would you feel safer at Patty's?"

"I'll be fine at home. Our prime suspect was just taken away in an ambulance, and his stalker is now in police custody."

Rob dropped me by my house, and I started working on my chore list. It was amazing how quiet and peaceful it felt being home alone. Jenny's laundry was finished and put away. Pulling out the mop and bucket, I started to clean the kitchen floor. There was a knock at the front door.

A large, rough-looking stranger stood there. "Meredith March?"

"Yes?"

"My sister said you've been asking questions about her."

"Your sister?"

"Belinda Harper—she works for the priest. She's a good person, she likes her job, and she likes living here. You're bothering her. I don't want you to bother her anymore. I don't want you to ask any more questions. Do you understand?"

As he spoke, his voice became softer and softer. Leaning closer, he stabbed his finger at my chest and moved well into my personal space. I backed up, quivering in fear. "Yes, I understand."

"I don't want to have this conversation again."

"Got it."

Turning on his heel, he strode to his car. As it pulled away, I vaguely took note of the fact that it was a black BMW. I slid down the door to the floor and sat there halfway inside the house.

A few moments later, Rob pulled into the driveway and rushed up the steps. "I saw the front door open. I was so worried. Why are you sitting there?"

I laughed somewhat hysterically. "I think I just met Belinda's brother."

"Father Tom's Belinda?"

"Yep."

"The brother who was in jail?"

"Pretty much certain."

"Let's get you up and into the house." Lifting me up, he held on to me as I wobbled my way in. Easing me down onto the sofa, he left to get some brandy. "Here, drink this."

I took a sip and immediately started coughing. He quickly retrieved a glass of water. When the choking subsided, I was embarrassed to find tears running down my face.

Rob said, "It's okay now. Try to drink some of the brandy."

I took another sip, then a healthy gulp, and pushed it away. "I'm okay."

"You don't look okay. You look white as a sheet."

"It was scary. I answered the door, and there he was, right in my face. He was so big!"

"I'll call Jay."

"No! He wants me to stop asking questions about his sister. I'm sure he wouldn't look kindly on me telling the police."

"We need to let him know. Keeping quiet will make things worse."

"Just give me a minute."

"Here, have another sip of brandy."

I slugged down some more. "I'm feeling better now."

"Good."

"I need to put the wash in the dryer. Wait. I think I already did that." I stood and tried to walk. "It's the oddest thing. The room seems to be spinning." Careening into the wall, I found myself sitting on the living room floor. "How strange."

"Maybe you've had enough brandy." He lifted me up and carried me to my room. He put me down gently on the bed and covered me with a quilt. "Take a nap. You'll feel better."

"I'm not tired." I was out like a light.

Waking two hours later, I sat straight up in bed. *Why am I lying down when it's light out?* With a start, I remembered Belinda's brother. Brushing my teeth and hair, I decided I looked as presentable as I was going to get and made my way downstairs. Jay and Rob talked softly in the kitchen.

As I entered, Rob stood and hugged me. "How are you feeling?"

"Better. Still a bit woozy. I don't think it was a good idea for me to drink all that brandy."

He smiled. "Next time I'll know to pour you a much smaller glass." He guided me to a chair. "Jay was bringing me up to date on the shooting."

"What happened?"

Rob said, "Paula lawyered up, and the official statement is that John tried to force his way into her apartment. She said she shot him in self-defense."

"Did she say why she was using an assumed name?"

"She didn't want John to know she was here," Jay said.

I frowned. "If she was so scared of him, why did she move? It's not like she works in town."

"She said she liked the town and wasn't going to let John determine where she lived."

Still a bit woozy, I didn't even attempt an eye roll. "That story has holes the size of big-eye Swiss cheese."

Jay nodded. "I agree. I'm just telling you the story she told us. Now, if you're ready, let's talk about your visitor this afternoon."

I sighed. "Remember when Sunday afternoons in this town were peaceful? They certainly aren't anymore." I told him what happened and shared the make and model of the car he drove. "Unfortunately, I wasn't able to get the plate number. Don't you have the addresses of convicted felons?"

"Some, especially if they are still on parole, but only if they haven't moved."

"They can move and not tell the police?"

"Happens all the time. Hopefully we have the information on this guy." Jay stood. "I wonder if I'll actually be able to have a hot meal at home tonight."

Rob smiled. "We'll be pulling for you."

"I'll increase the patrols in this area. Stay safe."

Rob gave me a kiss. "I'm trying to track down the school board president for a quote on John. Pizza for dinner?"

"I need to do something with my hands, so I'll cook. Are you okay with chicken? I'll see what I've got to go with it."

"That would be great, but only if you think you are up to it."

"I am. Dinner will be ready in about an hour."

"Do you mind if I use your office for my calls?"

"Have at it." I rummaged through the freezer. Finding some boneless chicken breasts, I put them in the microwave to defrost. Luckily I had gotten some packaged salad the last time I was at the store, so a vegetable was covered. Rice would work as the starch. Opening a can of mushroom soup, I whisked it with shallots, cream, thyme, and a few real mushrooms to create a nice sauce.

Rob came back into the kitchen. "John is on paid administrative leave pending the results of the investigation."

"I don't know how I feel about that."

"How so?"

"If Paula is lying through her teeth, it seems a shame he's getting punished."

Rob's mouth dropped open. "With all that you know about John and the things he's done, you think he's innocent?"

"I didn't say he was innocent; I said he may not have threatened her. Her behavior was pretty weird last night. On the other hand, John was slamming doors, so he may have some anger management issues."

"I'm sure Jay will get to the bottom of it. What's for dinner? Something smells terrific."

I told him and asked him to set the table. As we ate, we talked about the impact to the school district. "Do you mind if we go over to Patty's tonight? I need to let Jenny know about John before she hears it somewhere else."

"No problem. I'll drop you off and come back here. I need to write this up and get the story online. You can call me when you're ready to come back."

We cleaned up, and then he dropped me at Patty's. As I came through the door, I was inundated with questions.

"What happened with the superintendent?"

"We've been hearing all kinds of rumors and crazy stories."

I held up my hand. "One at a time. Let's all sit down." I told them what I knew. They were amazed that their superintendent might have threatened his ex-wife. I ended by saying, "Remember, innocent until proven guilty."

Jenny rolled her eyes. "Yeah. That's why he was your prime suspect."

"He may have been my prime suspect for the murders, but that doesn't mean he did this."

Patty's eyebrows rose. "I don't think you are alleviating any concerns the girls have."

"I may not be making a bunch of sense. At any rate, that's all I know."

Patty said, "Girls, upstairs. It's a school night."

They ran upstairs. She crossed her arms. "What else?"

"Nothing."

"Don't *nothing* me. I know you better than you know yourself. What else happened today?"

I told her about my visitor, and she shivered. "Be very careful, Merry. Best friends are hard to find."

I was going to text Rob to pick me up, but I wanted some fresh air. Kissing Patty goodbye, I left. I closed my eyes and relished the cold night air caressing my skin. It was one of those nights where the moon is so new you can't see your hand in front of your face. Thanking the heavens for streetlights, I quickened my pace, eyes darting left and right, seeing danger in every shadow. *I probably should have called Rob.*

A stick cracked behind me. I ran. I didn't stop until my feet hit the front porch. Breathing hard, I had my key ready to go and was pushing the door open when it swung inward. I landed on my knees and looked up at Rob. "I should have called you."

"Yes, you should have. What happened?" He helped me up.

"I think I just spooked myself. I didn't actually see anything."

"When are you going to learn? There are dangerous people out there."

I gazed into his green eyes. *I could get used to him picking me up. I feel so safe in his arms.* I shook myself out of it. "I'm sorry. Believe me, next time I'll call. Did you finish your story?"

"Yes. It's online now. Feel like a movie?"

"No. It's late. Let's just watch some TV. I don't feel like concentrating."

We channel surfed until we agreed on one of the home shows. We put our feet up on the coffee table, and Rob put his arm around me. I settled in against his chest. My mind started churning. *Do I believe Paula shot John? Who knows what goes on in people's marriages, or divorces, for that matter? He was mad last night. Did he threaten her? And why? They are divorced. And what is the deal with Belinda's brother?*

The last thing I remembered was a couple debating the three houses they considered. I woke up the next morning on my bed, covered with a quilt. Smelling coffee, I took a quick shower and made my way downstairs.

"Good morning." I gave Rob a quick kiss.

He grinned. "Sleeping beauty is awake."

"I'm starting to get used to being carried to bed."

"Too bad you don't remember it."

I smiled. "True. Thanks for your support. I must have been more tired than I thought."

"It was a stressful day. And you didn't sleep in—it's only seven. Want some eggs?"

"Love some, but then I need to get a move on. I have a meeting at eight thirty."

"I need to get moving too. I want to check on John's status. I'm not sure if he was admitted to the hospital, and I need to see if Paula's still in jail."

"Do you think I should visit John?"

Rob stopped in his tracks, his mouth open. "Why on earth would you do that?"

"He can't harm me if he's in the hospital, and I might be able to get some information from him, especially if they've given him drugs."

Rob frowned. "You can be devious."

I smiled. "Sometimes."

"I'll text you as soon as I know where he is."

"Thanks. I'll let you know when I'm going. Now, I have to leave or I'm going to be late. And thanks for breakfast." I gave him a kiss, picked up my briefcase, and headed out the door.

Midmorning, Rob texted me, "John still at hospital. Should be there at least one more day."

"Going to see him at two."

"Be careful!"

I sent a smiley face emoji in return. At one forty-five, I left for the hospital, picking up some flowers on my way. The visitor's desk gave me a tag and told me he was in room 315. Knocking, I poked my head around the door. John was in the bed, asleep. Tiptoeing in, I put the flowers on the table and sat. John looked so vulnerable. *Could he be a killer?*

The phlebotomist entered, and I jumped. "John, need to draw some blood."

He started awake, and his eyes fixed on mine. "Merry? Surprised to see you here."

The phlebotomist drew blood and left quickly.

John shook his head. "I have no idea what they do with all that blood. It seems like they take it every five minutes. I'll probably leave here anemic."

I chuckled. "It does seem excessive." I moved closer to the bed. "I heard about the shooting and wanted to make sure you were okay."

"That's kind of you. Are the flowers from you as well? I don't think they were there when I went to sleep."

"Yes. I thought they might cheer up your room."

"You cheer up the room."

I blushed. "What happened?"

"That woman is so frustrating."

"Who?"

"My ex. I purposefully didn't tell her where I was moving. She showed up at the town I lived in before and made my life a living hell. I eventually had to leave so I could get some peace. It worked for a while but not long enough. I couldn't believe it when I recognized her at church on Saturday."

"So you didn't know she had moved to town?"

"No."

"Why would she do that?"

"She's nuts. She wants to make my life miserable. She has it in her head that I used her. Do I look like the kind of guy who uses people?" His blue eyes stared straight into mine, waiting for an answer.

I shifted in my chair. "No, of course not. Why would she think you used her?"

"I worked for her dad at the mine he owned. I did right by him, put in long hours, and was quite successful there. Then he suggested I take advantage of the company's educational program. He didn't think mines were my passion long term."

"He suggested it?"

"Yes." He sat straighter in the bed. "Why would you question that? What have you heard?"

"I wasn't really questioning. I was repeating what you said to make sure I understood." I took a deep breath. He seemed so suspicious. *Stop asking questions and just let him talk.*

"Oh, okay. Sorry, the pain medication is making me paranoid." He collapsed back on the bed. "Anyway, I followed his advice and obtained my advanced degree. Right about then our marriage started to fall apart. Paula was always so defensive and seemed to think I had limited her opportunities. I decided I would be better off on my own, so I filed for divorce. It wasn't my fault the mine failed and her dad died right after that. I liked the guy."

I nodded to show I was paying attention.

"Hey. What's the deal with you and Rob Jenson? He said you were living together."

"We are...temporarily."

"What does that mean?"

"After Nancy was murdered, it was scary to be next door with just my daughter."

"I would have helped. You could have called me."

"It's complicated."

"So you're not involved?"

"We are. We just haven't gotten as serious as living together."

"Were you involved when you came to dinner with me?"

"We had been seeing each other but not exclusively."

"I liked you, Merry. I thought we might have something together. It makes me sad to think you were just stringing me along."

"What? I was not."

"What would you call it? You were seeing us both at the same time."

"I think I better leave. You need your rest."

"I don't like playing second fiddle, Merry March. And people who play with me get burnt." His face turned bright red and the blood pressure alarm squealed.

A nurse ran in the door. I slid out as she came past.

Taking the elevator to the main level of the hospital, I got off, and Rob met me. "How'd it go?"

"Not well. Let's get out of here.

CHAPTER 22

I asked Rob to take me back to work, even though my head was pounding. Just thinking about the discussion with John made me queasy. I'm not the type of person who strings people along. Is that what I have been doing?

"You're being really quiet," Rob said. "Are you going to tell me what happened?"

"Yes, but I'm going to need a drink and food to make it through the story."

He glanced at me. "Now you are worrying me."

"There's nothing to worry about. John will be in the hospital till tomorrow at the earliest." Rob pulled up in front of my agency, and I leapt out. "See you at five. And thanks for the ride."

The rest of the day was spent on personnel matters and getting up to speed on assignments. Satisfied things hadn't gone too far awry, I focused on my call lists. Candy Johnson was on my list as a prospect for auto and renter's insurance. Dialing her number, I was pleased when she picked up the phone. "Hello, Ms. Johnson, this is Merry March from the Meredith March Insurance Agency. I understand you are in the market for insurance."

There was a pause. "I might as well tell you. We've met, Merry. I'm actually Paula Sanders."

I feigned surprise. "I'm sorry. They had your name down as Candy Johnson. I apologize for calling the wrong number."

She sighed. "It's not the wrong number. I live here in Hopeful now. I was using a different name. Look, it's complicated, and I wouldn't mind talking about it. Can you meet me tonight?"

"Sure. Let's talk over dinner at six at the Iron Skillet. Do you know where it is?"

"Yes. I've been by there."

"I'll treat. Do you mind if I bring Rob with me?"

"If you're buying, you can bring anyone you want. The only exception is that lying ex-husband of mine."

"We'll see you there."

I texted Rob: "Dinner plans tonight IS at six with PS."

"Meet you in your office at five thirty."

I moved back to working the call list and didn't see any other names I knew. At 5:20 p.m., my phone alarm sounded. Pulling the mirror from my desk, I quickly replenished my makeup.

Rob was right on time. "IS?"

"Iron Skillet."

"PS?"

"Paula Sanders."

One of his eyebrows lifted. "We're having dinner with Paula Sanders? How did that happen?"

"She turned up on my call list under her assumed name. I was surprised she was home. I thought she'd still be in jail."

"Jay turned her loose this morning. Her lawyer was raising a stink, and John Gordan refused to press charges."

"Why? He said she shot him. Why would he change his story?"

"Why indeed. Let's get Paula's story tonight. And speaking of that, we should get a move on."

"This isn't quite how I planned on spending my evening. I was looking forward to some dinner and then a long soak in the tub."

Rob pulled me closer. "How big is your tub?"

"Don't be getting any ideas! It's a tub for one!"

178

He smiled. "A fella can hope..."

Rob opened the door to the Iron Skillet. Paula waved to us from the back. We made our way through the crowded restaurant.

She stood to shake our hands. "I bet you are surprised to see me."

I nodded. "You'd win that bet. What are you doing in Hopeful?"

"I was worried about what John was up to, and I wanted to keep an eye on him."

"By shooting him?" I asked.

"Oh, you heard about that." She looked down at the table.

"Yes. You'll find that news travels fast in this town."

Rob nodded. "Speaking of that, is there anything you'd like to say to my readers to set the record straight?"

Her eyes narrowed. "My lawyer said not to talk to anyone. I forgot you were a reporter, or I would have told Merry not to bring you."

"Okay," Rob acquiesced. "This will all be off-the-record. I'll be here as Merry's friend."

I kicked him under the table. "So what happened? Why did you shoot John?"

"Well, since I may still be in trouble, I'm not saying I did and I'm not saying I didn't." She scooted her chair closer to the table. "If I did, it was because he showed up at my apartment shouting at the top of his lungs for me to leave him alone. He said he would kill me."

I said, "Sounds like he thought you were stalking him."

"With everything he put me through, was it wrong for me to make him uncomfortable?" She sat back and crossed her arms. "I think not."

"He mentioned you harassed him at his last town as well."

"It sounds like you're on *his* side."

"Not at all." Rob flashed a thousand-watt smile. "We're just trying to figure out what really happened. Let's grab the waitress and get you a drink." He flagged her down. "What would you like, Paula?"

"A mojito, if they make them here. I love the mint."

"Merry?"

"A glass of the house white would be good."

"And I'll have a mojito too."

Paula smiled at him and instantly looked ten years younger. "You have good taste." She slid her chair closer to his.

I started a slow burn as Rob amped up his charm. "I've never understood why such a good-looking woman like you ended up with John."

She preened. "It was because I was young and foolish. But I'm not now." Paula batted her eyelashes at Rob.

Shifting in my seat, I started to object. Rob kicked me. "Paula, why don't you tell us what *really* happened the other night?" He lifted his glass to toast her.

She scooted even closer, which I didn't believe was possible. "I was very young when I first met John. He dazzled me with his charm and wit. I didn't realize he was just using me." She fluffed her hair. "You may not know it, but I was quite sought after in town. In fact, I was the homecoming queen. I thought he was truly attracted to me the way the other men were." She looked down at the table and traced the wood grain.

"I can certainly understand that." Rob touched her shoulder. "You don't look a day over eighteen now, and I think you would still give the other women a run for their money."

She practically purred. "Then you can understand why I was so scared last night."

"Oh yes. Would you like another drink?"

"If you'll join me."

"Sure."

Rob ordered two more drinks. I was definitely going to need a shower when I got home because it had gotten so deep. I watched, annoyed, as Rob stared deeply into Paula's eyes. The waitress delivered the drinks.

Rob raised his glass to Paula. "To our newest and prettiest neighbor." They didn't bother to clink glasses with me. Then Rob asked, "So what *really* happened last night?"

"If you promise you won't tell..."

Rob actually crossed his heart and motioned zipping his lips.

"Well, if you're sure."

He nodded. "I am."

Her eyes darted around the room. Satisfied that no one else was close enough to hear, she began. "I went to the evening Mass on Saturday and was shocked to see both of you standing with Father Tom. I was even more shocked to see my ex. I drove out of there like a bat out of hell because I was worried John would follow me home. I swerved into the McDonald's parking lot and ducked down behind the wheel. When I thought it was safe, I drove home. Later that night, I went over to John's house. When we divorced, he made off with some candleholders my mother left me. He's so brazen that he has them displayed on his mantel like they were his! I looked around to see if there was a way to get in, and then he came into the living room. I jumped. I was so scared he'd see me that I crept back to my car and drove away.

"The next day, I went to his house, and his car wasn't there. Circling around back, I saw that the basement door padlock was unlocked. I snuck in, got my candlesticks and some other items that should have been mine, and left a note telling him I took them." She smiled smugly.

"I didn't think he'd be able to find out where I lived, so I thought I was safe. I was wrong. He showed up, and, boy, he was pissed. He started banging on the door and threatening to kill me, like I told you before. When I saw him through the peephole, I could tell he was about to explode. I ran into my bedroom and got my gun from the safe. Running back to the door, I told him I had a gun, and he said he didn't care. He was still going to knock the door down. So I aimed for the middle of the door and pulled the trigger. The police say a few inches to the right and John wouldn't be alive today. My lawyer says it's a classic case of self-defense."

I asked, "Did your lawyer know about your breaking and entering earlier in the day?"

She studied her nails. "No. I didn't see any reason to bother him with that detail."

"Weren't you afraid John would tell the police?"

"If he did, then I would have said he stole them from me." She smiled. "How would it look if the fine, upstanding superintendent of schools stole things? It's bad enough the school board now thinks he threatened me."

I frowned. "Couldn't he just say they were his and that you stole them from him? And that he momentarily lost control when he realized they were missing?"

"I have the receipts from my mother, and besides, what parent wants their children to be around someone who momentarily loses control? Get with it!" She sat back with a self-satisfied smile and toyed with her glass. "Rob, are we going to have another drink?"

Rob shot me a sidelong glance and then thought better of it. "I think not. I need to get Merry home."

Paula pouted. "What about me? I thought we were getting along just fine."

"Here's the number for a cab if you don't want to order an Uber." Rob flicked the card down on the table. He paid the tab, and we left.

I gave Rob a long look in the car. "Is that how you get all your stories? You get the women drunk and fawn over them?"

"Not normally, but I thought it might work in this case." He rubbed my arm. "I'm sorry if I made you uncomfortable."

"I was mad until you kicked me."

"I'm sorry for that too."

"Paula and John are quite the pair."

"Yes, they are. It's almost like they were made for each other."

We drove home. The message light was blinking on the answering machine when I opened the door. I pressed play. "Merry, it's Melissa. The police finally released Nancy's body, so the wake will be on Thursday at two and six and the funeral at ten on Friday. I just wanted to make sure you will still be able to do a reading at the service."

My smile drooped. "I'd better get back to her."

I called Melissa and assured her I would be honored to do a reading and told her to let me know if there was anything else I could do.

Suddenly exhausted, I rubbed my eyes. "Bath and bed for me." Giving Rob a quick kiss, I ran lightly up the stairs.

I drew a bath, poured in some stress-relieving bubble mixture, and eased myself into the tub. As I relaxed, my mind kept going back to my conversation with John. *He seemed so nice when I started to get to know him. Now I don't have any respect left for him. Am I destined to continue to meet people who aren't what they seem?*

Climbing out of the tub, I trudged to bed and burrowed under the covers. The minute I hit the sheets my eyes opened. Tossing and turning, I finally gave up and went downstairs to fix some warm milk. I put the mug in the microwave and stared out the window. *What evil lurks there? Will I ever feel safe again?* The microwave beeped.

Rob came up behind me. "Are you okay? I heard you going down the stairs."

"I'm so sorry. Did I wake you?"

"No. I couldn't sleep."

"Me either, hence the warm milk." I gestured to my mug. "Want some?"

"I've never been a fan. But, if you don't mind, I might have a splash of your brandy."

"Help yourself." I sat at the counter and waved toward the cupboard.

He did and joined me. He rubbed my back. "You feel tense."

"I am tense. I don't know why we can't figure this out."

"Just relax." He stood behind me and massaged my neck and shoulders.

"That feels so good. I was relaxed when I got out of the bath, but two hours in bed tossing and fretting tensed all my muscles up again."

"Don't talk. Just relax."

"I'm going to relax right into this counter."

He laughed. "That's okay. I can always carry you up to bed again."

I smiled. "This is getting to be a habit."

"It's a habit I'd like to get used to." He kissed the back of my neck.

"Now you're making me tense again."

"In a good way I hope."

"The best." I kissed him. He kissed me back, and before long we were on the couch. I laughed when I came up for air. "We always seem to end up here."

He eyed me speculatively. "We could go upstairs and be more comfortable."

My body longed for me to say yes, but I didn't want to get hurt again.

He stroked my hair. "When you're ready. I'm okay with waiting for what I want." Pushing himself off the couch, he held out his hand. "Come on, sleeping beauty. Time for you to get back into bed," he paused for dramatic effect, "alone."

We went upstairs, and I gave him one last kiss. He groaned and pushed me away. "I'll see you tomorrow."

I floated back to my room and crawled into bed. As I drifted off to sleep, happy thoughts of Rob played in my head.

CHAPTER 23

Stretching like one of my cats, I woke feeling great. A smile on my face, I caught sight of the clock. It was ten. Screeching, I jumped out of bed, threw on my robe, and ran down the stairs. Rob worked peacefully at the kitchen table.

"How could you let me sleep that long? I have things to do, meetings to attend."

"First, you needed the sleep. If you remember, we were up late last night. Second, I called Cheryl and told her you wouldn't be in till one. She rearranged your schedule."

I had the good grace to blush as I remembered our early morning rendezvous. "Thanks. You really are too good to me."

"Coffee's hot, and I ran out for some bagels. They're in the bag, and the cream cheese is in the fridge."

"You *are* too good to me, and I'm going to take every advantage of it." I grinned, kissed his cheek, and made a beeline for the coffee, filling my mug. "What are you working on?"

"I'm writing a follow-up to the Paula/John story. I checked with the hospital, and he's going to be released today. There's going to be a special board meeting next week to discuss his administrative leave."

My hands around the hot mug, I shivered.

Rob stood and wrapped his arms around me. "Are you cold?"

"No. I never had a chance to tell you what happened when I talked with John. I was going to tell you at dinner, but we met up with Paula. And then afterward, I forgot."

He pulled me close. "What happened?"

I whispered into his chest, "He threatened me."

Rob held me at arm's length. "Say again?"

"He threatened me. He said I was stringing him along. Then he told me he'd make me pay for it."

Rob hugged me tightly. "I won't let him get to you."

"Hopefully he'll be so busy with the board he won't have time to think about me."

"Eat your bagel. I need to finish this." He ushered me to one of the counter seats. "Oh, by the way, Father Tom called about the reading for Nancy's funeral. He gave me a suggested list; it's by the phone."

"How did you explain being here so early?"

"He didn't ask, and I didn't tell."

"Great." I took a bite of the bagel and frowned. Father Tom was going to want an explanation the next time I saw him. I grabbed the list of readings and scanned them. "For Nancy's funeral, what do you think about Ecclesiastes 3:1–8?"

"Is that the one the Byrds turned into a song?" He sang a few bars.

"Yes." I smiled at him. "You have a good tenor."

"Thanks. I think Nancy would have liked that reading."

"Me too. It reminds me of gardening, and she loved to garden."

"Then it's perfect. Are you going to call Father Tom?"

"No. I'll stop by on my way to work. Speaking of work, I need to get a move on since I've been such a sloth all day already."

With that, I kissed Rob on the cheek and ran upstairs to shower. I finished quickly and raced back down the steps. Stopping to give Rob a quick peck on the cheek, I scratched the cats and was out the door.

Belinda answered the rectory door. "Merry, I'm glad you stopped by. I want to apologize for my brother." She looked down at the ground and shifted her feet. "I know he can be intimidating. He's very protective of me, but he would never really harm you."

"Thank you for the apology. I hope you know this whole town appreciates the important role you play in the church and wants you to stay. I'm just trying to get to the bottom of this mystery." I grimaced. "I will say he is a very forceful man."

"He has been all his life." Adopting a more businesslike tone, she asked, "Were you looking for me or Father Tom?"

"Father Tom."

"You're in luck. He has a few minutes before his next appointment, and I know he wanted to speak with you about the reading for the funeral." She led me back to his office.

He got up to greet me warmly. "I hope you are here to tell me you'll do the reading?"

"Of course I will. Thank you for leaving some suggestions for me."

"Yes, Rob was nice enough to take them down." Father Tom arched an eyebrow.

Feeling like a teenager who'd been caught, I blushed. "Yes, he's been kind enough to stay with me while the murderer is on the loose. He's been sleeping in my guest room."

"Merry, you don't have to explain anything to me."

"He really has been sleeping in the guest room."

"I believe you."

My shoulders sagged, releasing some tension. "I was thinking about Ecclesiastes 3:1–8."

"That's a great selection. I'll make sure to mark it in the program." I stood, and he held up a hand. "One last thing, Merry."

"Yes?"

"I expect to see you at confession this Saturday."

Shaking my head on the way out, I crashed right into Belinda. I jumped back. "I'm so sorry. I should pay more attention to where I'm going. I hope I didn't hurt you."

She patted my shoulder. "No harm done. Why are you so jumpy? You're not still concerned about my brother, are you?"

"Nope, no, I'm just fine."

I headed for the exit. I definitely did not want to get another visit from him. Waving and trying my best at a normal smile, I shut the door behind me.

I braced myself against the door and took a few deep breaths. Then calmer, I made my way to the office. My afternoon was busy, so I concentrated on business for a change.

At seven, there was a knock on my office door. Rob stood there with takeout bags. "I thought we might want to eat here since we need to be at the school at eight."

"Why do we need to be at the school? Crap. Tonight is Jenny's ballet recital."

"Yes. I know. She asked me to remind you."

"She asked you?"

"She said you've been distracted lately."

I sighed. "Super. I'm going to go down as the worst mom ever."

"No, you won't. I even brought you flowers to give her."

I hugged him. "You are a nice man."

"I'd let you thank me properly, but we need to eat." He grinned.

I smiled back. "Later. Let's go to the conference room. My desk is a mess, and I'm afraid I'll get food on everything."

He laid the meal out on the table. "I wasn't sure what you wanted, but I saw a fried chicken food truck and decided on that. We have chicken, biscuits, mashed potatoes, gravy, and some coleslaw. I also picked up coffee."

"Looks like a feast!"

After digging in and some embarrassing moans of ecstasy from me, he said, "I guess this chicken place is a winner."

I held up the chicken leg I was eating. "You better believe it. I need to figure out the food truck's route so I can stalk it. Of course, that means I'll need to exercise a ton more. On a lighter note, how was your day?"

"Not too bad. There's a big brouhaha going on with regard to the Christmas decorations."

"What about?"

"The chamber of commerce submitted their recommendation, but one of the town selectmen insists on wreaths for the streetlights. Another wants small hanging trees. And then there is the question of bulb colors. They'll be looking for public comment prior to finalizing the decorations."

My eyes widened. "Do they know two people died? Where are their priorities?"

"Christmas is not that far off, and decorations have been proven to bring in shoppers."

I put my head in my hands. "Don't remind me. I haven't even started shopping." When I looked up again, the table was nearly empty of food. "I can't believe how much we ate. Let's put the trash out back so the office doesn't smell tomorrow."

Arriving at the high school, we settled in our seats. The production started, and the dancers were terrific. Jenny and Cindy seemed to float by when they were on stage. *Jenny must have gotten her grace from Drew. I have two left feet.* After the ballet ended, Rob and I fought through the crowd to the backstage entrance and were quickly joined by Patty and Patrick.

I gave Patty a hug. "Does your family think you've adopted Jenny? I'm hopeful it won't be too much longer."

Patrick replied, "She's a lot of fun to be around. Everyone will be sorry when she goes home." He turned to Rob. "Nice flowers."

Rob handed them to me. "Merry got them for Jenny."

Patty arched her eyebrows. "Nice save."

The girls came out talking a mile a minute, and we all heaped praise on them. Pulling Jenny aside, I gave her the flowers. "I'm so proud of you." I hugged her fiercely.

"They're so beautiful. Thanks, Mom."

Patty joined us. "We're going for ice cream. Do you and Rob want to come?"

I gave him a questioning look. He nodded, and I said, "We'd love to. Jahn's?"

"Of course."

"We'll meet you there. Jenny, do you want to come with us?"

"Yes." She hugged Cindy. "I'll see you there." Jenny bounded in front of us.

Rob and I exchanged a glance. I smiled. "We may have to tether her to the ground."

Jenny twirled and laughed. "I'll slow down for you old folks."

I dashed up behind her and grabbed her in a hug. "I'm not old!"

We both laughed as we pushed out the doors into the cold. Rob caught up and gathered us both in his arms. "I'm only slightly old." This sparked more hilarity.

Jenny froze.

"What?" I looked over my shoulder.

"Mr. Gordan," Jenny said. "I thought you were still in the hospital."

John scowled at us, his arm in a sling.

"John, should you be out in the cold so soon?" I asked.

His eyes narrowed. "Probably not. I just came to get some papers."

"I thought you were on leave?" Rob said. "Should you even be entering the school?"

Shooting Rob a look of pure hatred, John got back in his car. "That's none of your business. I suggest you and your *friends* go on your way." He glared at us through the window.

I pulled on Rob's arm. "We were just leaving."

Rob looked like he was going to argue, but then he noticed Jenny's pale face and trembling body. He held his hand out to her. "Come on, Jenny. Let's go."

She took his hand, but her eyes never left John. The three of us walked toward town.

"Mom, he was so mean. Why doesn't he like us anymore?"

"He's had a tough time; he was shot. If you can, you should avoid being around him."

"I will. He's scary."

I held her face. "Are you still in the mood for ice cream?"

She smiled. "Absolutely!"

We arrived, and Patty, Patrick, and Cindy waved us over. Their celebratory mood lifted ours. At the end of the evening, we hugged Jenny goodbye as she got into the Twilliger's car.

Patty said, "We could drive you."

I smiled. "Yes, but then we wouldn't have a chance to try and burn off the banana split you thought was such a good idea."

"What can I say? I'm such a temptress, but you didn't have to say yes." She winked as the car pulled away.

Rob and I strolled for a while, both lost in our own thoughts. Rob abruptly stopped. "What do you think was so important that John went to the high school just after being released from the hospital?"

I shrugged. "I have no idea. He said he was looking for some papers."

I opened the door to the house. "Let's call Jay," Rob said. "He may want to know about this."

After a few minutes, Jay called back. "I spoke with the board president. He's given me permission to search John's office. I shouldn't let you, but do you want to meet me there?"

Rob didn't hesitate. "Yes. We'll be there in ten minutes."

I stared at him. "Don't we need a search warrant?"

"I guess if you have permission, you don't need one."

"Good thing. It looked like John was going to leave after you challenged him. Do you think he doubled back after we left?"

"I guess we'll find out."

Rob drove to the high school. I frowned. "It's weird to be here this late. There's no one around."

"I think that's the point."

Headlights came our way. Jay parked next to us, and we got out of the car.

He joined us. "The board president told me the district's offices are on the second floor on the east side. The night janitor is supposed to meet us to let us in."

We came to the doors, and the janitor opened them. "How long are you going to be?"

Jay replied, "Not sure yet. Give me your cell number, and I'll text you when we leave."

They exchanged numbers as I looked around. Only the night lights were on. The school was so dark it was spooky. I started when Rob put his hand on my arm. "This way."

We ran up the stairs and into John's office. I asked, "Where should we start?"

"Look for a briefcase or backpack." He pointed toward the closet. "You can start over there, and Rob and I will look through his desk."

Opening the closet door, I muscled some coats out of the way. A backpack peeked out from behind a stack of paper. I lugged it out and placed it on one of the armchairs. Pulling the other chair up, I sat and rummaged through the pack. A few files, some receipts, and then I removed a velvet bag. I opened it and gasped. It was a beautiful twenty-four-inch pearl necklace. And it looked real. I held it up. "Who leaves a valuable pearl necklace in their backpack?"

Rob's eyebrows rose. "Maybe someone who already had their house burgled."

Jay frowned. "I think I missed a chapter."

Rob filled him in on our conversation with Paula. Jay said, "I'm going to have a chat with her. And I'd wager we found what John was coming to get. Thanks for the info and for meeting me here. I'll text the janitor. You two better go home now."

Rob and I scurried down the hall past all of the gray lockers standing sentinel in the darkened hall. Our steps echoed. I shivered.

Rob put his arm around me. "Are you cold?"

"No. Nervous, I guess. Feels like someone just walked over my grave."

"Let's get you home. I'll make some hot chocolate for us."

I smiled. "That's just what I need tonight: more calories."

We slid into the car. I bit my lip. "How mad do you think John is going to be when he finds out the necklace is gone?"

"Very mad. I'm glad we're not going to be there when it happens."

As we pulled out of the parking lot, John's car drove past. I ducked down. "Do you think he saw us?"

"I couldn't see him, so I doubt he could see me. And I don't think he knows my car on sight. Good thing Jay is still at the school."

✳ ✳ ✳

As I went to work the next morning, Jay's car pulled up next to me. The passenger-side window slid down. I leaned in. "Good morning. It seems like I just saw you."

"You did. We've got to stop having these early mornings after late nights."

I laughed. "You're right. We are getting too old for this. Hey, I have a question for you."

"What?"

"What did John say when you saw him last night?"

Jay frowned. "I didn't see him."

"That's strange. He pulled into the school parking lot as we were pulling out."

"He didn't come in or I would have seen him. I was talking to the janitor by the front door."

"I guess he didn't want to run into you."

"Well, he's going to run into me today. I need to ask him about those pearls you found."

I waved. "Good luck, and have a good day."

"Likewise." He drove away.

I texted Rob, "Do you think we should call Paula re: pearls?"

"No. Let Jay handle."

I sent him a thumbs-up emoji. The morning was busy, and I had just enough time to dash over to the Morning Pastry to grab a sandwich to eat at my desk. As I stood in line, I noticed Suzie looked worried and seemed distracted. I had to repeat my order several times.

After the third time, I said, "Suzie, are you all right?"

She nodded. "I'm just out of sorts. There's a lot going on."

"Call me if you want to talk."

Picking up my tuna on sesame bagel, I grabbed a drink and left. Suzie still seemed out of it. *I wonder what that's all about?* I shook my head and returned to the office.

At five thirty, Rob poked his head around the door. "Finishing up? Or should I come back later?"

"Finishing up, but you shouldn't feel we're joined at the hip."

He smiled. "What's wrong with being joined at the hip?"

"Nothing, I guess. I'm just wondering if you are getting tired of babysitting all the time. Don't you want a night off?"

"From you? Never."

I raised one eyebrow. "If Jay doesn't solve this thing, we're eventually going to have to go back to normal. Jenny needs to come home soon. I miss her, and I don't want Patrick and Patty's hospitality to run out. You must miss your house and routines as well."

He looked pensive. "I do, but I'd never forgive myself if something happened to you. Were you able to clear some time on your calendar for Nancy's wake tomorrow?"

"Yes. I thought we'd stop by for a few minutes at two and then stay for the whole time tomorrow night. I also had Cheryl clear my calendar for Friday morning so we'd be able to go to the funeral."

"Are you going to want to go back to work after the funeral?"

"It's going to be a light afternoon, so we'll play it by ear."

As we went to my house, Rob's phone rang. After listening for a few minutes, he covered the phone. "Jay wants to come by at eight. Is that okay?"

I nodded. "Works for us. We'll put the coffee on," Rob said and then hung up.

"I wonder what he wants."

We had a quick dinner and focused on tidying up some business odds and ends until Jay knocked at the back door. Rob let him in and poured the coffee.

Jay took a mug and sipped it. "I spoke with both Paula and John today. What a piece of work they are."

"Was the necklace Paula's?" I asked.

"Yes. Apparently, it was a Tiffany heirloom from her mother. She reported it stolen five years ago when she was still living with John. I guess we now know who took it."

Rob asked, "Why would he have taken it?"

"Paula told me she thought it was spite. She said he was always jealous of the expensive things she got while growing up. I'm surprised he didn't sell it."

"How much is it worth?" I asked

"A conservative estimate is $50,000 to $60,000."

Rob whistled. "Wow. That's a lot of money for one necklace."

Jay nodded. "It sure is."

Rob frowned. "Did you arrest him?"

"No. She's refusing to press charges. She says she must have forgotten he had it. She's just happy to have it back."

"Do you think that's why Ben was blackmailing him?" I asked.

"Hard to tell. It might have been, since the police report was a public record." Jay stood. "Thanks for the coffee. Let me know if you hear anything else."

Rob accompanied him to the door. "Thanks for letting us know what happened." He shut the door. "Curiouser and curiouser, as Lewis Carroll would say."

CHAPTER 24

As I donned my black suit and white blouse, I cried. I remembered how kind Nancy was to me and Jenny. She took care of the cats on a moment's notice and kept an eye on my place. I sighed. I would miss our coffee klatches on her front porch and the way she always had her finger on the pulse of the town. It would be tough getting through the next few days.

Jenny was excused from school on Friday so she could attend the funeral with us. *Need to take her clothes to Patty's.* Wiping my eyes and smoothing the creases in my skirt, I trudged slowly down the stairs to the kitchen.

Rob looked up when I entered and came over to give me a hug. "Feeling blue?"

"How could she be gone? She was so full of life."

"She was a good friend to you. It's natural for you to feel down. After you leave, I'll go home and get my suit."

I studied him with a wry smile. "I thought you looked a bit casual."

"Don't worry. I won't embarrass you."

"I'll see you at two?"

"Yes, I'll be there."

I gave him a quick kiss and left. Staring up at Nancy's porch, I automatically looked up for her wave. Shoulders sagging, I continued on to work.

At one forty-five, I left the office, walking to the funeral home. Rob waited outside the door. He hugged me, and we went in together. Even though we had gotten there early, a line had already formed of people waiting to pay their respects. It went quickly, and before I knew it, we were standing in front of the open casket. I knelt and said a prayer, tears running down my face. Touching her hand, I said goodbye.

Rob put his arm around me, and we made our way over to Melissa and her girls. I hugged them. "I'm so sorry she's gone. I miss her every day."

We stayed a few more minutes, talking with other people, and then made our way toward the door. Rob asked, "Are you going to be okay going back to work?"

"I want to keep busy."

"I'll pick you up at five. We'll have an early dinner and then head back over here."

I gave him a quick kiss. "Thank you for your support. It means more than you know." I returned to the office and tried to concentrate without a lot of luck.

At four, Cheryl stuck her head in the door. "You don't have any appointments for the rest of the day. Why don't you go home? We all know how hard this is for you."

I gave her a half smile. "Thanks for looking out for me. I'll just finish up a few things and then try to take a nap before the wake tonight."

"Remember, we pretty much cleared your calendar for tomorrow. Text me if you want me to move your three o'clock."

I tidied up my desk. *A nap would be most welcome.* Leaving, I traipsed slowly back to my house. Again, I stared up at the empty seat where Nancy should have been. With a heavy heart, I pushed open the door. I trudged up the stairs, tumbled into bed, pulled the covers over my head, and fell instantly asleep.

I woke abruptly after something pounced on me. Courvoisier had decided my feet moving under the blankets constituted a threat to be vigorously defended against. Groaning, I glanced at the clock and saw I had just enough time for a quick shower before Rob got home. I gave the cat a quick pet and apologized for taking away her game. I looked down and realized I would have to find something else to wear, as my suit was now hopelessly wrinkled. *Serves you right. Next time remove clothes before napping.*

A pair of black slacks and a subdued sweater hung in my closet. Donning them, I contemplated makeup and decided it was pointless. I headed downstairs to join Rob.

"Something smells good," I said as I rounded the corner into the kitchen.

"I picked up eggplant parmigiana. It felt like a comfort food kind of night."

"Thanks. Let me put a salad together." I set out plates and cutlery. "How was the rest of your day?"

"It was good and relatively uneventful. Yours?"

"I left early and came back for a nap."

He kissed me on the forehead. "That's good. You probably needed it."

"I did. I feel much better now."

At the funeral home, we greeted Melissa and her daughters again and sat down to watch a tribute tape they had put together. It was fun to see the younger pictures of Nancy and the ones of her and her nieces as children. They also had some nice pictures of her gardens over the years. I was impressed to see how much it had grown and filled in even since I'd been living next to her. Quite a few people stopped by and shared their remembrances.

I was paging through one of the photo albums when Rob's hand tensed on my shoulder. I followed his gaze to John Gordon in the receiving line. "What's he doing here? He didn't know Nancy."

"I don't know. She didn't have any children, so he wouldn't have known her from the school either."

Jay stared at John too. John finally made it to the front of the line and briefly knelt in front of the casket. I could have imagined it, but he seemed pleased as he bent over Nancy's body. I shuddered. Standing, he scanned the crowd. His eyes settled on me.

Making his way to my side, he held out his good arm. "Merry, I know how close you were to Nancy. Although I didn't know her that well, I wanted to attend to offer you my deepest sympathies."

I shook his hand. "Thank you for coming. I wasn't aware you even met Nancy."

"Sadly, I met her only once, briefly. I congratulated her on her beautiful garden."

"I'm sure she appreciated it. Her garden was her pride and joy."

He moved closer to me and whispered, "Sorry I missed you at the school last night. I just hate to let precious things go." He tightened his grip on my hand. I gasped, and he said more loudly, "Well, I need to be going. I'm sorry to see you under these sad circumstances. Merry, let's catch up soon." He nodded to Rob and gave my hand one last hard squeeze as he left.

I rubbed my hand. Rob frowned at me. "What happened? What did he say?"

I explained, and his face tightened. He started to go after John, but I grabbed him. "Not tonight. Tonight is all about Nancy."

He swallowed hard. "He's not going to get away with this."

Jay joined us. "Everything okay?"

I nodded. "Everything's fine. We'll catch up tomorrow after the service."

He gave me a hard stare. "Good. I look forward to it."

Father Tom came forward and led us in a prayer for Nancy prior to closing the coffin. Reflexively, I rubbed my hand as he spoke, but my thoughts were all about my kind neighbor.

After the prayer, we said our goodbyes and got in the car. Rob noticed me holding my hand and flushed. "We'll get some ice on that when we get back."

I went upstairs to change into my sweats and rejoined Rob in the living room. He motioned with a glass in his hand. "I hope you don't mind, but I needed something strong."

"I don't mind at all. Please pour me one too." Sinking down onto the sofa, I tucked my feet up under my legs. Rob came back with my drink and an ice pack. Taking the drink in my left hand, I tried to balance the ice pack on my right.

"Let me help." He sat next to me. Putting his arm around me, he used his hand to steady the pack. I took a sip of my drink and let my head sink onto his chest.

"Now I feel better," I murmured.

"It was a tough day, and it didn't help that John showed up. You should have let me go after him."

"I needed you to stay with me. I didn't want to worry about you. Who knows what that nut is capable of?"

"I could take him!"

"I know you could, but we don't know if he's armed."

Rob stood and paced. "I can't believe he hurt you. And right in front of me."

"I guess the good news is now we know it's not safe to be around him, even in public places. If you want to feel some satisfaction, focus on the fact that we got the necklace back. He obviously valued it. I think that's what got him so riled up."

He punched his fist into his hand. "He better hope he doesn't run into me in a dark alley."

"Let's not waste our evening talking about him. Would you mind listening to me practice the reading for tomorrow? I'm afraid if I don't try it out loud a few times, I'll completely break down."

201

After rehearsing, I felt better and thought I might actually be able to keep myself together. Rob and I finished our drinks and decided to make it an early night.

The next morning, I woke in time to do some meditation and stretching. My hand still hurt but didn't look too bruised. Taking a quick shower, I dressed and made my way downstairs. I was surprised to see Rob making pancakes in the kitchen.

"I need to keep you around. My only regret is that Jenny isn't here. She loves pancakes." I hugged him.

"Coffee's ready. Pancakes will be done in a few minutes. Would you mind heating up the maple syrup in the microwave?"

"The least I can do." I filled the pitcher and put it in to heat. As I turned, I blinked. The table was set for three. "Did you miscount?"

"Nope. We forgot to drop off something for Jenny to wear last night, so Patty's bringing her by any minute now."

"I can't believe I forgot!"

"You had a few things on your mind."

Jenny came in the back door. "I can't believe you forgot my outfit, but all is forgiven since Mr. Jenson told me he was making pancakes."

I laughed. "Is that how he lured you over here?"

"You bet. Pancakes first or getting dressed first?"

Rob looked over my head. "Pancakes."

"Works for me." Jenny hugged me as she sat.

I picked up the orange juice to pour it and almost dropped it.

"Is it too heavy for you, Mom? I guess you haven't been working out much lately." She smirked.

"She hurt her hand last night," Rob said.

Jenny picked up my hand. "It's bruised. What happened?"

"You know me—just clumsy, I guess."

Rob frowned at me, and I shrugged. "Pancakes are ready." He put a large stack on the table.

Jenny grabbed three. "You don't have to tell me twice."

The rest of the breakfast went quickly, and Jenny filled us in on all of the things that had been going on in school since we last were together. When Jenny stood to help clean up, I shook my head. "Nope, you need to get ready. We have to leave in fifteen minutes." Jenny rolled her eyes and ran up the stairs.

Rob looked at me. "Why didn't you tell her what happened?"

"I didn't want her to worry. She's concerned enough."

He sighed. "Your call. Do you mind finishing down here so I can do a few things before we leave?"

"No problem. Remember, we need to leave in fifteen."

"Got it."

I finished cleaning up. At the appointed time, Jenny came running down the stairs and almost bowled into Rob coming out of the office. He asked, "Drive or walk?"

"Walk!" Jenny and I said together.

"Well then, let's hop to it."

Jenny and I strode in front, arms around each other. "Mom, are you okay?"

"As good as I can be. It's going to be a sad day."

"I'm going to miss her."

"She was a good person and a good friend. I'll miss her too."

When we got to the church, we sat in the third pew. After a minute, Father Tom and Melissa motioned for me to come to the altar. They told me my reading would be second and that I would follow Melissa's daughter Kate. I joined Rob and Jenny in the pew, and the service started. I was pleased I was able to get through my reading without crying. When we moved to the gravesite, Jenny and I dropped two roses on the casket together. Afterward, we went back to the church basement for refreshments with the rest of the mourners. I was happy to have Jenny and Rob stationed on either side of me so they could delicately keep people from shaking my already sore hand.

On the way home, Rob told me he had texted Cheryl to tell her I wouldn't be in for the rest of the day. I crossed my arms. "I could have gone in."

"You could have, but would it have been worthwhile?"

I sighed. "It probably wouldn't have been. Thanks."

We stopped at Patty's house, dropped Jenny off, and picked up her laundry. Patty said, "We need a girls' night out soon."

"I agree. Soon." We hugged, and Rob and I left for home.

Courvoisier and Drambuie were waiting for us and were vocal about wanting to be let out in the backyard. I complied like the servant I was and took the wash in to sort.

Rob poked his head into the laundry room. "I hope you don't mind, but Jay's going to come by this afternoon."

"Why?"

"He wants to ask you some questions about what happened last night, and I have some questions for him."

"Fine, I guess."

I took some frozen cookie dough out to thaw. If this was going to continue to be a depressing day, I was going to need chocolate. The first batch had just come out of the oven when Rob wandered back in.

He gave me a hopeful smile. "Do I smell cookies?"

"You do, but they are still hot." I swatted his hand away.

He pulled me to him for a long kiss that I felt all the way to my toes. He smiled. "Almost better than cookies." He reached behind me to grab one and bit into it. "Ouch. That's hot."

"Serves you right. 'Almost' indeed!"

He gave me another kiss, this one chocolate scented. "Yum, you taste even better now," I said as I kissed him back.

The back door opened, and we jumped apart. Jay stared at us with his eyebrows raised. "If I'm interrupting, I can come back later."

I blushed and retrieved a coffee mug. "You aren't interrupting anything."

Rob put a hand to his heart. "Cut me to the quick, woman. That was surely something."

My face flamed as I put the cookies on the plate. "Anyone like one?"

Rob grabbed another, along with a napkin and his coffee.

Jay snatched one as well. "Don't mind if I do."

I regained my composure. "Why did you stop by today, Jay?"

"I wanted to know what happened last night. You and John looked pretty serious. What did he say?"

"He told me he was sorry he missed me at the high school."

"So that was his car you saw."

"Apparently."

He fixed me with his policeman's eyes. "I don't think that's all of it."

Rob nodded. "Show him your hand, Merry."

Embarrassed, I held it out. Jay said, "That's quite a bruise you have there. Did John do that?"

"Yes. He shook my hand quite energetically."

"What she meant was viciously," Rob said.

"Do you want to press charges?" Jay asked.

I stared at him in disbelief. "For shaking my hand too hard? Lots of men don't know their own strength and squeeze much harder than they should. I don't think I'd have a strong case."

"Just letting you know you could file," Jay said. "Between injuring your hand and the tone of his comment, I think he was threatening you."

"I'm not saying you're wrong. I just don't want to overreact."

"Keep me posted if anything else happens."

"I promise you I will."

"Rob, you mentioned you had a question for me?"

"Yes, I did. I saw on the wire that there was a dead body found outside of Urbana the other day. I was wondering if they had identified the person."

Jay nodded. "I heard about that too. They found the body on the outskirts of the Cedar Bog. From the report, it looks like it had been there for a couple of years. What's the interest?"

"I'm just curious. I wanted to see if there was a story there. Would you do me a favor and keep me posted?"

"Will do. Merry, do you mind if I take a few more of these cookies with me? I have a feeling it's going to be a long shift."

I retrieved a paper bag and filled it with several cookies and napkins. I also gave him a to-go cup of coffee. He smiled. "This should keep me going till I get home tonight."

I saw him to the door. "Anything I can do to help our local law enforcement."

After the door was shut, Rob said, "Did you have to give him so many?"

"Don't worry. I have more in the freezer." Somewhat mollified, he took another and ate it slowly. "Why are you so interested in the Urbana death?"

"It's relatively near to us. I'm just curious about it and figured my readers may be too."

"If they even know about it. Well, this laundry isn't going to wash itself. I better get after it. I need to do some grocery shopping too. The refrigerator looks pretty sparse."

"Do you want me to go with you?"

"No need. You stay here and work. I've been asking for a lot of your time lately."

"If you are sure..."

"I am. However, if you want to help me unload the car when I get back, I'll be a happy camper."

"You got it!"

It felt so normal to go grocery shopping. It was almost a treat, "almost" being the key word. Grabbing a cart, I perused the produce department. As I squeezed a few avocados to test for ripeness, a cart stopped next to mine. Paula Sanders stood there.

"Paula, you startled me."

"Detective Ziebold told me you helped get my necklace back. I want to thank you."

"I didn't really do anything."

"He said you found it. So thanks."

"You're welcome. Can I ask you a question?"

"You can ask."

"Why didn't you press charges against John for stealing it?"

"Because he didn't."

I frowned. "I'm confused. You reported it stolen a few years ago."

"I did."

"So how did John end up with the necklace if he didn't steal it?"

She gave me a knowing smile and left me with my avocados. Shrugging, I swiftly moved through the store, hoping I wouldn't run into anyone else I knew.

I called Rob as I neared home. "Ready to stock my shelves?"

"You talk so dirty." He chuckled. "I'll be right out."

I drove in and parked. He waited by the trunk as I popped it open and grabbed a bag. "I'll bring them in and hand them to you."

Working as a team, we made short work of putting everything away. *I've missed this.* "You're hired."

"I'd like to think I'm a keeper for more than my car-unpacking abilities." He wiggled his eyebrows as he sidled up close to me.

"You are. You definitely are." I pulled his head down, and my mouth found his.

After a cold shower, I puzzled on my conversation with Paula. The cats joined me on the bed, and I moved my feet into better positions for them. Their soft snores lulled me to sleep.

It was gray and drizzling the next day. After performing some quick stretches, I made short work of getting dressed. Moving downstairs, I was surprised that Rob was not there. I spied leftover Italian bread and decided on French toast. As I made breakfast, my thoughts drifted to John and Paula.

Why did Paula say John hadn't stolen the necklace? She'd seemed happy enough to get it back. Suddenly, I hit on a scenario that worked. Pleased, I turned the coffee on, put the French toast in the oven, and set places at the counter.

Rob came through the back door. "Oh, you're up."

"I thought you were still asleep. Where were you?"

He displayed his suitcase. "More clothes. I was getting tired of washing everything out."

"If we don't solve this thing soon, I'm going to have to bring Jenny home."

He looked at the oven. "What's that fantastic smell?"

"Breakfast. It will be done in about five minutes."

"Let me run upstairs and put my bag in my room."

I poured him a cup of coffee and warmed the syrup. Rob made his way back downstairs, and I slid two slices onto his plate.

"That looks great." Slathering it with butter and syrup, he bit into it and closed his eyes. "Heaven."

Smiling, I put a slice on my plate and went through the same ritual. "Yes, it is good. It beats the heck out of my normal yogurt. I forgot to tell you I saw Paula yesterday in the grocery store."

"Paula Sanders?"

"The same." I told him what she said and then explained my theory. "We know she needed money at the time. Her dad was dying and had a lot of bills. John had left her, and she owed him money due to the divorce. We also know she reported the necklace stolen and filed a police report. My theory is she faked the robbery to get the insurance company to pay on the necklace. I have my expensive jewelry insured, and I sell a lot of that type of insurance. Is there any way we could find out if she filed a claim and collected on it?"

He nodded slowly. "So you think John was in on it?"

"Maybe she told him that was the only way she could pay him what he was due under the terms of the settlement. And maybe he didn't return it like he was supposed to after he got his money."

"That certainly would give him a reason to be involved, and it would explain why he hadn't sold it. Let me give Jay a call and see if he knows if the insurance company paid out."

Rob dialed Jay's number and put it on speaker. Jay answered, "What?"

Rob shook his head. "You really need to work on your phone etiquette."

"Who, me? It's a Saturday, and it's raining. I didn't think you were calling me to play golf, so it has to be work."

"You must be a detective." Rob explained what we were looking for.

"If your theory were true, they'd be guilty of insurance fraud. I'll look into it. Oh, on a different subject, I checked with the Urbana police on the dead body they found. They identified him. He's a man by the name of Paul Devlin. His prints were on file from when they hauled him in for beating his wife."

I shrugged. No one I knew.

Jay continued, "The interesting part is that Suzie Krump's married name was Devlin. She started using her maiden name when she moved here from Urbana. They've asked me to interview her to see if she knows anything. Got to go now."

Rob whistled. "Well, that explains how she was able to get away from her abuser. He was dead."

CHAPTER 25

The next morning, Rob and I decided to take a walk over to the Morning Pastry after breakfast. Both of us were full, but we figured we could order a coffee if we had to. The blinds were closed, and there was a sign on the door: "Due to a family emergency, we will be closed Saturday and Sunday."

I groaned. "I'm glad I don't have to have another cup of coffee, but I wanted to see how Suzie was doing. Losing someone is tough no matter what the circumstances."

"He was abusing her, but I guess she hadn't gotten divorced."

"I wonder what the cause of death was."

"I'll call Jay later to find out. I don't think he'd welcome another call so soon after the last one. What do you want to do now?"

"Let's go over to Patrick and Patty's. I want to see how Jenny is. I really miss her."

We strolled for another two blocks. I smiled up at Rob. "I like walking in the rain. Thank goodness it's not too cold out."

Rob pulled me closer under our shared umbrella.

I opened the back door while Rob shook out the umbrella. Patty was reading the paper at her counter. I pushed it aside. "We have news for you!"

As I told her everything that had happened, she looked as astonished as I felt. Once I finished, she said, "I think we need to bring comfort food to Suzie."

"It'll be weird cooking for a chef. What if she doesn't like our food?"

Patty rolled her eyes. "The point is to show we care for her, and if we get more information, even better."

"Shouldn't I come too?" Rob asked. "I'm a newsman, and this story is happening in our town."

I rubbed his shoulder. "It is, but she may clam up if you're there. I'll tell you everything we find out."

"I guess that'll have to work."

"Why don't you stay here with Patrick? That way you can catch up on your football."

He smiled. "Now, that's an idea." He left to join Patrick in the den.

"What should we make?" I asked Patty.

She stuck her head in the refrigerator. "I have some chicken breasts, mushrooms, and sour cream. How about making a casserole using that and some penne?"

"Sounds great. You direct; I'll assemble." I took a casserole pan and the penne out of her pantry.

We worked together smoothly, benefitted by the fact that we cooked together as a team on many occasions. After putting the casserole in the oven, she poured us both a cup of coffee. "So what's going on with you and Rob? The looks you give each other scream couple."

I smiled. "We have grown close. I'm enjoying being with him. He makes me feel safe."

"Just safe?"

"Safe, warm, and hot."

"Hot?"

"Yes, hot, really hot, not that we're doing anything about it."

"You're in the same house alone, you think he's hot, and you're both over twenty-one. Why haven't you done anything about it?"

I rubbed my forehead. "What if the relationship doesn't last? My history of picking losers precedes me. I feel deeply for Rob, but I'm scared to commit further. What if he has skeletons I don't know about? What if his character is flawed?"

"Those are all great questions." Patty pierced me with her warm brown eyes. "You and I are old enough to know that there are no guarantees in this life. So we need to choose if we are going to live it or if we are going to sit on the sidelines. I think if you decide the latter, your life will be boring and you'll give up on any chance of happiness. I don't know if Rob is 'the guy' or not; only you can decide that. And if he isn't, a girl can have fun while she figures it out." She winked.

I hugged her. "You are one smart lady. What would I do without you?"

"Hopefully you won't have to find out. Now, let's get this casserole over to Suzie."

We poked our heads into football central and told everyone where we were going. Jenny was curled up against Rob, watching the game.

Patty and I left, and she said, "Looks like Jenny approves."

"He's been so nice to her. He invited her over for breakfast the other morning and was one of her biggest fans at the ballet recital."

She grinned. "He may be a keeper."

We drove up to Suzie's condo. Since Patty carried the casserole, I rang the doorbell.

Gloria, Suzie's mother, answered. I asked, "Suzie lives here, right?"

"Yes."

Patty moved up next to me on the stoop. "We brought her a casserole." She held it in front of her. "We wanted to give her our condolences in this difficult time."

"He was a jerk. I'm glad he's dead. Come in. Suzie's upstairs. I'll let her know you're here."

She went upstairs. I mouthed, "Wow." Standing there awkwardly, Patty still held the casserole. Suzie came slowly down the stairs with her mother trailing her.

In a monotone, Suzie said, "Oh, hi, Patty, Merry."

Patty pushed the casserole forward. "We brought you a casserole. We were so sorry to learn of your husband's death."

"Thanks. It's been hard. Mom, could you put this in the fridge?"

Her mother complied. We stood there silently until Suzie waved us toward the living room. "Sit, please sit. Would you like some coffee or tea?"

"No, we're good," I replied.

We sat, and Suzie joined us. "It was all such a shock."

Patty asked, "Were you married long?"

"Five years, but then I left town. I hadn't heard from him since I moved here. I thought it was strange, but I figured he got over me. He was a good man, unless he drank. And he drank a lot." She rubbed the arm Rob told me her husband broke.

I shivered. "Sounds like you were well rid of him."

She looked up, her eyes wide. "Maybe, maybe not. I miss the good times."

Her mother came back into the room. "What good times? The man was a schmuck! He treated you badly. All the times he beat you! I could just cry. Good riddance to him." She sat next to Suzie and put her arm around her.

"He was a human being, and he was the man I was married to."

Patty asked, "You never thought of divorcing him?"

"One time, when it got real bad. But when I took counseling with our priest, he told me I should stay and try to work it out. He said if I was a better wife, Paul wouldn't drink."

"That priest sounds like he shouldn't be counseling anyone." I shook my head and rolled my eyes at Patty. "What made you decide to leave?"

"It had been a really bad week. Paul was having trouble at work, and money was tight. Then a man was killed at my restaurant. I couldn't prove it, but I always thought Paul had something to do with it. The customer was one of my regulars, and Paul didn't like the way

213

he looked at me. Paul called him out on it once, and the customer told him he was crazy."

I gasped. "Did you tell the police that?"

"Yes, but again, they had no proof. That's when I knew I had to leave. It was bad enough he was beating me but then to kill someone else? I knew I had to get out of there." She sobbed.

"Thank God you did." Her mother held her tighter and rocked her gently back and forth.

Patty frowned. "Didn't you think it was strange he let you go?"

"No. I was just so thankful he was out of my life!"

Suzie's mother glared at us. "Why are you asking all of these questions? Can't you see what it's doing to her?"

I grimaced. "We're just trying to understand. Suzie, we'll go now, but if you need to talk, please call us. We'll let ourselves out."

Patty and I made a hasty retreat and shut the door quietly behind us. "What do you make of that?" she asked.

"If she killed him, she's a heck of an actress!"

"Maybe she is. I find it hard to believe she'd be concerned about someone who beat her on a regular basis."

"It takes all kinds of people in this world."

"Luckily one of the bad ones is gone."

We spent the rest of the day at Patty's watching football and enjoying tasty things. Jenny and I claimed one of the couches and snuggled up to watch the game. It was nice to have a normal Sunday. Sated and sluggish, Rob and I bid the Twilligers and Jenny farewell for the evening. The brisk air revived us as we strolled home.

Rob asked, "Are you going to tell me what happened at Suzie's?"

"She appears to be mourning Paul's death. However, her mother was quite vocal about being glad he was dead."

"He beat her daughter."

I shuddered. "I get it. If someone hurt Jenny, I don't know what I'd do, but I do know it wouldn't be pretty."

Opening the front door, I turned back to ask Rob if he wanted coffee. Drambuie sailed past, and Rob caught her just as she was making her escape.

"Good catch."

"Does she do this a lot?"

"Not that often. It usually only happens after she has a disagreement with her sister." He put the cat down, and I shut the door. "Speaking of Courvoisier." I pointed to the top shelf of the bookcase. "You know you're not allowed up there."

Rob lifted her up and deposited her on the floor. I shook my head. "Would you do me a favor and feel around to see if there is a fake mouse?" He moved his hand around and grabbed something. "I knew it. That's Drambuie's toy. Bad girl." I shook my finger at Courvoisier and tossed the toy to Drambuie. "Thanks for the assist, Rob."

"Life as a cat owner sure is interesting."

"You have no idea. Coffee?"

"No, I think I've had enough caffeine for the day."

"I have decaf."

"No, I'm good." He sat on the couch and patted the seat next to him. I sat, and he put his arm around me. "Fun day."

"Yes, it was good to just relax like real people."

He nuzzled my hair. "You know something else real people do?"

"No, what do they do?"

"This." He nibbled my ear. "And this." He turned my face toward his for a long, slow kiss.

"I'll be a real person any day," I told him as we came up for air.

"Be quiet." He kissed me again.

"Let's go upstairs and be more comfortable."

Rob's eyes widened. "Are you sure?"

"As sure as I'm going to be."

He lifted me off the couch and started carrying me up the stairs. A sharp knock echoed from the back door. I groaned. "Not now."

He put me down and kissed my nose. "I'll get it. Just give me a minute. I'll get rid of whoever it is." He opened the door. "What?"

Jay said, "You need to work on your etiquette. Can I come in?"

"I guess."

Disappointed, I trudged back down the stairs and into the kitchen. "Evening, Jay. Coffee?"

"Would love some. You wouldn't happen to have any of those cookies from the other day, would you? I didn't get dinner yet tonight."

"Are you sure you wouldn't like something more substantial? I could cook you an omelet." Over Jay's shoulder, Rob shook his head no and motioned toward the door. I ignored him.

Jay smiled. "If you're sure it's not any trouble."

"No trouble at all." I retrieved the ingredients and poured Jay some coffee. Taking the cookies out for Rob, I put them in front of him. Frowning, he sank onto one of the chairs and took one.

Rob glared at Jay. "What's up?"

Jay held his hands up to Rob as if to stop him. "Someone's in a mood."

"Ignore him. What's going on?"

"I received some additional information from the autopsy on Paul Devlin. It looks like he was in the ground around three years, and the cause of death was a blow to the head. From the indentations on the skull, it looks like someone swung at him with a baseball bat."

Grimacing, I put Jay's omelet in front of him.

He dug in. "The grave wasn't that deep; that's why the hikers found him. Some critters had gotten at him too." He looked up. "Good omelet, Merry."

The blood drained from my face. "Glad you like it."

"Three years? Rob said. "That would put him in the ground right around the time Suzie left."

"The timing's certainly interesting. I'm going to have another chat with her tomorrow." He grabbed a cookie and his jacket. "Thanks again for the omelet, Merry. I appreciate it. Oh, I nearly forgot, Paula Sanders did file an insurance claim, and the company paid out on the necklace. We've alerted them that the necklace was recovered in her ex-husband's possession. I'm sure charges will be filed shortly."

The door closed. Rob pulled me to him. "Now, where were we before we were so rudely interrupted."

I gently untangled myself. "I hate to say it, but all this talk of death and duplicity has ruined the mood. I'll see you in the morning." I gave him a kiss and headed for the stairs.

"Crap," Rob said.

The next morning, I felt much better. Running down the stairs, I turned the corner into the kitchen and gave Rob a big kiss. "I'm so sorry about last night. I'm also sorry I left everything a mess." My eyes widened. The kitchen was spotless. "I guess I also owe you thanks for cleaning up."

"I know how you can make it up to me." He winked.

"Let's talk about that later." I grabbed a yogurt from the refrigerator. "Dinner out tonight?" I picked up my briefcase.

"Sounds good." He waved. "I'll come get you at five thirty."

Blowing him a kiss, I left. The day started peacefully enough, but at four, I received a text from my daughter: "Can't take it here anymore! I'm coming home!"

I hit Patty's speed dial. "What's up?"

"Teenage angst. Cindy wouldn't let Jenny borrow one of her favorite sweaters, so the world is at an end."

"Sorry about that."

"Not your fault. Jenny stalked out a few minutes ago, so you may want to head home."

"On my way." I grabbed some things to work on at home and headed out. I called to Cheryl over my shoulder, "Daughter trouble. Call me if you need me."

Five minutes later, I was in my house, hugging Jenny as she sobbed. "I only wanted to borrow the sweater tonight. I can't believe she wouldn't loan it to me. She's so selfish."

I patted her back. "How about I make some hot chocolate?"

"Do you have any cookies?"

"I might be able to manage that." I smiled as I handed her some tissues. Sliding the cookie jar in front of her, I put the milk on to heat.

"I just want to come home! Nothing's happened in a while. I don't understand why I can't be in my own room." She paused and looked stricken. "Unless you don't want me here."

"Of course I do! I miss you terribly. Things are still up in the air, but I think we've narrowed down the players enough that, if we're careful, you can come home." I gave her a kiss on the cheek and a big hug.

She smiled. "I think the milk's done."

After stirring in the chocolate, I handed her a mug. I raised mine. "To being together again."

The back door opened, and Rob entered. "Cheryl told me you came home?"

I hugged Jenny. "Jenny was homesick, and I decided it was time for her to come back."

His face fell, but Jenny's back was to him. He recovered quickly. "That's great. I'll take you both out to dinner to celebrate."

Jenny asked, "Fiorella's?"

"Fiorella's it is. I think there is some garlic bread with your name on it." He kissed my forehead. "If you'll excuse me, I'll call and make a reservation." He disappeared into my office.

Tears forgotten, Jenny said, "I better get changed." She ran up to her room.

"Be ready by six."

Rob came back out. "Is the coast clear?"

"For a few minutes."

He gave me a kiss. "I'm glad she's home, but it does put a damper on things."

"Yes, it does, but I've missed her so much."

"I know." He kissed me on my nose. "Before she comes back down, I have something to discuss with you. I spoke with Jay today, and it seems there is some confusion about the necklace. We have our theory, but it could be true that Paula didn't know John took it. He could have stolen it. Since Paula seems to like me, Jay wanted to know if I would be willing to wear a wire and take her out. I told him I'd have to talk with you first."

"So you're going to ply her with alcohol and charm the truth out of her?"

He nodded. "That's the plan. How do you feel about it?"

"Seems slimy, but it would be good to know what really happened. You'll be careful?"

"Safety is my middle name."

I gave him a stern glance. "It better be. I'm going to ask Jay if I can listen with him."

Jenny thundered down the stairs. "Ready?"

"For a ballerina," I said, "you're not very light on your feet."

She punched my arm playfully and grinned. "Let's go."

CHAPTER 26

Rob and I rendezvoused with Jay at the Pickled Herring. He showed us the tiny back office where he and I would be stationed. The owner had installed hidden cameras in the restaurant so he could make sure his staff performed to his high standards.

I said, "Wow." There were six different screens. "Remind me to behave myself the next time I'm here." Rob chuckled. I told him, "Remember, I'll be able to see everything you do."

He gave me a quick kiss. "Don't worry. I'll be on my best behavior."

Jay handed Rob a tiny listening device. "Stick this onto the side of your phone and leave your phone on the table between you. That way we'll be able to listen and record your conversation."

Rob gave him a thumbs-up. "I could think of a few other uses I might have for this."

"I need to return it once we're done, so don't get too attached. It's almost time for you to meet Paula. You should probably go up front."

Rob kissed me goodbye. He moved toward the front of the restaurant, his head still bent over the tiny device on his phone.

Jay and I went back into the office and tried to get comfortable on the folding chairs. He pointed toward the screen to a table in clear view of the camera. "I told Rob to sit at that table. That way we'll have a clear view of the action."

Camera one showed Paula coming in. She looked around at the décor, and when Rob joined her, she smiled. She took his arm as they walked to the table.

Paula pointed to the plastic fish hanging over the bar. "Early rustic."

"It's one of my favorite watering holes. Let's sit at one of these corner tables. That way we won't have to shout."

She smiled at him as she slid into the booth. Rob joined her and put his phone down where he had been told.

"I was surprised to hear from you," Paula said.

"Why?"

"I thought you were sweet on Merry."

He paused for a minute, gazing at camera two. "She's a good friend." He turned to more fully face Paula. "But I'm interested in you."

Paula scooted closer to him. "That's nice to hear." Her voice lowered. "Has anyone ever told you how good looking you are?"

Rob cleared his throat. "Let's not talk about me. Let's talk about you. But first, let's order a drink."

Rob waved the server over. "I'm in the mood for a martini—a dirty martini. How about you, Paula?"

She looked at him suggestively. "A dirty martini works just fine for me."

"While she's getting the drinks, why don't we take a look at the bar menu?" They perused the single menu, heads almost touching. "Do you see anything you like?"

"Mmm, I love sauerkraut balls." She licked her lips. "Why don't we get some of those and the cheese sticks?"

"Sounds great!" The server came back with the drinks, and they ordered the food. Rob raised his glass to Paula. "To you, blue eyes."

"That's so romantic." They touched glasses.

In the back, I rolled my eyes at Jay. "This is tough to take. I can't believe she's buying this."

"Merry, you need to keep quiet. I'm trying to listen to them, not you." He glared at me, and we returned our attention to the screens.

Rob took a healthy gulp of his martini and looked to see if she did the same. "Tell me more about yourself, Paula. I find you fascinating."

"Did I tell you I was the homecoming queen in my town?"

"You may have mentioned that."

"Well, I was." She smiled. "It was so perfect. I had the most beautiful dress, and my hair was styled just so. All the boys were after me. It was such a fun time in my life." She swigged down almost half of her martini. "Now I'm divorced, I work in a bank, and I'm all alone." She finished her martini.

Rob raised his hand for the server. "Another round please."

The server brought the new martinis and the food. Paula said, "Do it again."

Face slack, Rob stared at her. "To you, blue eyes."

She laughed and sipped her drink. "Now, where was I? Oh yes, I was talking about my life. Getting my necklace back made me happy, though. Who would have thought you and Merry would help me get it back?" She raised her glass. "Thank you. It means a lot." She slugged down a good portion of her drink.

"I was only too glad to help."

"See, that's what I like about you, Rob." She put her hand over his.

"Rob, Paula, how nice to see you here," Father Tom said.

Startled, they looked up. Rob pulled his hand back. "Good to see you as well, Father.

Paula grinned. "Howdy, Padre. Rob and I are just getting to know each other better."

Father Tom nodded at them, a stiff smile on his face. "Paula, we still need to talk about you coming to town under an assumed name.

Rob," he paused and frowned at him, "I'll see you at confession." He left.

Paula reclaimed Rob's hand and stroked it. "Isn't it nice he stopped by? He's been encouraging me to get out more and make friends."

"Yes, it was." Rob gave her a sickly grin. His shoulders tightened. "Now, where were we? Oh yes, you were talking about your necklace."

"I was saying how glad I was to have it back. It's so pretty, and it's worth a lot."

"You must have been very unhappy when it was taken."

"Not really." She shrugged and gulped her drink.

"I'm confused. Why weren't you upset?"

She looked around cautiously and put her finger to her lips. "You won't tell?"

"Scout's honor."

"Money was really tight, and John was pressuring me to give him his divorce settlement. I told him I only had part of it, and he came up with the idea to have my place look like it had been robbed. Needless to say, I couldn't keep the necklace at my place. The police would have found it. So he said he would hold it for me until I gave him the insurance money. What a fool I was. I gave him the money, and he kept the necklace anyway. What an ass!"

"Why didn't you turn him in?"

"I filed the claim and collected the money. If I told about him, I would have gone to jail. He had me over a barrel."

"Why didn't he just give it back? He couldn't sell it."

"Spite, pure and simple." She stroked his arm and pressed against him. "You wouldn't do something mean like that, would you?"

"Never." Rob edged away. "Well, this was fun. We'll have to do it again someday."

"It's still early!"

"Not for me. I have to be up with the chickens tomorrow. Sorry. Can't be helped. Let me get you a cab home." Rob stood, hustled her up, and escorted her out.

"No kiss?" She pouted and pointed to her lips.

"No time. Great to see you." He closed the cab door and watched it drive away.

Rob returned to the restaurant. Jay and I escaped the cramped room and joined him. Rob asked, "Did you get it?"

Jay nodded. "Clear as a bell. We'll be putting warrants out for both John and Paula. Hopefully we can pit them against each other and use this to get them to talk about the murders."

Rob took the bug off his phone and handed it to Jay. Jay shook his hand. "Thanks for doing this. It makes my job a lot easier."

"Always glad to do my civic duty," Rob replied as we headed for his car.

Rob rounded the car to the driver's side. "Hold up, buster," I said.

"What's wrong?"

"Exactly how much did you have to drink?"

Jay smiled. "He didn't drink. We told the server to give him water flavored with a little bit of olive juice for color."

I laughed. "Good thinking. See you around, Jay."

We drove back to my house. I smiled. "I'm very interested to hear what you're going to say to Father Tom the next time you see him."

Rob groaned.

I chuckled and then yawned. "It's been a long day. I'll see you in the morning." Rising on my toes, I kissed him good night.

CHAPTER 27

As I strolled to work the next morning, John's car screeched to a halt next to me. "Merry, get in quick. It's Jenny; she's been in an accident. A car took the curve on Crescent too sharply and plowed right into her. If you jump in, we can probably beat the ambulance there."

I raced around the car and climbed in. "Let's go. How bad did it look?"

He smiled and sped down the road. "Not bad at all."

After fastening my seat belt, I gripped the hand strap and held on. "Aren't we going the wrong way? Crescent's to our left."

He glanced at me. "I lied. I haven't seen Jenny today, but I knew you'd get in if I told you she was hurt. You've been avoiding me, and this was the only way I could think of to make you listen. Rob Jenson has been lying about me, and you believe him."

I took a deep breath to steady my nerves. "Just to confirm, Jenny wasn't in an accident?"

"What piece of this don't you understand? I just said that to get you in the car."

Anger surged in my chest. My heart pounded. "I can't believe you did that!"

"Focus, Merry! Rob has been telling you lies about me."

"What lies, John?"

"Paula gave me that necklace as part of the divorce settlement. I can explain everything. I was never going to hurt her when I went to her apartment, but then she shot me and my life became a living hell."

"Could you slow the car down a bit?" I slammed my feet to the floor when we rounded a curve way too quickly.

"Why? I like going fast."

I weighed my limited options and decided we were going too fast for me to open the door and roll out. "Okay, well, could you pull over and park somewhere so you can tell me what I missed? I'm finding it hard to concentrate, and I want to believe you."

He studied me. "I'll pull over when we get to the park if you'll promise not to get out."

"I promise."

A few moments later, he screeched into the parking lot, almost taking out the park sign. Luckily he braked in time to stop the car before we plowed into one of the shelters. Shaken, I turned to him. "Talk."

"The police found a necklace in my office at the school." He gave me a sidelong glance. "They didn't say, but I think you may have been involved in finding it." He paused. I didn't say anything, so he continued. "Paula gave me the necklace because she didn't have the money to pay me for the divorce settlement. I wanted it over and done with, so I took the necklace as payment."

"Why didn't you sell it? You couldn't wear it."

"I didn't need the money right away, and I thought it would be a lovely gift for a future bride." He pulled my hand to his heart.

I yanked it back. "Why was Ben blackmailing you?"

"How did you know?"

"The book I found. The book you were looking for when you ransacked my house."

His face went slack. "I didn't ransack your house, but Ben was blackmailing me. He threatened to tell the school board how badly

Paula felt I treated her. She sent me a letter detailing her accusations and implied there was some mystery around the way her father died. I thought the envelope looked like it had been opened. I was correct. Ben copied the letter and used it to blackmail me. It was all a fabrication, but I had to think of my standing in the community. I paid him off. I didn't kill him."

"What about the insurance?"

"What insurance?

"The insurance payment on the necklace."

John looked confused. "I don't know what you are talking about."

"Paula filed a claim with the insurance company and told them the necklace had been stolen."

"But that's fraud!"

"Yes, it is." As I finished my sentence, the parking lot was awash in police cruisers, all with their lights flashing.

A megaphone blared, "Come out with your hands up."

John took a deep breath. "We better comply."

We eased out of the car, working hard to keep our hands visible at all times. Two policemen came at us with guns drawn, and then they frisked us. John was handcuffed, and they moved to cuff me.

"Merry?" I turned. Jay stared at me. He told the officer, "Hold off on her." He joined me, frowning. "What are you doing here?"

I sagged, and he caught me. "It's a long story."

The officers took John away. I sat in the front seat of Jay's car. I told him how John tricked me into getting into his car and the story he told about the necklace and Ben. "Did you believe him?"

"I don't know what to believe. There's a lot going on. He seemed truthful when he talked about Ben, but who knows? He's also the man who threatened me twice, bruised my hand, and abducted me."

"I'll take you home."

"Thanks. Please keep us posted."

Dropping me off, he watched until I was inside. By focusing on the door, I was able to get there without collapsing. The minute the door shut I sank into the nearest chair, sobbing. When John told me Jenny was hurt, I was so scared. Then being abducted! It was all too much. The back door opened, and I started, putting my hands up to protect myself.

Rob rushed in and gathered me in his arms. "Jay called me. I'm so sorry. I should have taken you to work."

I choked back tears. "You can't always be there."

"I want to try. I want you to be safe with me."

I kissed him. "I do feel safe when I'm in your arms." He kissed me back and held me. I started to shake, and my teeth chattered.

"Delayed shock."

He held me closer and tried to give me some of his body's warmth. I continued to shake. He carried me up the stairs. Putting me down on the bed, he piled blankets on and around me. He squatted down next to the bed. "I'm going to draw you a bath. Hopefully that will enable your body to relax. You've had a bad adrenaline rush. Will you be okay for me to leave you for a minute?"

I tried to nod, but it was a difficult task since my head was shaking so much already.

The water turned on. He came back to the bedroom and climbed onto the bed, holding me and rubbing his hand up and down my back. After a few minutes, he ducked back into the bathroom and shut off the taps. "Can you get undressed by yourself?"

I tried to get up and take my shirt off, but my body didn't seem to be obeying any of my commands.

"I'm going to have to help." Quickly undressing me, he lifted me gently into the tub. He picked up the washcloth and rubbed my back with small circles.

Feeling the warmth of the water and his massage, my muscles started to unclench. My teeth stopped chattering, and I stopped shaking. "Feeling better?" he asked.

"Yes, thank you. However, I'm pretty embarrassed. I didn't think this would be the way you'd see me naked the first time."

He chuckled. "Do you want me to put some more hot water in? The tub seems like it's cooling."

I blushed. "I think I can handle it from here. You're not going to leave, are you?"

"I'll be right outside the door. Anything special you want for lunch?"

"I'm not really hungry."

"You should eat something."

"Surprise me."

He shut the door, and I added more hot water to the tub. Leaning back, I tried to block the events of the day from my mind. All but the last part when Rob washed my back. That was something to remember. Sighing, I lifted myself from the tub and dried off. I considered reapplying my makeup but decided it wasn't worth it. Putting on my sweats and a T-shirt, I came back downstairs.

Rob put my lunch down in front of me and gave me another hug. "Chicken noodle soup and a peanut butter sandwich on rye with a glass of milk. You looked like you needed some serious comfort food. Oh, and I called Cheryl and told her you wouldn't be in for the rest of the day. She's rescheduling your appointments."

"What would I do without you?"

"Hopefully you will never have to find out." He rubbed my back. "Feel like talking about it?"

"Not really, but I guess I should."

"What happened? What on earth possessed you to get into a car with him?"

"It wasn't like I decided to go for a joyride." I faced him. "He told me Jenny had been in an accident. I wasn't thinking. I just wanted to get to her as quickly as possible."

"She hadn't been in an accident."

I gave him a dirty look. "I found that out after I was already in the car."

"I understand, but, Merry, you need to be more careful than that. You can't hop into cars with homicidal maniacs no matter what they tell you."

"He may not be a murderer. He admitted Ben was blackmailing him, but he said he didn't kill him."

"And you believe him because he's such an upstanding citizen?"

"I'm not that naïve. I'm just saying it is a possibility. He also had a different story than that woman *you* took for drinks last night."

"Paula?"

"Was there another woman?"

"Merry, there isn't another woman. There's only you. I'm sorry I made you mad, but you scared the heck out of me. I couldn't bear to lose you."

I stood. "I was more scared than I've ever been in my life. It makes me mad that he picked the exact right ruse to get me in the car."

Rob hugged me. "How about some cookies."

"I'm thinking a scare this bad chewed up a bunch of calories, so why not."

He took the cookie jar out of the pantry and held it out to me. "Need some more milk?"

"Nope, I'm good. Aren't you going to have some?"

"Don't mind if I do." He poured himself a glass of milk and took two cookies out of the jar. "So you don't think John did it?"

"I don't know. What if Paula did it to frame John?"

"I wouldn't put it past her, but how would she have known Nancy? And how did she know Ben had been framing John? And why would she care if he was?"

"Those are all good questions."

"I guess we'll know more after Jay finishes interrogating them. He said he'd try to stop by later to give us an update. How are you feeling?"

"I'm really tired but much better than I was."

"Do you mind if I borrow your office for a while? I need to follow up on some things for a story I'm writing."

"Have at it. I'm going to clean."

Rob glanced around at the sparkling house and then at me. "You're tired. Why don't you take a nap?"

"Nope, cleaning lowers my stress level." I smiled at him and picked up the dust rag.

Shaking his head, he went into the office and shut the door. I made short work of the kitchen and then decided to make blueberry scones as an afternoon snack for Jenny. I was just taking them out of the oven when she got home.

"Mom, what are you doing home? And what's that great smell? Oh, scones. Yum!" I came around the counter and gave her a tight hug. She hugged me back and then squirmed out of my embrace. "I love you, Mom, but I also love oxygen. Give a girl some room."

"Sorry. I'm just glad to have you home."

"Glad to be home." She grabbed a glass of milk and put a scone on a plate. She blew on her fingers. "Ouch! These are still hot! Got a test tomorrow. Need to study. Love you!" She disappeared around the corner.

Shaking my head, I put some coffee on to brew and sat at the counter. I opened the paper. The wake for Suzie's husband was scheduled for the following evening. Debating going, I decided Suzie needed my support. I poured myself a cup of coffee. The scones were calling my name, but I was determined to resist them.

Rob ambled into the kitchen. "What is that wonderful smell? Oh, scones, my favorite." He grabbed one and took a bite, savoring it.

I poured him a cup of coffee as he sat. "Paul Devlin's wake is tomorrow."

"So?"

"We need to go."

"He was a wife beater."

"Wakes are to help the living, not the dead. We need to go to support Suzie."

"I guess you're right."

The back door opened, and Jay came in. "Do I smell coffee?"

"I just made a fresh pot. Blueberry scone?"

He smiled. "Twist my Gumby arm."

"I'm assuming that's a yes." I laughed as I put one on a plate and slid it in front of him.

Jay took a bite, and his eyes lit up. "Wow, that's good."

I smiled. "I'm glad you like it. What happened with John and Paula?"

"We caught up with Paula at the bank today. We escorted her out in handcuffs. You know where we found John."

Rob asked, "What did they have to say?"

"Paula said it was John's idea to take the necklace and get the money from the insurance company. John claims he didn't know anything about Paula reporting it stolen and that Paula gave him the necklace in lieu of the money she owed him from the divorce. It's early days yet, but we'll unravel the story. Both of them have lawyered up, so it's going to be slow going."

"What about Ben and Nancy?"

"They're both claiming they didn't have anything to do with the deaths. John did admit to paying Ben blackmail money. It doesn't look good for him."

CHAPTER 28

Since we had to be at the funeral home at seven, I decided to order a pizza. Jenny made us a salad so it wasn't all carbs. Even so, I felt my waistband tightening. I told Jenny, "I'm sorry, honey, but you'll need to come with us. I don't want you to be alone."

She rolled her eyes. "Fine, but I'm not going anywhere near the body. And I get to use my phone."

"Deal. We'll find somewhere unobtrusive for you to sit."

As we headed for the wake, I told Rob, "That pizza was delicious, but I'm going to need to think about dieting. I can't continue to eat this way."

He put his arm around me. "I think you look great. However, I've noticed that I've put on a pound or two since I've been living at your house. Maybe we should exercise together."

Jenny giggled. "The couple that exercises together stays together."

I glared at her. "I'm not sure our relationship has progressed that far yet."

He laughed. "Not far enough to see you sweat?"

We entered the funeral home. Finding Jenny a seat in one of the other rooms, we entered the parlor for Suzie's husband and made our way to the casket. Luckily it was closed, due to the condition of the body. I placed my hand on the coffin and said a prayer.

We then made our way over to Suzie and her mother. "Suzie, I'm sorry for your loss."

She nodded at me sadly. Gloria leaned over. "I don't even know why we are having a wake for that bastard. I'm glad he's dead!"

Appalled, Suzie put her arm on her mother and pulled her back. "Mother, control yourself!"

Rob and I nodded to Suzie and made our way to the back of the funeral home where Patrick and Patty sat. I said, "Wow. Her mother had no use for Paul."

Patty nodded. "She sure didn't. She called him a bastard."

"She said that to me too." I giggled. "I wonder when she's going to tell us what she really thinks."

Patty snorted and gave me a dirty look. "Don't make me laugh at a wake."

I smiled. "I couldn't help it. Are you going to stay much longer?"

"I thought I'd say hello to Father Tom."

Gloria bent over Father Tom's ear. "Are you going to interrupt him?" I asked.

She followed my gaze. "No. I don't think so. Let's go."

Patty and I picked up Jenny, and we left together. Patrick and Rob followed.

Patrick said, "Rob and I were thinking about going for a drink. Would you both care to join us?"

"After that, I could use one," I admitted. Patty concurred, so we made plans to rendezvous at the Pickled Herring.

"What about me?" Jenny asked.

Patty said, "We didn't forget about you. My mom is making cookies with Cindy and the other kids. Would you like to join them?"

"Definitely."

"Then we'll drop you off and meet your mom and Rob in a few minutes."

Rob and I arrived first, so we claimed a booth. Patrick and Patty arrived, and we waved them over. After ordering drinks, Rob and

Patrick decided on a game of pool. We assured them we'd cheer them on from afar.

Patty looked across the table at me. "I heard you had some excitement this morning."

"It scared me, Patty. I was glad the police caught up to John when they did."

"I can't believe he was the school superintendent. It seems like there should have been a more thorough background check."

I shrugged and took a sip of my wine. "I don't think they would have found anything. Think about it. I actually went out with him." We both shuddered. "Hopefully that chapter of my life is over."

"Speaking of chapters in your life, anything new to report on you know who?" Her gaze flicked to Rob.

"Same status, other than the fact he gave me a bath this afternoon."

"What?"

"Doesn't count. I was in shock, and he was administering first aid."

She stared at me. "I don't know whether to laugh or be worried."

"You can laugh. I'm safe now. It looks like we'll be platonic for a while with Jenny being home. I'm so happy to have her back, but it does kind of put a crimp in the romance department."

"If it's meant to be, it's meant to be."

"You have such a way with words."

She grinned. "I do, don't I?"

Patrick came back to the table. "Anyone want to play the winner?"

Rob did a little victory dance by the pool table. I shook my head. "Nope. I think I've had enough fun for one day. I'm tired." I motioned Rob over. "Do you mind if we go home?"

He finished slapping himself on the back. "We can leave if you want to. Are you sure you don't want to play the winner?"

I laughed. "Home, James, but don't forget we need to pick up Jenny on our way back."

Patrick said, "We'll give you a lift."

Picking up Jenny, we decided to walk home from there. The air was chilly, and leaves blew around us. Bundling through the door, I was happy to feel the heat blowing through the vent.

"Make me some hot chocolate, Mom?" Jenny asked.

"You know how to make it."

"I know, but I don't know how to make it as good as you do." She batted her eyes and gave me a hug.

I looked over my shoulder at Rob. "I think I'm being played."

"Make me some too?"

I sighed. "Three hot chocolates coming up. Rob, could you light the fire in the living room?"

"I live to light your fire."

"Gross." Jenny followed him into the living room.

I made the hot chocolate, grabbed some cookies, and headed for the living room. I was cheered to see the fire going. I handed Jenny and Rob their mugs and sat on the floor by the fire, leaning against the sofa. "This feels great." I stretched my feet out.

Jenny smiled. "The hot chocolate is delicious, Mom. I'm so glad *you* made it."

I rolled my eyes. "I'm glad you like it, dear."

Rob chimed in, "Mine's great too."

"I'm happy you are both pleased. You can clean up when we are done."

"Anytime," Rob said.

"Mom, Bobby Ziebold texted me while you were gone. He said you got into some sort of trouble this morning. What happened?"

"Nothing really happened. Let's enjoy the fire and our hot chocolate."

Jenny shot me a troubled look but decided to enjoy the moment. "It's so nice to be home." She sank down next to me on the floor and put her arm around me.

"Yes it is," I agreed.

* * *

Feeling slightly guilty for neglecting my staff, I decided to run by the Morning Pastry to see if they were open the next morning. I was surprised and pleased to see they were. Suzie ran the cash register. She looked tired, her skin had a grayish cast, and there were bags under her eyes. Her uniform looked like it hadn't been ironed. Reaching the front of the line, I asked for a vanilla latte, a raspberry Danish ring, and a loaf of pumpkin bread. The server packaged the items as I paid Suzie.

"I was surprised to see you were open this morning."

"The funeral's not till tomorrow, and I can't be closed that long. I need the money."

I nodded sympathetically. "Please let me know what I can do to help."

"Thanks for coming to the wake yesterday. I'm sorry if my mother upset you."

"She seemed pretty vehement."

"What can I say? I'm her only child, and he treated me badly. The line's getting longer, so I need to get back."

"Thanks. Please remember you have friends. All you have to do is let us know if you need help."

I waved to her, and she smiled wanly at me. When I reached my office, I was greeted warmly. I preferred to think it was because they missed me, but the baked goods may have had some impact. The staff meeting went well, although it was filled with questions about John. I answered the ones I could and was upfront about the ones I couldn't. I gently guided everyone back to work-related issues. Business handled, I retreated to my office to return client calls.

Jenny texted me, "Don't forget basketball tonight."

Groaning, I tried to figure out what to do. I had planned on doing a Facebook Live segment on the value of life insurance, and Cheryl had already teased it to our clients several times.

I texted Rob, "Any way you could watch Jenny's bball game tonight at seven?"

"Love bball. I'll be there."

That handled, I settled down to write the script for the segment. Finishing the first draft, I ran over to the Morning Pastry to pick up a quick lunch. Suzie's mother was behind the counter, and I ordered a cup of the split pea soup and a small salad.

As I waited, I said, "We haven't really had a chance to chat. How are you enjoying living in Hopeful?"

"It's fine. Suzie's happy here, which makes me happy."

"What did you do in Urbana?"

"I worked in a butcher shop. I made friends with the farmers who supplied our meat, and the butcher taught me a lot of his trade. It's tough work. You have to be plenty strong, but I really enjoyed helping customers get the cuts they were looking for and introducing them to new ones. Here I'm helping to prep the food and wait on customers. My experience and connections mean Suzie gets better deals for this place."

"I'm sure she appreciates it."

"She does. Suzie and I have always been close, even when that scum tried to drive a wedge between us in Urbana."

"How's Suzie doing? She looks like she's having a tough time."

"She'll be fine. It was just a shock, them finding that jackass Paul's body and all."

My order came out, and I thanked Gloria for the chat. As I was leaving, Suzie grabbed my arm and pulled me into her office. "What did Mom tell you?"

"We were just chatting about what she did in Urbana. She didn't say anything out of the ordinary."

"Okay. That's good." She looked relieved. "Thanks." She let go of my arm.

I glanced around the small office. "I've never been back here before."

"It's not much, but it's a quiet place for me when everything is chaos in the kitchen."

A plaque hung over her desk. I edged closer so I could read it: *Top Batting Average 2005 .730.* "Wow. Your school must have been happy to have you on their team."

She smiled. "They were. We were state champs three years in a row." Eyes widening, she took the plaque down and turned it upside down on her desk. "That was a long time ago, but it was the best time of my life. Thanks for stopping by, Merry. I appreciate your business."

I hurried back to the office. Why was Suzie so nervous about what Gloria and I discussed? It must be rough for Suzie to be mourning her dead husband while her mom made snide comments about him. But I wouldn't have liked him either.

CHAPTER 29

Rob entered my house with a bucket of chicken. I gave him a big hug. "You're a lifesaver. I was trying to figure out how I was going to make dinner and get you and Jenny off on time, and you came through for me. Problem solved."

Jenny ran down the stairs in her gym attire. "What smells so good?"

"Rob brought fried chicken. We had it the other night, and it was terrific."

She smiled at him. "You are now my favorite out of all the men my mom is dating."

He raised an eyebrow at me. "All the men?"

I tapped his shoulder. "It was her idea of a joke, dear. I don't have time to date any other fellows."

"I have a good mind to hog the chicken, Jenny."

She wrapped her hand around the bucket. "Don't do that. You know I was only kidding."

I smacked her hand. "Why don't you set the table? We're under a bit of a time crunch."

"Will do. Thanks for the chicken, Mr. Jenson."

I glanced at Rob. "How fancy do you want to be? Should we put everything on platters?"

"Nope, let's rough it and serve out of the containers."

"A man after my own heart."

We made quick work of dinner, and they left shortly thereafter for the game. I put the dishes in the dishwasher and threw out the containers. Kitchen clean, I set my iPad up in the center of the island. I put a flip chart behind me with some drawings I created to illustrate the benefits of life insurance. Just before seven, I signed on to Facebook and went live.

"Good evening, everyone. I'm so glad you tuned in to learn more about the importance of life insurance. Don't forget; if you miss something, you can always find these sessions catalogued on my Facebook page. The last educational session was about pet insurance, and everyone remembers Drambuie, right?" I picked up the cat and waved her paw at the screen.

"Let's talk about life insurance, shall we? I have life insurance because, as many of you know, I have a fabulous daughter who brings a lot of joy into my life. Here's a picture of her." I moved a picture onto the screen so everyone could see it. "She's the best thing in my life, and I want to make sure she's protected. If something were to happen to me, I want her to be able to stay in this same house and attend the school she wants to attend. That's why I'm passionate about the benefits of life insurance for the loved ones we leave behind."

Someone knocked at the back door. Startled, I decided I would work whoever it was into the presentation. I told the audience, "You'll have to excuse me for a moment while I answer the door."

Suzie and her mother stood there with Patty's clean casserole dish. I sighed. "I'm sorry, but this is not a good time for me."

Gloria pushed her way past me. "Too bad. You're going to have to make time."

"I don't understand."

Suzie came in behind her mother. "I'm sorry, Merry."

I frowned. "That's Patty's casserole dish, not mine, and are you sure we can't do this another time? You see I—"

Gloria backhanded me across the face. I fell on my butt. "No, we will not do this another time. You know too much, and I want to make sure my daughter is safe." She grabbed a knife from the butcher block and casually picked up a tomato from a dish I had on the counter. Holding it gently, she slashed it with the knife. It made a clean slice. "Sharp enough."

I rubbed my aching cheek. "Sharp enough for what?"

"To silence you."

I was amazed that the iPad captured the drama happening in my kitchen. "So you killed Ben and Nancy."

Gloria nodded. "Ben was blackmailing my baby. She had paid him more than enough to keep her secret. He would have bled her dry. I couldn't believe it when I stopped by that night to drop off the coffee ring and saw him talking to Belinda in the church. I knew God was telling me it was time. I snuck into the rectory, grabbed the butcher knife, and hid behind the side door to the church. When he came out and started down the stairs, I stabbed him." Regret flashed across her face. "I didn't get a chance to enjoy it, though, because your daughter and her friend came out a moment later."

She smiled coldly. "Then I heard you found something at Ben's house. I ripped this place apart but didn't find it." She made a stabbing gesture toward me with the knife.

I scooted backward. "I gave it to the police."

"Busybody. Just like Nancy. Nancy stuck her nose where it didn't belong. She asked to use the phone in Suzie's office to call you. She pretended someone in the store was not who she said she was."

"That was the truth!"

"It doesn't matter. We fixed her. Then you come along all neighborly: I'm so concerned about Suzie, yada, yada, yada, and it was all a pretext to get into her office."

"I don't understand. What is so special about her office? Oh. I saw the batting trophy." I turned to Suzie. "Your husband was killed with a baseball bat."

Tears streamed down her face. "Yes. He was drinking at the local tavern that night. When he got home, something set him off. I don't even remember what it was. Might have been the towel wasn't straight in the washroom. The littlest things set him off. He began to beat me, and then when he got tired, he sat down at the table and demanded I get him a beer. I limped to the refrigerator and got one, worried my hands were shaking so badly the beer would foam when I poured it. I carefully twisted the cap off, and luckily it was okay. He chugged it, and when he was done, he put his head down on the table and fell asleep.

"That's when I got the bat. I picked it up and felt its weight. I took a few practice swings and then walked over to where he was sleeping. I said a prayer; you know the one: 'Now I lay me down to sleep, I pray the Lord my soul to keep...'"

I nodded slowly to indicate I knew what she was talking about.

She continued, "I pretended I was at the plate and had gotten the signal to swing for the fences, and I did. I looked down and couldn't believe it at first. But he was dead, really dead. I called my mom, and she drove over. We rolled him up in a carpet and drove him over to the Cedar Bog. I dug as best I could, and then we unrolled him, dropped him in the grave, and covered him up. We tossed the carpet in an apartment dumpster on the way back. I used a whole bottle of bleach washing down that kitchen. Who knew it would take the police three years to find him or that there would be anything left to find?"

I asked, "How did Ben find out?"

"He didn't. He was blackmailing me because I didn't want people to know someone was poisoned in my last place, the Purple Plum." Her eyes welled. "Paul did that, you know."

"Paul poisoned the man?"

"Yes. I told you the other day. It was the last straw. He thought Dennis—that was the guy's name—was putting the moves on me. I got a black eye over that one, and Dennis got dead."

"You should have gone to the police after you killed your husband. You could have claimed self-defense."

"Killing a sleeping man? Get real. He made my life a prison while he was alive. I didn't want to live in a prison after he was dead."

I arched my eyebrows. "So you killed two more people?"

"I didn't kill them. Mom did. She didn't want me to go to prison either."

"Enough talk." Gloria edged closer to me with the knife. "Nobody is going to hurt my daughter ever again."

She was about a foot away when my back window shattered, a brick sailing through it and landing on the floor. We all jumped. I seized the moment to kick the knife out of Gloria's hand. It flew across the room. A second later, Rob leapt through the window as Jay barreled through the back door.

Jay tackled Gloria, and another policeman came in and cuffed Suzie. Jay read them their rights.

Dazed, I stood and looked at the camera. "Thanks for tuning in, folks. I'll complete this educational session another evening. Don't forget to click on the follow button if you like what you've seen tonight. Signing out, this is Merry March of the Meredith March Insurance Agency." I closed the session and fainted.

When I came to, I was lying on the living room sofa being fanned with a newspaper by Rob as Jenny held ice to my cheek. "What happened?"

"You fainted," Rob said.

"How'd you know I was in trouble? I was never so glad to see my kitchen window smashed in my life."

Jenny said, "You know you were still broadcasting, right?"

"Yes. I thought I'd get rid of whoever was at the door or try to work them into the broadcast. Suzie and her mother forced their way in. I tried to tell them I was in the middle of the show, but they didn't give me a chance."

"It was a good thing. That's how we knew you were in trouble," Rob said.

"But you couldn't have been watching it. You were at Jenny's game, and Jenny was playing."

"My phone blew up with texts. I knew something was going on, so I logged in to watch. Seeing the two of them threaten you, I called Jay. He had already heard from three other people. Needless to say, I grabbed Jenny, and we hightailed it over here. I was never so scared! Are you sure you're okay?"

"I'm fine." I struggled to get to my feet. Feeling woozy, I sat back down. "Maybe not a good idea yet. That adrenaline rush is a killer. Ha ha, a killer, get it?" I dissolved into hopeless laughter and then tears.

Rob touched Jenny's arm. "I'm going to go get some brandy. Stay with your mom?"

"I'm not leaving her." Jenny sat and put her arm around me. "It's okay, Mom. All the bad guys are locked up now. Plus, there is a positive side."

My mouth sagged. "Positive side?"

"I checked your stats. You normally average about twenty people per session, right?"

"Yes."

"Well, you started out with eighteen people watching at 7:05 p.m., and by the time Rob threw the brick in the window, over two hundred thousand people were on, and nearly one hundred thousand of them are now following you. You're famous. And who knows how many people are viewing the replay right now?"

Rob returned with some brandy. "Now take this slow. You know what happens when you drink it too quickly."

I took a sip and then carefully put it down on the coffee table. "What a day."

CHAPTER 30

Jenny insisted on sleeping with me. She said she was worried about me being scared. I think she was a little scared too. Seeing the morning light play on her face, I marveled to be so blessed. I felt incredibly happy. I survived everything that happened the night before and was alive on this lovely morning with my amazing and talented daughter within reach. I watched her slow, deep, even breathing and felt at peace with the world.

The door banged open. Rob stood there with a large tray full of blueberry pancakes. Jenny jolted awake. "Hey, we were sleeping!"

"I'm so sorry. I'll take your pancakes back downstairs." He backed out the door.

She sat up quickly. "No need to trouble yourself. You can leave them here with us."

Smiling, he set the tray down at the foot of the bed and handed me a mug of coffee.

"Heaven," I said as I sipped. "Pure heaven."

He gave us both napkins and silverware. "There seems to be only one tray, so one of you is going to have to balance your plate."

I pointed toward the dresser. "If you look behind it, you'll see another one."

He brought it over and set Jenny's place. Jenny and I made ourselves comfortable against the pillows and headboard, and he deposited a tray on each of our laps.

Jenny closed her eyes and chewed slowly. "Pancakes and hot chocolate in bed. Best morning ever."

"It's got to be up there."

"Text when you're done, and I'll get the trays. FYI, Jay will be stopping by around ten thirty." He shut the door.

Jenny held up her mug. "To the best mom ever."

I smiled and raised my mug. "To the most fabulous daughter ever."

We both drank and finished our breakfast. "I hate to say this, but I need to get going if Jay is going to be here soon."

"Party pooper." Jenny got out of bed. "Why don't you jump in the shower? I'll take the dishes down to Mr. Jenson."

I stood in the shower, letting the hot water stream over me. Suzie might have had such a different life if she had never met Paul. All of this ugliness might never have happened. Our lives are forever changed by those we choose to love. Like mine. I thought Drew and I would be together forever. That didn't work out. Rob would, though. He'd shown he could be counted on when it mattered most. Drying off, I swore that from now on I would leave murder investigations to the police.

Jenny knocked on the door. "Jay's here. And it's a good thing because you must be a total prune by now."

I poked my head around the door. "That's a laugh, oh ye of the marathon showers. I'll be down in a minute."

Jay was sitting at the counter eating a pancake and drinking coffee when I came into the kitchen. "It looks so dark in here with the window boarded up," I said. "Who cleaned the mess up last night?"

Rob raised his hand. "Me, once the crime technicians were done. The window people will be out later this afternoon to take measurements. Hopefully they have one in stock."

"Thank you. I appreciate you cleaning up and calling them." I gave him a quick kiss. Then I took a step back and touched his face. "What are all these cuts?"

"The window won last night. Don't worry. The EMTs cleaned me up."

I kissed him again. "Thanks for sacrificing your good looks for me."

Rob kissed me back. Jay cleared his throat. "I'm still here."

Heat flooded my face. "Jay, what happens now?"

"Both Gloria and Suzie have gotten attorneys. They are going to have an uphill battle on their hands with such a public, recorded confession. Paula and John are also still in jail, although it's likely John will make bail in the next day or so. I've issued a restraining order against him coming anywhere near you."

"Thanks. I wonder if he'll give Paula the money so she can make bail too."

Rob and Jay both gave me an incredulous look. "Doubtful," Rob said.

Jay stood. "Merry, I'll need you to come down to the station today to make a formal statement."

"I'll bring her there," Rob promised.

"And thanks for breakfast." Jay made his way out the door.

Rob pulled me into his arms and gave me a long, slow kiss that I felt all the way to my toes. Hugging him even tighter, I returned his kiss with vigor.

Jenny cleared her throat and looked down at the floor. "Ahem, this is so embarrassing."

"What happened to your clomping down the stairs? You could give people a bit of warning," I said.

"I came down the stairs the way I always come down the stairs. I can't help it if other people had their minds on other things. I'm going over to Cindy's. Her mom said you owe her a call. Love you, Mom. Thanks again for the pancakes, Mr. Jenson." She left.

Rob's eyes brightened. "No one else is here, right?"

I laughed. "Not to my knowledge."

"Good. Let's pick up where we left off." He swept me into his arms and started to carry me up the stairs.

The doorbell rang. He groaned. "Do we have to answer it?"

"Every piece of my body is screaming no, but with everything that's been going on lately, we probably should."

I ran down the stairs, opened the door, and gasped. "Drew! When did you get out?"

ABOUT THE AUTHOR

Eileen Hammond is an author who recently retired from a successful marketing career in the insurance industry. She and her husband share the house with two cats that are determined to train them. Rounding out the household are two koi, Daisy and Rose, as well as assorted shubunkins and minnows. Tending to this menagerie, writing, and rescuing the frog population from certain death in the pool keep her busy.

32635886R00156

Made in the USA
Middletown, DE
08 January 2019